THE WORKS OF LIANG YUCHUN

梁遇春

著译全集

5

第五卷

李力夫 商昌宝 主编

本卷总目

潘新可夫 …………………………………… 1
The Red Flower
红花 ……………………………………… 57
Esther
厄斯忒哀史 ……………………………… 121
The Poet's Portmanteau
诗人的手提包 …………………………… 199
The Three Strangers
三个陌生人 ……………………………… 251

潘新可夫

屠介涅夫　著
梁遇春　译

"欧美名家小说"丛刊，上海北新书局，1928年3月初版

潘新可夫

一

这事情发生在圣彼得堡，一个冬天，狂欢节的第一天。一个同学请我赴他的宴会。这人年青时候，享有同少女一样谦虚守礼的好名声；但是他后来的行为，可不见得很规矩。他同我的大多数同学一样现在已经死了。这回宴会除我以外还有两个人：君士坦丁·亚力山都乐非取·亚生诺夫同一个当时的文豪。这位文豪使我们等了好久，最后送来个信说他不能到会。刚好来了一个躯体短小头发轻松的先生填了这位文豪的空位。他是个照例的不速之客，这种人圣彼得堡有的是。

这一餐吃得很久；我们主人对于酒是很舍得的，所以我们的头都渐渐受影响了。我们平常深存心中的事情——谁的心中没有点秘密呢——都跑出外面来了。我们主人脸上那种谦抑，深沉的神情忽然消去；他眼光中闪着厚颜的傲慢；他的嘴唇弯成卑鄙的狞笑。那位头发轻松的先生微弱地哂笑，喉中无意义的作响。但是最使我奇怪的是亚生诺夫。谁也知道他平常最讲礼节的，可是他现在忽然常用手摸他前额，做出煞有介事的神气，夸讲他的亲戚，时刻提起他有一个叔父，一个非常重要的人物……我真应该不认得他；他是毫无意义地在讥笑我们……他明显的表示他看不起我们，不过没有说出就是了……亚生诺夫的无礼使我气愤起来。

"听！"我对他讲；"你既这么瞧不起我们，干脆走开，找你那位鼎鼎大名的叔父去。恐怕他未必见你。"

亚生诺夫不答我，还是用手摸他的前额。

"这一班什么东西！"他又说；"他们从来就没有到过上等社会，一个上等女人也不认得。看我这里，"他大声嚷，一面迅速地从边袋里拿出一个小本子，将手轻轻拍一下，"一大包的信，都是一个你们在世界上找不出第二个比得上的女子写的。"

我们主人同那头发轻松的先生没有注意亚生诺夫后面那句话；他们互拉着纽扣在那里各诉事情；但是我却激起了耳朵。

"呵，你吹牛，名人的侄儿先生，"我走到亚生诺夫面前讲；"你一封信也没有。"

"你以为没有么？"他反驳我，又高傲地看着我；"那么，这是什么？"他打开那小本，取出差不多一打封面上写着他的名字的信给我看……这字迹我很熟，我想……现在我还觉得我满脸绯红……我的自尊心难过得很……自认从前的丑行是谁都不愿意的……但是这也顾不到了：当我着手写这篇东西的时候，我已经知道写到中间我一定会羞红得连耳朵也红了。所以我要硬下心肠老老实实承认……

好，这便是当时的情形：亚生诺夫一不小心，信就落在那沾了香槟的桌布上；我欺侮亚生诺夫醉了，（我的头也是一样的狠晕了），狠快的将中间的一封信瞧了一下……

我的心停止了……唉！写信给亚生诺夫的女子就是我所钟情的人。我现在不能不信她是爱他的。信是用法文写的，从头至尾都表现着柔情与诚恳……

"我亲爱的朋友君士坦丁！"那信是这样开头……结尾几个字是："你要同从前一样小心，我若不是你的，我就决不属于旁人。"

给雷打了一般，好几分钟我坐着不动；后来我心中清醒了，我跳起来，跑出了屋子。

一分钟后我回到我住宿的地方了。

资乐力思基是我从莫斯科到圣彼得堡最先认识的一家人。他们家有父亲，母亲，二个女孩同一个儿子。父亲头已经花白，身体仍然强壮，从前曾经入过军队，这时还有一件重要的差事，早上在政府机关办公，吃完饭睡一忽，晚上到他的俱乐部打牌去……他不常在家，很少讲话，就讲也狠勉强的样子，目光由眉毛下射出看人，带有半是愤怒，半是什么也不理的态度。他除游记同地理书外不看别的书。有时候他觉得不好过，他就自己关在房子里，画点小图画，或者弄弄老鹦鹉波普卡。他的妻是一个身体孱弱患痨病的妇人，她有一对深陷的眼睛同尖利突出的鼻子，常接连好几天不离她的沙发，总在绣幕布垫面。就我所能的观察看起来，她似乎狠怕她的丈夫，好像从前她曾得罪过他似的。那个大女儿樊樊兰是一个肥胖，脸色嫣红，头发美丽的十八岁的姑娘，常坐在窗户旁边，看街上走路的人。儿子在官立学校念书，只有星期日才回家；他也是不爱讲话的。就是那小女孩苏菲亚，我所钟情的姑娘，性情也是偏于沉默的。所以资乐力思基家里没有时候不是静悄悄的；打破这种静默空气的只有波普卡刺耳的尖声叫唤，但是客人对这声音很快就听惯了，随即又觉得那永远寂寞的压迫了。但是资乐力思基家里并没有很多客人，他们的屋里太沉闷无味了。就是那器具罢，客厅中印黄花的红色花纸，饭厅里的几只芦苇作垫的椅子，沙发上绣着七孩同狗的退色的毛垫子，枝歧的灯架同墙上阴气森森的相片……样样都引起无奈何的愁闷，没有一样东西不含着冷意与无味。当我到圣彼得堡的时候，我想我应该去拜访他们；因为资乐力思基是我母亲的亲戚。我极不自在地挨着坐了一个钟头，隔了好久我才再去找他们。但是我渐渐地比较常到他们家里了。我是被苏菲亚引去的，虽然起先我不大注意她，最后我却钟情于她了。

她是个细长，可以说是单瘦的女子，中等身材，脸色苍白，厚厚的黑发，还有一对大的棕色的常是半开半合的眼睛。她那端整严肃的姿态，尤其她的紧闭的嘴唇，表现出她意志的坚强和毅力。在家里他们都知道她是个凡事都有她自己的意志的姑娘……

"苏菲亚同她的大姊加大林那一样,"资乐力思基夫人一天当我同她二人对坐着的时候讲;(在她丈夫面前她是不敢提起这加大林那名字的)"你不知道加大林那;她现在在高加索,已经出嫁了。你想想才十三岁她就爱上了她现在的丈夫,她那时就对我们声明她是绝对不嫁旁人的了,我们用尽方法——都不济事。她到廿三岁,敢犯她父亲的盛怒,终于嫁给她的崇拜的偶像去了。谁也不敢说苏菲亚将来什么事干不出来!希望上帝保佑她使她不要这么顽强!但是我真替她担心;她才十六岁,已经管不住了……"

资乐力思基先生进来,他夫人立刻不讲了。

我爱苏菲亚不是爱她的意志力——不是;但是不管她怎样神情冷淡,不活泼,想象力不丰富,她有她特别的美丽,譬如她的直率爽快的态度,真实诚恳的感情,同洁白无瑕的心地。我敬她同我爱她的程度一样……我觉得她对我好像也有特别的好感;把我心中存着她爱我的幻景打破,而确实证明她爱了旁一个人,这是对我一个大打击。

这个预料不到的发现更使我觉得奇怪,因为亚生诺夫并不常到资乐力思基家去,比我少得多,他又没有现出特别看重苏菲亚。他是个很美,皮肤带黑的少年,面貌很有表情但是略带呆重的样子,有光亮,凹出来的眼睛,宽大雪白的前额,和美丽髭须底下猩红的嘴唇。他是个非常小心的人,不过行事很严厉,对自己所讲的话和下的批评都很自信,沉默的时候也有一种尊严的态度。这是很显明的他是非常自重的。亚生诺夫不常笑,笑起来闭着牙齿,他从没有跳舞过。他的躯干并不平整,还颇有些笨拙。他曾在第……团服务过;人家讲他是个很能干的将校。

"奇怪的事情!"我躺在沙发上想;"怎么我一向没有看出一点痕迹?"……"你要同从前一样小心":我忽然记起苏菲亚信中这几个字。"唉!"我想;"这么一回事!多么狡猾一个歹小女人!我还以为她坦白,诚恳。……不要紧,等一会看;我总要叫你知道……"但是我想到这里,若使我现在记得不错,我狠痛心哭起来,整夜都没有睡觉。

第二天下午二点钟我到资乐力思基家里。父亲不在家,母亲也不坐在她平日坐的地方;从前天的薄饼节以来,她就有些头痛,躺在她卧室里。樊樊兰肩膀靠着窗子站着看街,苏菲亚双手抱在胸前在房子里走来走去;波普卡大声叫着。

"呵!你好。"樊樊兰看见我进房子,慢吞吞地说,接着她放低声音说,"这里去过一个农夫,头上顶只盘。"……(她看见过路人有一一对自己报告的习惯)

"你好。"我回答;"你好,苏菲亚·力可利夫那,大提安那·花新力夫那在那儿?"

"她躺着去了。"苏菲亚答道,仍旧在房子里走。

"昨天我们吃薄饼,"樊樊兰说,并没有转过头来,"你为甚么不来?……那个书记是那里去的?"

"呵,我没有空。"("举起手臂来,"鹦鹉尖声地叫唤。)

"今天波普卡叫得多么利害！"

"他总是这样子叫，"苏菲亚说。

我们暂时都不做声。

"他跑到门里去了，"樊樊兰说，她突然坐上窗台去，打开窗子。

"你说谁？"苏菲亚问。

"那儿有一个叫化子，"樊樊兰答道。她弯下腰，由窗子上捡起一个值五可贝的小铜币；安息香的灰色残灰还粘在铜子上；她就将铜子丢下街中去了，随后她把窗子砰的一声关上，狠重地又跳到地板上。……

"昨天我过得狠有趣，"我坐在圈手椅上说道。"我同我一个朋友吃饭去了；君士坦丁·亚力由都乐非取也在那里……（我瞧苏菲亚一眼，她脸上一根眉毛也不动。）"我要承认"我接着说，"我们喝了好多酒；我们四个人喝了八瓶酒。"

"真的！"苏菲亚安静地一字字说着，又摇了一下头。

"是的，"我往下讲，对她的安若无事觉得有点不快："你知道吗，苏菲亚·力可利夫那，'酒醉出真言'这句话好像是不错的？"

"怎么这句话是不错的？"

"君士坦丁·亚力山都乐非取把我们都引笑了。你想想，他忽然这样用手摸他的额，一面讲：'我是个漂亮的人！我有一个有名望的叔父！'……"

"哈，哈！"我听见樊樊兰短促的笑声。

……"波普卡！波普卡！波普卡！"鹦鹉大声回应她。

苏菲亚还站在我面前，直着眼睛看我。

"你，你讲什么呢？"她问；"你还记得吗？"

我止不住红起脸来。

"我记不清了！大概也是胡说一阵罢。喝酒还真是危险，"我故意加重声音；"一个人一喝醉立刻就乱谈起来，狠容易讲出旁人不应当知道的话。后来一定会追悔，但已经太迟了。"

"你漏出什么秘密没有？"苏菲亚问。

"我不是讲我自己。"

苏菲亚转过头去，又在房子里走来走去。我瞪着她，心里发气。我想，"她确实只是个小孩子，一个婴孩，但是多么有把握的样子！她简直是个铁石心肠人。但是，不忙……"

"苏菲亚·力可利夫那……"我大声说。

苏菲亚停住。

"什么事？"

"你弹下钢琴给我听，好不好？"我沉下声音加上；"我还要告诉你一些事情。"

苏菲亚，一字不说，走到另一间房间里去；我跟着她。她到钢琴旁边站着。

"你要我弹什么？"她问。

"你爱什么就弹什么……就是初宾夜曲的一段罢。"

苏菲亚开始弹夜曲。她按的不大妙，但到〔倒〕很带有点情感。她的姐姐只会奏波兰舞蹈曲同二人旋舞曲，就是这二种也很少弹。樊樊兰有时候懒洋洋地走到钢琴旁边，坐下来，随她的外衣由肩膀落到肘节上（我没有看见过她没有穿外衣）大声地弹波兰舞蹈曲，一只没完又按别只，忽然长叹一声，站起来又到窗旁边去了。樊樊兰真是个怪物。

我坐在苏菲亚旁边。

"苏菲亚·力可利夫那，"我开口道，很用心地从一边看着她。"我应该告你一个新闻，一个使我不高兴的新闻。"

"新闻？什么新闻？"

"我现在讲给你听……我一直误解了你，完全误解了。"

"怎么误解？"她回答，还是在按琴，她眼睛注视着她的手指。

"我以为你是坦白；我以为你不会做假君子，隐藏你的情感，不会骗人……"

苏菲亚俯着脸更近她的乐器。

"我不懂你。"

"而且，"我接着说："我绝对想不到你这样年纪居然作假作得这么好。"

苏菲亚手在乐键上微微颤动。"你为什么讲这话？"她说，眼睛还是不望我；"我做假？"

"是的，你做假。"（她微笑着……我心中觉得很愤恨。）……"你对一个人假装毫不关心的样子……你实在一面写信给他，"我低声加上。

苏菲亚脸变白了，但是她并不转向我；她一直把夜曲弹完，立起,把琴关好。

"那里去?"我迷乱地问她。"你没有话回答我吗?"

"我怎样能回答你?我就不知道你讲的是什么……我又不会假装……"

她把乐谱搁在一边。

我的怒气直升上来。

"不;你知道我讲的是什么?"我讲,也站起;"不然,若使你愿意,我还能引给你听你一封信上的话:'你要同从前一样小心'……"

苏菲亚稍稍吓了一跳。

"我万不想到你会这样,"她最后说。

"我也万不想到你,"我反抗说,"苏菲亚·力可利夫那,会留意这个人……"

苏菲亚狠快扭过头向我;我自然而然退几步;她那平素半开半合的眼睛睁得非常阔大,在紧蹙的眉下含怒地闪着。

"呵!就是这个,"她讲,"那让我告诉你罢,我爱那个人;你对他同对我的爱他作何意见,于我都是丝毫无关系的,这与你有什么相干的?……你有什么权力同我讲这事情?我若心中决定了……"

她不讲了,赶快跑出房去。我站着不动。突然我觉得羞耻,心中非常不好受,我把手遮了脸。我明白我所做的事情是不合理的,卑鄙的,我给羞耻和悔恨压住我的心头,好像丢了脸样的呆立着。"天呵!"我想,"我干的什么事!"

"安敦·力岂提取，"我听见女仆在外房里讲，"倒杯水来，快点，给苏菲亚·力可利夫那。"

"什么事？"那人问。

"我想她哭了……"

我跳起来，走到客厅里拿我的帽子。

"你同苏菲亚讲了什么？"樊樊兰随便地问我，停了一会她又低声讲："那个书记又来了。"

我开始告别。

"干吗就走？待一会罢；妈妈就要下来了。"

"不，我现在不能待了，"我说："还是下次来看她罢。"

在这时候使我战栗，苏菲亚一步一步很安定的走进客厅来。她脸比平常更苍白，眼皮有点红。她一眼也不瞧我。

"看，苏菲亚，"樊樊兰说道；"那里有一个书记老在我们房子前面走。"

"一个侦探，或者……"苏菲亚冷淡，鄙薄地说。

这使我太难过了。我走开，我真不知道我怎么走到家的。

我觉得非常难受，形容不出的苦恼与愁闷。廿四小时中受两次这么痛心的打击！我知道苏菲亚爱的是别人，我又从此给她看不起。我觉得非常失败和丢脸，连对自己愤怒的能力都没有了。面向壁躺在沙发上，我正在尝着新的失望的苦痛，我忽然听见房中有脚步声。我仰起头来，看见我一个最亲密的朋友耶克夫·潘新可夫。

我本来打算对于那天进我房子的无论何人都要发脾气的，

但是对潘新可夫我是不能生气的。完全相反,不管愁苦怎么熬煎我的心,我看见他来,心中却暗暗地欢喜,同他点头。他照他的习惯在房子里转两转,清一清喉咙,把他的长的臂和腿伸一伸;他对我默默站了一分钟,又一声不响地坐在房角里。

我认识潘新可夫已经很久,差不多从小孩时候起。他也是在那私立学校内长大的,一个德国人温特弃缕尔办的学校,在那里我曾经住过三年。潘新可夫的父亲是一个退职的穷少佐,人很老实,可是脑筋有点糊涂,当他儿子七岁的时候,他就带他到这德国人学校里;预先缴了一年的费用,他后来就离开莫思科,从此没有人看见他过……时时有些关于他的奇怪的模糊的谣言。过了八年我们才确实知道他在经过儿提取的时候,给大水淹死了。他为什么到西伯利亚去,只有上帝才知道。耶可夫没有旁的亲人,母亲早已死了。所以他就此搁在温特弃缕尔的手上。不错,耶可夫还有个疏远的亲戚,一位姨妈;但是她太穷了,她起先不敢来看她的外甥,怕的是照顾他的责任要推到她的身上来。她这恐惧实在是无须的;那位好心肠的德国人依旧留耶可夫在家里,让他同旁的学生一块念书,给东西他吃。(但是,除非礼拜,耶可夫是没有饭后果点吃的,)把他的母亲不要的便衣——多是鼻烟色的——裁下做衣裳给耶可夫穿,他的母亲是里方力亚地方的妇人,虽然年纪很大,还是狠敏捷爱动。因为这几种情形,多半因为耶可夫在学校中低下的位置,他的同学待他很随便,藐视他,叫他做"妈妈的便衣","小帽的侄子,"(他姨妈总是带一个奇怪的小帽,帽上笔直地插着一束黄缎带像是圆蓟），有时候叫他做"也马的儿子"（因为他父亲同这英雄一样在儿提取淹死的）。然而不管他这么多的绰号，滑稽的衣裳，和穷光的境况，谁都高兴他，我们实在不能不爱他；在世上从来没有性情比他再温和高尚的了，他念书也狠好。

我最初见他的时候，他是十六岁，我只十三岁。我是一个娇养坏了的自私自利的小孩；我是生长在一个比较富裕的家庭，所以一进学校我赶紧同一位小王子——温特弃缕尔对于这小王子特别用心招呼——同还有别的两三个贵族子弟结交；对于其他我则大排架子。潘新可夫我连瞧也不瞧一下。我把这躯干高大，带些乡气，穿着不成样的衣衫，狠短的裤子，露出他的粗线袜的小孩，当是小仆家奴看待——至多也不过一个工人阶级的人。潘新可夫对人非常客气，虽然他并不有意同谁要好。人家待他不好，他既不怎么下声低气，也不怎么发怒；他就走开，脸上略带悔恨的样子，像在那里待时而动的神气。这也是他对我的法子。过了两个月，一个晴明的夏天，我偶然在热闹的跳蛙戏后走出游戏场，于花园中踱着，我看见潘新可夫坐在高大的紫丁香树下长凳上。他正念书。我走过时候把书的外皮看一下，上面写《薛来尔全集》（Schiller's Werke）。我站住了。

"难道说你还懂得德文吧？"我问潘新可夫。

我记起那时声音的傲慢，我现在还觉得惭愧……潘新可夫轻轻举起那小而能表情的眼睛，望我一眼。

"是的，"他答道："你呢？"

"我希望我也会！"我说，心中觉得这句问话很有侮慢的口气,正想走我的路,好像有什么东西留住了我。

"你念薛来尔的什么?"我还是同一骄傲的口吻。

"刚才念《顺服》,一篇好诗。你要我念给你听吗?来,同我在这长凳一块坐。"

我迟疑一会,还是坐下。潘新可夫开始念。他的德文程度比我好。他还解释几行的意义给我听。我对于自己的无知识和他之比我高明觉得不用惭愧。由那天起,由我们在花园紫丁香花荫下同念书那时候起,我爱潘新可夫,得他的欢心,完全受他的指导。

我对他那时候的外貌有狠明显的记忆。后来他的形状没有多大变更。他身体瘦长,四肢构造略似笨拙,长背窄肩,胸部凹陷,因此他显得狠文弱的样子,虽然在健康方面他并没有毛病。他那像圆屋顶的大头稍斜一边;他软黄的头发松松地散在细长的颈旁。他的脸生得不美,或者人家看见还觉得丑陋,因为他那又长又大又红的鼻子差不多把他扁宽的嘴全都遮了。可是他那开展的眉是轩昂的,他微笑的时候,小灰色的眼睛发出温和亲热的慈爱神情,谁看见他心中都会高兴,也觉得亲热。我还记得他的声音,细柔恬静,含了一种甜蜜好听的沙声。照例他不大说话,说时带狠困难的样子。然而当他起劲的时候,他的话和水一般自由地流着,并且——讲起来实在奇怪——他的声音更细柔,他的目光仿佛向内看,没有了那种火气,他的全脸却稍稍发红。在他口里"慈爱""真理""生活""科学""恋爱"这几个字,讲得无论怎么热烈,似乎总没有过分之嫌。

不用勉强，不费力气，他走到理想的境界；他那洁白的灵魂无论什么时候都可以站在"美之圣龛"前面；只等那欢迎的呼唤，同别一个灵魂的接触……潘新可夫是一位理想主义者，我命中得遇的最后的理想主义者的一个。我们都知道理想主义者现在已经不存在了，无论如何目下青年里头是找不着的。这是现在青年的不幸！

我和潘新可夫相处三年，真是所谓"心心相印"。他很信任我，告诉我他的初恋。我多么感激他的信任，同情地注意听着！他所钟情女子是温特弇缕尔的侄女，一个头发狠好看很美丽的德国少女，脸子肥胖短小好像小孩子的面孔，还有一对表示信人的温柔的蓝眼睛。她性情仁慈又易动情；他爱读麦提逊（Mattison），温兰（Uhland），薛来尔（Schiller），常用她胆怯和谐的音调背诵他们的诗歌。潘新可夫的爱情是纯粹属于精神的。他只在星期才看见他的爱人，在这天她常来同温特弇缕尔的小孩玩"罚"戏，他同她也不多谈天。但是有一次她叫他"我亲爱的，亲爱的雅各先生！"他心中充满了快乐，以至于整夜没有睡着。他在那时候简直忘了她无论对他那一个同学都叫"我亲爱的。"我还记得他的愁苦同丧气，当他得到费得利小姐——这是她的名字——快嫁给克力土司的消息，一个发财屠宰铺的老板，人狠漂亮，受过完全教育，并且知道她不仅是从父母之命，并且是为爱而嫁他的。这给潘新可夫一个痛心的打击，在这一对少年夫妇头一次来访时，他的苦痛特别重。从前的费得利小姐，现在是太太，介绍他与她的从头到脚妆得很漂亮的丈夫，又叫他一回亲爱的雅各先生；她丈夫的眼睛，向上卷着的黑发，前额，牙齿，衣衫的纽扣，背心上挂的表练〔链〕，无论那件东西一直到那阔大的特式的皮鞋，都发着光亮。潘新可夫握了克力士司的手，祝他有永久美满幸福。（我相信这祝望是诚恳的，）这是我亲眼目击的。我还没有忘记我当时怎样地赞叹和同情地望着他。我以为他真是好汉！……后来我们有多么愁惨的谈话。"到艺术中去安慰罢，"我对他讲。"是的"，他回答我；"还有在诗歌里。""在友谊上也可以，"我加道。"在友谊上也可以，"他照着我说。呵，那种快乐的日子呵！……

我离开潘新可夫是一件很大的苦痛。在我离校以前他费了好多力气经了好些难关，还有一种发笑的通信，他终于得他生辰和受洗礼的证明及护照，进大学去了。他一切费用还是由温特弃缕尔负担。不过他不穿那家里自做的小衫同裤子了，他有了普通的衣服，这是他教几个小学生的代价。一直到我离开学校潘新可夫待我总是一样，虽然我们年龄的不同渐渐明显地现出来，我记得我对他的新朋友有些妒忌。他的影响是对我非常有益的。他的影响不能再继续下去了，这是狠不幸的。举一个例罢：小孩时候我有扯谎的习惯……在耶可夫面前我却讲不出假话。我特别爱同他两人一块儿散步，或者房里跟他来去地闲踱，听他眼睛不看着我，用那细柔兴奋的声音，朗读诗歌。我仿佛慢慢地离开人间，飞入了灿烂光明神秘的境界……我记得一晚上我们俩在那紫丁香树下坐着；我们很爱这个地方。同学都睡了；我们轻轻地起来，穿好衣裳，暗中摸索，偷偷地跑到外面"做梦"去。户外很温暖，但是有时一阵凉风吹来使我们紧紧地贴着。我们谈天，谈许多话，狠热烈的谈着——热烈到二个人的话抢起来，虽然我们并没有辩论。天上闪着无数明星。耶可夫仰起头来，握我的手，他低唱：

"在我们头上

天上有永久的星……

在星的上层有他们的创造者……"

我觉得一种敬畏的情绪穿过我的心里；我全身冰冷，倒在他肩上……我心中被情感充满了……这种快乐现在那儿去了？唉！在少年人那里。

八年后在圣彼得堡我又碰着耶可夫。我刚被派得军队中一个位置，旁人替他在别的部里找了一个小差事。我们的会见非常快乐。我再不会忘记那个时候，当我独坐在家里忽然听到走道里他的声音……我怎样惊喜；心如何跳突，我跃起来，倒在他的颈子上，也不等他把皮大氅围巾脱去！我怎么样由我那不能自制的晶明的眼泪里钉〔盯〕着眼睛看他！在这七年中间他老了些；绉痕，很细的好像是针画的，散在他的额上，双颊向内略凹，头发也稀少了一点；但是他的须并没有增多，笑容还是同从前一样；他的大笑，一种轻柔，向内，好像没有出气的大笑，也是不变……

天呵！那天我们什么不讲！……我们念诵我们心爱的诗歌！我求他搬来同我同住，但是他不肯。他却答应每天来找我，他后来真守他的话。

精神方面潘新可夫也没有变。他仍是我从前所知道那样的理想主义者。无论生命的冷酷，阅历的艰苦的冷酷，怎么样压迫他，他童年时代心中所开的柔嫩的花仍然保存它洁净的美丽丝毫不损。他心中没有悲忧的痕迹，就是愁绪也一丝没有；他总是那样的安静，心中老永是喜悦的。

在圣彼得堡他好像住旷野一样，不计将来，差不多一个人也不认识。我带他去资乐力思开家里。他后来也常去。因为他不觉得自己为众人所注目，所以他的态度不忸怩，不过，在那里好像别的地方一样，他很少说话；但是他们都喜欢他。就是那讨厌的老人，大提安那·花新力夫那的丈夫，对他也有好感，那一对静默的少女同他也熟起来了。

有时候他到他们那里，在衣衫后袋里放一本新出版的书，好久不敢拿出来念，只斜伸着脖子像鸟一样，仿佛问，"可以吗？"最后他坐在一个房间角里（他总是爱坐角里）取出书来，开头细声地读，以后声音渐渐大起来，有时还加点短评和叹赏。我看出樊樊兰比她妹妹更愿意坐在旁边听，虽然她不大懂得；文学不是她的专长。她坐在潘新可夫对面，手托下颔，睇着他——不仅是看他的眼睛，是看他全面——一声不响，不过忽然大声长叹一下。在晚上有时我们玩"罚"戏，特别是礼拜和放假日玩的时候，我们还有二位资乐力思开的远亲，一对又矮又胖非常爱笑的姊妹，同几个陆军学校的学生，脾气和善举动安详的童子。潘新可夫常坐在大提安那·花新力夫那旁边，帮她决定赏罚的人要怎样受罚。

苏菲亚不爱常用的接吻这一类的罚法；樊樊兰当找东西或猜东西时候就出现烦恼的样子。那一对姑娘不停地笑——那仿佛是用魔术引出来的——我有时看着她们，心中觉得生气，可是潘新可夫微微一笑，摇摇头。老资乐力思开不加入我们的游戏，并且有些不赞成的样子，从他的书斋门口看我们。只有一回，完全出人意料，他来向我们提议，下一个无论谁受罚要同他作一次"旋转舞"；我们自然同意。刚好大提安那·花新力夫那受罚。她的脸全红了，忸怩地好像是一个十五岁的少女；但是她丈夫立刻叫苏菲亚按琴，自己走到他妻子的前面，同她跳二圈那旧式的三度旋转舞。我记得他那沉闷的含怒的脸孔同那没有开过笑眼的眼睛怎样地一出一没，当他舞的时候，他那严肃的形容没有一丝放松。他舞时是一个长步后一个短跳，他的妻子却跳得很快，把脸靠在他胸前，仿佛害怕的样子。他把她送到她本来坐的地方，鞠躬一下，依旧回他的书房去，关上门。苏菲亚正要站起，樊樊兰吩咐她再按下去，自己走向潘新可夫，伸出手，用一种难看的笑容问他："你高兴不高兴也来舞一下？"潘新可夫吓了一跳，但是他立刻站起——谁也知道他是最讲究礼节的——抱了樊樊兰的腰，不幸他头一步就摔倒，手离开了他的舞伴，一直滚到放鹦鹉的架子底下……架子倒了，鹦鹉惊叫起，"拿过手来！"众人大笑……资乐力思开站在书斋门口，含怒地看我们，又将门砰的一声关了。以后只要有人在樊樊兰面前提到这事，她立刻大笑，看着潘新可夫，好像想不出比他那回的行为更有趣的事了。

潘新可夫非常爱音乐。他常求苏菲亚弹小歌，坐在一边听着，有时遇着特别动情的地方他用微细的声音唱和。他特别喜欢舒伯尔（Schubert）的《星空》。他常说当他听见这调子的时候他总想像许多长的青苍色的光线随这声音从天上一直射到他身上来。就是现在每当我望着晚上无云的天空，众星闪动着，我总忆起舒伯尔的乐调同潘新可夫……我又记起我们一回郊外的旅行。我们全体雇二辆四轮车向派哥路服出发。车子是服拉的麦司基的：车身很旧，漆加蓝色，有圆的钢簧，坐位很大，里面塞着干草；那棕色的声嘶气促的一对马慢慢拉着我们，每匹都跛了一只脚，虽然所跛的脚不同。我们在派哥路服外边松林中蹓跶了好久，土瓶里盛着牛奶，喝了一回又吃了些糖浸野草莓。天气非常好。樊樊兰不爱走长路，通常很快就倦了；这次却赶得上我们。她脱去帽子，头发垂下，面上也不见了往常沉闷的样子，双颊发红。后来碰着两个农家的女孩，他忽然坐在地上，招呼她们，和气地叫她们坐在一边，苏菲亚隔不多远冷笑地看她们，也不走近她们。她和亚生诺夫走着。资乐力思基说樊樊兰是爱坐着的。樊樊兰站起走开了。她在散步的时候，她好几回对潘新可夫说道："耶可夫·伊凡里取我有话同你讲，"但是她要讲的是什么——始终没有说出来。

可是我现在应当回到我的故事去了。

我看见潘新可夫心中狠喜欢；但是一记起我前日干的事情，心中非常惭愧，我的脸又向壁上去了。过一会耶可夫问我身体有什么不好么。

"我很好，"我回答，从齿缝里；"不过有点头痛。"

耶可夫没有答话，拿起一本书。一点多钟过去了，我正要向耶可夫自招一切的时候……忽然我的平房门外的铃子响起来。

朝楼梯的门推开了……我仔细听……亚生诺夫问我的仆人我在家没有。

潘新可夫立起；他不愿意理亚生诺夫，低声同我说他要去我床上躺一躺，就入卧房里去了。

一秒钟后亚生诺夫进来了。

一看他红涨的脸，很快很冷的点头，我猜着他不是没有目的来的。我想，"发生什么事情呢？"

"先生，"他开口说，很快地坐在一张圆手椅上，"我来这里请你解释一件怀疑的事情。"

"什么事？"

"就是：我想知道你是不是个诚实的人。"

我发起怒来。"你讲的是什么意思？"我诘问。

"我告诉你那是什么意思，"他反答，沉重着声音，仿佛在每字底下都画个注意的线号一样。"昨天我拿个本子给你看，里面有一个人写给我的信……今天你就对那个人提起，而且还加以责难——加以责难，听着——信中的话，你没有一点这样的权力。我很想知道你对这事能够有什么解释？"

"我也很想知道你有什么权力可以这样盘诘我，"我答道，愤怒与惭愧使我全身战栗。"你要夸奖你的叔父，你的通信；同我毫不相关。你的信并没有丢，有没有？"

"信是没有丢；但是在我昨天的情形之下你很容易能——"

"总而言之,先生,"我故意尽我的力量大声说,"请你不要来扰我,听见没有?我不愿意听这样的事情,我也不预备给你什么解释。你可以去找那个人解释去!"我觉得我的头昏起来。

亚生诺夫看我一眼,他想在这一眼中表示出他看透一切与蔑视我的神气,捋着他的上髭,慢慢站起。

"我现在明白了,"他说道;"你的脸就是反对你自己的最好证明。我告诉你这不是体面人做的事情……狡猾地偷看旁人的信,再去窘苦一个体面的女子……"

"滚你的!"我嚷道顿脚,"找个决斗副助手来;我不同你讲话。"

"你还是不告诉我怎么办好,"他冷冷回答;"但是我一定找个副手来。"

他走了。我倒在沙发上,手掩着脸。有人把我的肩膀触一下;我拿开手——潘新可夫站在我面前。

"这什么?这是真的吗?"……他问我。"你看了旁人的信?"

我没有气力回答,我只点头承认。

潘新可夫走到窗边,背向着我说道:"你看了一个女子给亚生诺夫的信。这女子是谁?"

"苏菲亚·资乐力思基,"我答道,好像因犯当审判时向法官招口供一样。潘新可夫静了好一回〔会儿〕。

"没有旁的只有爱情可以在相当范围内原谅你,"末了他说。"你爱这小资乐力思基么?"

"是的。"

潘新可夫又静默一会。

"我早就看出了。你今天去责骂她了？……"

"是的，是的，是的！……"我绝望地说。"你现在可以蔑视我了……"

潘新可夫在房子里踱了两转。

"她爱他么？"他问。

"她爱他……"

潘新可夫眼睛朝下，呆看了好久地板。

"好，这事要弄好才对，"他讲，抬起头，"事情不能让它这样下去。"

他拿起帽子。

"那儿去？"

"亚生诺夫那里去。"

我从沙发上跳起来。

"可是我不许你去。天呵！你怎么能去！他将作怎样想？"

潘新可夫看我一下。

"怎样，你想这样错下去，使你名誉扫地，使那女子丢脸倒好些么？"

"但是你要同亚生诺夫说什么？"

"我想向他解释一番，我要对他讲你求他恕罪……"

"但是我不愿意向他谢罪！"

"你不愿意？为什么，不是你错了？"

我注视潘新可夫；那平静严肃，虽然悲愁的面容给我一种很深的印象；这是我从来未见过的。我不敢回答，坐在沙发上。

潘新可夫出去了。

我多么焦急等他回来！时间多么残忍不肯快点过去！最后他回来了——很迟。

"如何？"我懦怯地问。

"感谢上帝！"他回答；"事情全办妥了。"

"你到亚生诺夫那里去了？"

"是的。"

"唔，他怎么样？——小题大做，我想？"我用力才发出音来。

"不，我不能这样说。我本来猜度要利害些……他……他并不是你所想那样的粗人。"

"唔，你还看见别人没有？"过一回〔会儿〕我问他。

"我去过资乐力思基家。"

"啊！……"（我的心急跳。我不敢正视潘新可夫的脸孔。）"唔，她呢？"

"苏菲亚·力可利夫那是一个讲道理好心肠的女子……是的，她是个好心肠的女子。起先她觉得不好意思，后来也就自然了。不过我们谈话只有五分钟。"

"你……告诉了她一切……关于我的……一切？"

"我对她说了必要说的话。"

"我将来绝对不能再去看他们了！"我失望地说……

"为什么？不，偶然你也可以去。正相反，你必须去看他们，才不现出痕迹……"

"啊，耶可大你现在要看不起我了！"我哭着，制不住眼泪。

"我！看不起你？……（他温和的眼睛很亲爱地发光。）看不起你……傻子！我不是已经看见这事使你多么难过，怎么苦痛吗？"

他伸出手来；我倒在他颈上呜咽起来。

过了几天，在那几天内我看潘新可夫精神非常沉闷，我最后下决心到资乐力思基家去。当我踏进他们客厅的时候，我心里是什么感觉，这是不容易用字表达出来的；我记得我简直分不清楚房子里头的人，我的声音也不随我的意了。苏菲亚也一般的不自在；她明显地勉强招呼我，她的眼睛躲开我的眼睛，同我的眼睛躲开她的一样，她每下行动，全身都表现出抑制，还合着——何必隐瞒？心中的厌恶。我尽力免去她同我自己这种感觉。幸喜这次相会是我们的最后一次——在她结婚之前。我生活上一种忽然的变动把我领到俄罗斯的别一端去了，我对圣彼得堡，资乐力思基一家，同使我最感苦痛的，亲爱的耶可夫·潘新可夫告一个长久的别离。

二

七年过去了。我在这时期所遇到的事情，可以不必详述了。我在俄境内不停地搬来搬去，曾走过最僻远的旷野，谢谢上帝我到那地方！旷野并不像人们所猜想那么可怕。在最隐密的地方，深林中堕枝腐叶的底下常开着芬芳扑鼻的花卉。

一个春天因为公务路过东俄边省的一个小镇，从我坐车的窄小的窗中我看见店前公地上站着一个很面善的人。我仔细地看一看他，我认得他是爱利赛，潘新可夫的仆人，我非常欢喜。

我立刻叫车夫停住，跳下车来，走去会爱利赛。

"哙！朋友！"我开口，压住我的心中的激动，"你同你主人都在这里吗？"

"是的，同我主人在这里，"他慢慢地回答，随即突然高声叫出来：

"怎么，先生，是你？我不认得你了。"

"你同耶可夫·伊凡里取一起在这里吗？"

"是的，先生，自然同他一起……我还跟旁的谁呢？"

"快点带我去看他。"

"当然当然！这儿走，请，这儿走……我们就住在此地旅馆里。"

爱利赛引我穿过公地，不断地讲——"好，现在，耶可夫·伊凡里取要高兴了！"

这个人，加鲁马族的人，面貌可厌，有点野蛮人的样子，心地却最善良，绝不是个傻子，非常忠于潘新可夫，做他的仆人已有十年了。

"耶可夫健康不健康？"我问。

爱利赛把他的忧愁枯黄的脸朝我。

"啊，先生，他很不好……很不好，先生！你要认不得他了……他恐怕不能活多久了。所以我们才停在这里，不然我们已到奥底沙去了，那里他可以静养。"

"你们是从那里来的？"

"西伯利亚，先生。"

"西伯利亚？"

"是的，先生。耶可夫·伊凡里取有职务在那边。他也就是在那边受了伤。"

"你是讲他入军队做事去了么？"

"呵，不，先生。他是个文官。"

"多么奇怪的事！"我想。

那时我们已经到了旅馆，爱利赛跑去报告我来的消息。我们初别的几年潘新可夫同我常通信，但是四年前我接到最后的一封，以后就没有得他的信了。

"请上来，先生，"爱利赛从楼梯上大声向我讲；"耶可夫·伊凡里取要立刻看见您。"

我很快跑上摇动的楼梯，走进一间又暗又小的房子——我的心沉下去了……潘新可夫倒在一个窄的床上，盖着皮外衣，同死尸一样的无血色，他伸出一只瘦得不像手的手。我抢上去亲热地抱住他。

"耶叉！"我最后叫着；"你到底有什么毛病？"

"没有什么，"他用微弱的声音答；"我稍为弱一点。你是为什么事到这里来的？"

我坐在潘新可夫床边的椅上，握着他的手不放，看他的脸。我认出我所爱的那个面貌；那眼睛同微笑的样子还没有变；但是病使他成了多么憔悴！

他觉出我看见他后所生的印象了。

"我已经三天不刮脸了，"他说道，"真的我头也好久没有梳洗，不然……我决不会显得那么不成样子。"

"告诉我，耶叉，"我说；"爱利赛刚才告诉我的……你受了伤吗？"

"呵！是的，这是一段故事，"他答道。"我以后可以讲给你听。是的，我受伤了，你想是受的什么伤？——一支箭。"

"一支箭？"

"是的，一支箭；不是神话的爱神的箭，是一支韧性的木的真箭，有锐利的箭……这箭射到的时候，尤其当它刺入肺里的时候，那真是很难过的。"

"这箭怎么会来？……"

"我来说给你听这是怎样发生的。你知道我一生本多狠古怪的事情。你还记得我为得护照那种滑稽的通信吗？我也是奇离古怪地受伤的。你想想在我们这文明时代，有那个自尊的人肯让自己受箭伤呢？不是偶然地——注意——不是什么游戏，是打仗时候受的伤。"

"但是你还没有使我明白……"

"不错，等一会，"他截住我的话。"你知道你离圣彼得堡后不久我就到诺夫哥乐去了。我在诺夫哥乐住了好久，我要承想我在那里真住得不耐烦了，虽然我在那里也曾碰到一个人……"（他叹口气。）……"别提这些事罢；二年前我得了个好位置,虽然这位置在儿卡思开省,这有什么要紧,我父亲和我好像生卜来就注定要到西比利亚去的。西比利亚是一个好所在!富饶,肥沃——谁也是这样告诉你。我很爱那地方。那地方里的土著就在我的管理之下;他们是一群安静的人;可是我运气不好,其中有十二人——只有十二人——想着偷运起违禁物品来。我被派去捉他们,我捉住了他们,但是有一个,大概是神经错乱,为保他自己,向我发一箭……我几乎死了,但是终于复原了。现在我快要医好了……政府——愿上帝给他们健康!负担一切用费。"

潘新可夫将头倒在枕头上,没有力气再说了,颊上出现红色。他闭了眼睛。

"他不能多讲话。"爱利赛说,轻轻地说,他没有走出去。

静默了一回,除病人苦痛的呼吸外,一点声音也没有。

"但是在这里,"他继续讲,张开眼睛,"在这个小镇上我住了两个星期……我想我受了寒。本区医生医治我——你快看见他了;他仿佛还懂得他的行业。但是我非常高兴我受了寒,不然我们怎么能够遇着呢?"(他拉我的手。原先冰冷的手现在发烧地热着。)"告诉我一点关于你自己的事情,"他又讲,将盖在胸前的外套丢在一边。"我们两人已经好久没见面。"

我即刻照他的话,开始述我的事情,因此可以使他不能讲话。他起先很注意地听我,要喝水,渐渐把眼睛闭着,头在枕头上不停地翻来翻去。我劝他睡一会,说等他舒服的时候我再继续讲下去,我告诉他我打算住在他旁边的房里。"这里龌龊得很……"潘新可夫又开始讲,但是我止住他的口,轻轻地走出来了。爱利赛跟我出来。

"什么一回事,爱利赛?怎样,他快死了,是不是?"我问那忠心的仆人。

爱利赛仅仅用手做个样子,就走了。

我打发了车夫,赶快将我的行李移到隔壁房里。我去看潘新可夫是不是睡着。在门口我撞见一个身体笨拙,高大的肥人。他那肥胖的麻脸上只表现着懒惰——没有别的;他那细小的眼睛好像胶着,他的嘴唇很光,仿佛睡了才醒的样子。

"让我问句话,"我对他说,"你是大夫吗?"

那胖子看我一下,好像要用他的眉毛抬起那下垂的额部一般。

"是的,先生,"最后他回答我。

"劳驾,大夫先生,可以不可以,请,到我房子里来坐坐?耶可夫·伊凡里取,我想,现在是睡着罢。我是他的朋友,我很想同你谈一下他的病势,他的病使我很不安。"

"好罢,"大夫回答,他似乎的神气说,"干吗讲这么许多话?我总是来的,"他跟了我走。

"请告诉我,"我等他坐下立刻就说道,"我的朋友病势很重么?你以为怎么样?"

"是的,"那胖子安闲地答道。

"是……很重吗?"

"是,很重。"

"所以他也许……会死么?"

"他也许。"

我看着这胖子差不多要恨他了。

"天呀!"我说;"我们应当想法子,找个大夫来商议一下,或者怎样。你知道我们不能看着他……上帝呵慈悲点罢!"

"商议?——办得到;可以?办得到的。请伊凡·儿佛来米取……"

医生说话有些困难,老是叹气。他讲话的时候,他的肚子看得出鼓起来,好像每字都用力说的一样。

"谁是伊凡·儿佛来米取?"

"本区医生。"

"我们去省里首县请不是更好吗?你想怎么样?那里一定有好医生。"

"唔!这也可以。"

"那里最有名望的大夫是谁?"

"最好的?那里有一个哥那不斯大夫……不过我想他已搬到旁的地方去了。但是我以为现在没有去请大夫的必要了。"

"为什么没有请大夫的必要?"

"就是天字第一号的大夫对你的朋友也没有用。"

"怎么,他病得这么重么?"

"是的,他一天一天弱下去了。"

"他到底是那里的毛病?"

"他受了伤……肺受了影响……后来他又受了寒发烧起

来……诸如此类。他现在体内没有一点余蓄力了；你知道体内没有余蓄的人是不能活的。"

我们静了一会。

"试一下轻济医法（Homobopathy）如何？"胖子说，斜着眼睛瞧我。

"轻济医法？怎么，你不是个对症医生（Allopath）吗？"

"什么？你以为我不懂得轻济医法吗？我同别人一样地懂得！我们这里制药师用轻济医法医人，他们什么学位也没有？"

"呵，"我想，"这不见有希望。……""不，大夫，"我说，"你还是照你平常的法子医他好了。"

"随你意。"

胖子站起来，叹一口气。

"你是到那里去吧？"我问。

"是的，我要去看一看。"

他走了。

我不跟他去；看他在我可怜的病友床边是我所不能忍受的。我叫我的仆人，盼咐他坐车到省中首县去打听那里最好的医生是谁，将他立刻请来。过道上有点声音，我很快地打开门。

医生已由潘新可夫的房里出来了。

"怎么样？"我低声问他。

"没有什么。我开好了一张方子。"

"大夫，我已决意到首县请医生去了。我对你的技术亦是很信任的，可是你知道两个头脑比一个要好些。"

"好，这是很好的办法！"那个胖子回答，他下楼梯去了。他讨厌我，这是很明显的。

我去看潘新可夫。

"你看见过本地的亚斯加拉卑亚斯¹没有？"他问。

"看见了，"我回答。

"我喜欢他那极端的定心，"潘新可夫说道："医生应当冷冷的不动情才是，是不是？这样才使病人不怕。"

我自然不反对他的话。

到晚上出乎我意料之外潘新可夫好像好些了。他吩咐爱利赛把茶炉排好，说他要请我喝茶，自己也想喝一杯；他是显得高兴点了。我想法要使他不讲话，我看见他不能静默，便问他爱不爱我念些东西给他听。"同在温特弃缕尔一样——你记得吗？"他答道。"你念，我很高兴。我们念什么？看，我的书在窗子上。……"

我走到窗前，随手拿起一本书……

"什么书？"他问。

"娄蒙土夫（Lermontov）。"

"啊，娄蒙土夫！妙极！自然普施金（Pushkin）比他更伟大些……你记得：'在这完全安静中，风雨又在我们头上聚合起来。'……或者，'最后一回敢在思想中拥抱你甜蜜的形相。'妙极！妙极！但是娄蒙土夫也很好。好，我要告诉你怎么办，亲

---

1 Asclepius 希腊之神医，能起死回生。（译者注）

爱的孩子：拿起那本书，随便翻开，念你所看见的！"

我翻开那书，心中不高兴起来；我翻着《遗嘱》那一篇。我想把那页翻过去，但是潘新可夫看见我的动作，很快地说："不，不，不！念翻出来那一篇。"

没有办法，我念《遗嘱》。

遗　嘱

我很想，兄弟
单单同你在一块；
他们告诉我，在世上
我待不久了，
你也快回家了：
看……不！对于我的命运，
讲直话，没有个人
真切关心的。

但是若使有人问……
好罢，无论谁问，
告诉他穿过我的胸
我是给子弹射中了；
我很荣耀的为皇帝死，
我们的医生太不高明，
对我的故乡

我送个低微的问好。

我的父亲同母亲，
你大概找不到他们还在人间……
我承认我心中难过
要使他们为我伤心；
但是若使他们还活着，
你说我懒得写信，
说我们团队奉命出去，
他们不要盼望我回家。

还有一个女子，他们的邻居……
你记得我同她离别
已经很久了……她不会
问我的消息……一样地
你告诉她真的事情，
不要宽容她空空的心——
让她哭一哭也好……
这不会使她过于伤心。

"好诗！"我念完了最后一首诗，潘新可夫说。"好诗！可是这很奇怪，"他停了一会之后加说道，"这是很奇怪你恰巧碰着这一首……奇怪。"

我开始念别的诗，但是潘新可夫不听我；他看着别处，两回反覆说"奇怪！"

我让那书落在膝上。

"还有一个女子，他们的邻居，"他低声说着，转过头问我——"我说，你记得苏菲亚·资乐力思开吧？"

我脸红了。

"我想我记得！"

"我猜她已嫁人了？……"

"嫁给亚生诺夫好久了。我曾写信告诉过你。"

"不错，你告诉过我了。后来他父亲宽恕她没有？"

"他宽恕了她；但是他不肯见亚生诺夫。"

"固执的老头儿！他们快乐不？"

"我不知道……我想他们是快乐的。他们——在乡下住。我老没有看见他们，虽然会从他们住的地方经过。"

"他们有孩子没有？"

"我想是有的……说起，潘新可夫……"我怀疑地问。

他看我一眼。

"老实说——你记得吗，你那时候不愿意答我——你有没有告诉她我爱她？"

"我告诉了她一切，……我从来是不对她扯谎的。对她作假是件大罪。"

潘新可夫停了一会不讲。

"来，告诉我，"他又讲："你不久就不想她了是不是？"

"不是很久，但是以后就不想了。无益的叹息有什么意思呢？"

潘新可夫转过头来，脸向着我。

"唔，兄弟，"他说——他嘴唇战动着——"这地方我还赶不上你，我到现在还是思念她。"

"什么！"我描写不出地惊慌地叫着；"你也爱她么？"

"我爱她，"潘新可夫慢慢地说，他将双手放在头后面。"我怎样爱她只有上帝知道罢。我没有对谁说过，我也不想对……但现在他们告诉我，在世上我待不久了。……这有什么要紧的？"

潘新可夫出乎意料之外的自由〔白〕使我很吃惊，我简直说不出话来。我只能诧异，"这是可能的么？怎么我没有疑心到？"

"是的，"他继续下去，好像对自己讲话，"我爱她。就是我知道她的心是爱亚生诺夫之后，我还是爱她。但是，我知道这事使我多么苦痛！若使她爱你，我最少还能为你欣喜；但是亚生诺夫……他怎么能使她爱他的？这不过是他的运气！她不能够反复她的感情，不能中途不爱他！一个真的心是不能变的……"

我回忆起了在那不幸的大餐后潘新可夫的来访与潘新可夫的从中斡旋，我不能自主地骇怪得舞起手来。

"那你还是从我这里听去的，可怜的人！"我喊道；"你还去见她！"

"是的，"潘新可夫又说，"这次的对她解释……我终身不能忘。在那时候我发现了那个字,我才了解从前我替我自己选定的那个字的意义:'默忍'。但是她还是我的梦里人,我的理想……活在世上的没有理想的人是可怜的。"

我看潘新可夫;他的眼睛好像注视着远处,微热似地发光。

"我爱她,"他联着讲,"我爱她,她,安详,真挚,没有错处,不能染坏;当她走的时候,我差不多苦疯了……从那时候起,我没有关心过旁人……"

忽然转过去他脸压在枕上呜咽起来。

我跳起来,弯着身向他,想设法去安慰他……

"这不碍事,"他说道,抬起头来,将头发摇到后面去;"没有什么;我心中有点难过有点忧愁……为我自己,这是……但是这都不碍事。这都是那诗引出来的。念点别篇快乐点的给我听罢。"

我拿起娄蒙土夫集,急忙地翻;但是仿佛运命预定了,我总碰些要扰动潘新可夫的心的诗歌。最后我念《提无烈的礼物》。

"悦耳的修辞!"我那可怜的朋友用教师的口吻讲;"但是也有好句子。兄弟,我们别后,我曾试做一首诗——《生命之杯》——但是没有做完!兄弟,我们是宜于欣赏而不宜于创造的……我有点疲倦,想睡一下——你以为怎样?睡觉是多么美丽的东西,想一想!我们一生是一个梦,我们一生中最好的东西也就是梦。"

"还有诗?"我问。

"诗也是梦,不过是天国的梦就是了。"

潘新可夫闭了眼睛。

我在床边站了一会。我想他不能就睡去,但是不久他的呼吸便渐渐齐匀而且迟缓了。我用足尖走出,到我房里,躺在沙发上。好久我细想着潘新可夫告诉我的事,说起好多事情,心中诧异;最后我也睡了。

有人动我一下;我跳起来;爱利赛站在我面前。

"到我主人那里去,"他说。

我立刻立起来。

"他怎么样?"

"他说谵语。"

"谵语?他从前有过没有?"

"有过,他昨晚也曾说谵语;不过今天有点吓人。"

我走到潘新可夫房里。他不是卧着,坐在床上,全身俯向前。他慢慢地做手势,笑着,谈着,用一种微弱空虚的声音讲话,好似芦苇的飒飒声。他眼中现着惊愕。那放在地板上的灯光被书遮着,射在天花板上成一块不动的黑阴;潘新可夫的脸色在这半黑中现〔显〕得更苍白了。

我走到他面前,叫他的名字——他不答应。我细听他的微语:他在讲西伯利亚,同那里的树林。有时他的谵语是有点意思的。

"多大的树啊!"他低语道;"直矗青天。上面多厚的霜!银白色……雪堆……这儿有小小足迹……这是一只兔儿一跳,这是白鼬鼠……不，这是我父亲带着我的证明书跑来了。他在这里！……他在这里！一定要去；月亮亮晶晶的照着。一定要去，找我的证明书……啊！一朵花，一朵红花——那里是苏菲亚……呵，钟鸣了，霜宪了地响了……啊，不；那是个傻大莺在灌木上跃着，低声叫……看，那群红颈鸟！冷……啊！这里是亚生诺夫……呵是的，自然，他是个炮，一个铜炮，他的炮车是绿色的。这是他所以能被人爱的道理。那是一个星堕下来的吗？不是，是一只射出来的箭……啊，多么快，一直穿入我的心……谁射的？是你，苏菲亚？"

他低下头，含糊地讲些不相连续的话。我看了爱利赛一眼；他站着，两手钩在颈后面，很悲哀地看着他的主人。

"啊！兄弟，所以你也变了成个注重实际的人了？"他忽然问，向我很清楚的有意识的一望，我不禁一惊，正要答应，但是他又继续讲："但是我还没变做注重实际的人，我还没有，我生来是个做梦者，一个做梦者！做梦，做梦。……梦什么？苏霸开亦取的亦夫——那是做梦。吓！……"

差不多一直到早上潘新可夫谵语不绝；后来他渐渐安静了，倒在枕上，睡了。我回我的房。我很难过地熬了一夜，精神衰颓，便很熟地睡去了。

爱利赛又把我叫醒。

"啊，先生；"他颤音地说，"我相信耶可夫·伊凡里取快死了……"

我跑到潘新可夫的房里。他卧着不动，在快天亮的光线底下他好似一具死尸。他认得我。

"再会,"他低声讲:"为我问她好,我快死,……"

"耶叉!"我叫;"瞎说!你会活的……"

"不,不!我快死了……这里,拿这个去做一件纪念物罢,"……(他指他的胸部。)……

"这是什么?"他忽然又说:"看:海……一片金黄色,上面有蓝色的小岛,大理石的庙,棕树,香……"

他不讲了……身子伸直了……

半点钟后他就死了。爱利赛倒在他的脚下哭。我把他的眼睛捻合了。

在他颈上有一个黑绳系的小丝袋。我把它收起。

过了三天他葬了……世上最高尚的心又一个永埋在墓中了。我最先抛一掬土在他上面。

三

一年半过去了,我又因事到莫思科。我住在一个好旅馆中。一天我在廊上走过,看见旅客名单的黑板,我惊愕得差不多叫出来了。同十二号相对用白垩明明白白的写着苏菲亚·力可利夫那·亚生诺夫的名字。近来我有时听见许多关于她丈夫的坏话。我听说他爱喝酒,赌钱,倾家荡产,一切行为都不对。谈到他的妻子人家都很尊敬……我心中很激动地回到房里。那早已经冷了的感情好似在我心中又动起来了,我的心也跳着。我决心去见苏菲亚·力可利夫那。"我们别离到现在已经好久了,"

我想,"她大概已经忘记从前我们之间的事情了。"

我打发爱利赛(潘新可夫死后我就收他做了仆人)拿我的名片到她的门口,叫他问她在家不在家,我可不可以会她。爱利赛很快回来说苏菲亚·力可利夫那在家,愿意会我。

我立刻去见苏菲亚·力可利夫那。当我进去的时候,她正站在房子中间同一个身体高壮的先生道别。

"随你的意,"他用洪亮老练的音声说;"他不是个没有害的人,他是个无用的人;在一个有秩序的社会里凡是没有用的人都是有害的,有害的,有害的。"

讲了这几句话,这位身材很高的先生走了。苏菲亚转过脸来对着我。

"我们别后已经很久了!"她讲。"请坐……"

我们坐下。我看着她。……相隔了好久又看见那曾经亲近过,或者爱过的面貌;认得它又好似不认得,仿佛在那旧的忘不了的脸孔上,有一个新的同旧的相像但又很新奇的样子,几乎不自觉地立刻看出岁月所留的痕迹;——这些思想都使人愁闷。"我一定也是同样地改变了,"各人心中想着……

苏菲亚·尼可利夫那并没有老了许多;虽然我最后一回看她的时候她才十六岁;这是九年前的事了。她面貌更端正严肃了;同从前一样它表现出情感的真挚和意志的坚强;可是从前的安详神态却换了一付隐隐看得出的秘密的悲痛和燥忧的表情。她的眼睛更深更黑了。她有点像她的母亲了……

苏菲亚·尼可利夫那先开口。

"我们两人都变了，"她讲。"你一向在那儿？"

"我是个滚动的石头，"我答。"你都在乡下住吗？"

"大部分我在乡下住。我不过暂时在这里。"

"你父母都好吗？"

"我母亲死了，但是我父亲还在圣彼得堡；我兄弟有职务，樊樊兰和他同住着。"

"你丈夫呢？"

"我丈夫，"她较快点说——"他现在在南俄罗斯赶马市去了。你知道他是最爱马的，他现在办牧马厂……所以……他现在买马去了。"

这时候一个八岁小女孩走进房来，头发结成辫子，面貌伶俐活泼，还有一对灰色眼睛。她看见我退了一步，忽忽地行过礼，就到苏菲亚·力可利夫那的身边。

"这是我的女儿；让我介绍她给你。"苏菲亚·力可利夫那说，把一个手指放在小女孩圆满的下额上；"她不肯在家里——要我带她来。"

那小女孩很快地把我看了一眼，又把眼皮低下了。

"她是个好小女孩，"苏菲亚继续地说："她什么东西都不怕。她念书也很好；我应当要这样讲她。"

"这位先生什么名字？"（原文法文）那小女孩低声地弯着身对她母亲说。苏菲亚·力可利夫那说了我的名字。那小女孩又看了我一眼。

"你叫什么名字？"我问她。

"我叫做梨笛亚,"那小女孩回答,勇敢地看着我。

"我想他们纵容歹你了,"我说。

"谁纵容歹了我?"

"谁?我想谁也是;你的父母,说起来,便是为首的。"

(小孩不讲话,瞧她的母亲。)"我想君士坦丁·亚力山都乐取,"我继续说……

"是的,是的,"苏菲亚·力可利夫那插嘴说,她的女儿眼睛钉〔盯〕着她;"我丈夫,自然——他非常爱小孩。"

黎笛亚伶俐的小脸上现出一种怪相,嘴唇稍呶出来;她低下头。

"告诉我,"苏菲亚·力可利夫那很快的说;"你是有事情到这儿来的吧,我想?"

"是的,我是有事情到这儿来的……你也是这样吗?"

"是的……在我丈夫走了的时候,你知道,我得照应一切事情。"

"妈妈!"梨笛亚开始讲。

"什么,我的乖乖?"

"没有——什么……我以后告诉你罢。"

苏菲亚·力可利夫那微笑,耸了耸肩。

"请告诉我,"苏菲亚·力可利夫那又讲;"你记得吗,你有一个朋友……他叫什么?他的脸色和气得很……他总是念诗;那么热狂的——"

"不是潘新可夫吗?"

"是，是了，潘新可夫他现在在那里？"

"他死了。"

"死了？"苏菲亚·力可利夫那问；"多么可怜！……"

"我看见过他没有？"小女孩低声快地问。

"没有，梨笛亚，你没有见过他。——多么可怜！"苏菲亚·力可利夫那反覆说。

"你可惜他……"我说，"若使你知道他像我知道他一样，还不知要怎样呢？但是，……你为什么问起他，我可不可以问？"

"呵，我也不知道……"（苏菲亚·力可利夫那垂下眼睛。）"梨笛亚，"她说，"找你的保姆去。"

"我可以回来的时候你叫我吗？"

"好罢。"

小女孩走了。苏菲亚·力可利夫那转过脸对我。

"你所知道关于潘新可夫的事都请告诉我。"

我就将他的事情告诉她。我用简单的话叙述我的朋友的一生；尽我的能力想说明他的心；详述我们最后的相会和他的临终情形。

"这样一个人，"我喊着，我说完故事之后——"离了我们去了，谁也没有注意他，他的好处差不多谁也没有了解！但是这不是大损失。人们的了解又有什么用呢？可是使我痛心的使我难过的便是，这样一个人有如此挚爱诚恳的心，终于至死不曾尝过受人报以爱情，是怎样的快乐，没有引起一个配得上他的女人对他发生一点意思！……像我这样的人可以不知道这种幸福；我们不应当得这幸福；但是潘新可夫！……然而一生中我不是碰着成千成万在那一方面都比不上他的人却常被人爱着吗？我们真要相信人的缺点——譬如骄傲或者轻浮是得女人的欢心所必需的？或者爱情怕完满，世间所能的完满，仿佛完满是一种奇怪可惊的东西？"

苏菲亚·力可利夫那听我一直说到底，没有移开那对着我的一付严肃穷究的眼睛，嘴唇也不动；不过有时皱起眉头来。

"你为什么相信没有女子爱过你的朋友？"她静默了一会之后说。

"因为我知道事实是这样。"

苏菲亚·力可利夫那好似要讲什么话，又止住了。她仿佛在同她自己的内心争斗一样。

"你错了，"她最后说；"我知道有一个女人曾经热烈地爱过你这已死的朋友；她爱他，直到现在还纪念他……他的死信将对她是个大打击。"

"谁是这个女人？我可以知道吗？"

"我的姊姊，樊樊兰。"

"樊樊兰·力可利夫那！"我惊奇地喊道。

"是的。"

"什么？樊樊兰·力可利夫那？"我重复地说，"那个……"

"我可以替你说，"苏菲亚·力可利夫那继续我的话；"那个女子，我以为是冰冷不动情的，她却爱了你的朋友；这是她不嫁和不会嫁的原因。到现在除我而外没有人知道；樊樊兰宁可死不肯吐露她的秘密。我们家里的人都是知道怎样暗地忍痛的。"

我很长久很注意地看苏菲亚·力可利夫那，自然想到她后面那句话的苦味。

"你真使我惊愕，"我最后说道。"但是你知道吗，苏菲亚·力可利夫那，若使我不怕提起令人不快的旧事，我也能够使你惊愕……"

"我不懂你的意思，"她慢慢地说，有点莫名其妙的样子。

"你自然不懂我的意思，"我说，急忙地站起；"让我送些东西给你看，替我口头解释……"

"什么东西？"

"不要怕，苏菲亚·力可利夫那，那是同我不相关的。"

我鞠躬一下，回到我房里，拿出潘新可夫身上取下的小丝袋，送给苏菲亚·力可利夫那，附上一封信——

"这是我的朋友常佩在胸前的，到他死时还在身上。里头存在着你写给他唯一的短札，内容很不要紧；你自己看罢。他佩它因为他热烈地爱你；他只在死前一天对我承认，现在他死了，为什么你不可以知道他的心也是你的？"

爱利赛很快仍将那遗物回来就带了。

"唔？"我问；"她告诉你什么话没有？"

"没有。"

我静默了一会。

"她看我的信没有？"

"她一定看了；那女仆拿给她看的。"

"没有错，"我想，记起潘新可夫临死的话。"好罢，你可以走了，"我大声地讲。

爱利赛奇怪的笑着不走。

"这里有一个女子……"他说，"要见你。"

"谁？"

爱利赛迟疑了一会。

"我主人没有告诉过你？"

"没有……什么？"

"当我主人在诺夫哥禾的时候，"他继续讲，手指门口，"他认得这个女子。现在这女子要来见你。有一天在街上我碰着她。我同她说，'来，若使我主人肯，我可以带你去见他。'"

"请她进来，请她进来，自然。但是……她是什么样子？"

"一个普通女子……工人阶级……俄国人。"

"耶可夫·潘新可夫喜欢她么？"

"是的……他爱她。她……当她听见我主人死的消息，她伤心极了。她是个好女子。"

"请她进来，请她进来。"

爱利赛出去，立刻回来。他背后跟着一个女子，穿着有条纹的棉布外衣，一方深色的头帕半遮着她的脸孔。她看见我很羞怯地转过头去。

"什么事？"爱利赛向她讲；"走上去，不要怕。"

我走前一步，拉她的手。

"你叫做什么？"我问她。

"马叉，"她柔声地答应我，偷看我一眼。

她看去有二十二三岁的样子；有一个圆圆的，坦白的，可爱的脸孔，柔软的双颊，温和蓝色的眼睛同很好看的平静的小手。她的衣衫也非常干净。

"你认得耶可夫·潘新可夫吗？"我接着问。

"我同他很熟，"她讲，拉下她的头帕，眼泪已在眼眶里了。我请她坐下。

她随即坐在一只椅子的边上，也没有什么虚文与客气。爱利赛走出去。

"你是在诺夫哥乐认得他的么？"

"是的，在诺夫哥乐，"她答道，双手在头帕下紧握着。"我前天才由爱利赛·提摸非取听到他死的消息。耶可夫·伊凡里取，当他去西比利亚的时候，应允写信给我，只写了两封，以后就没有了。我要跟他到西比利亚去，可是他不喜欢这样办。"

"有你亲人在诺夫哥乐么？"

"有。"

"你同他们在一块吗？"

"我从前常同母亲和我已经出嫁的姐姐同住；但是以后我母亲常恼我，我的姐姐家中又太挤，她有一大群小孩子：所以我搬了。我的希望就在耶可夫·伊凡里取身上，不想旁的，他对我也非常好——你可以问爱利赛·提摸非取。"

马叉停一下。

"我有他的信,"她往下讲。"看这里。"她从她口袋里拿出几封信,交给我。"你看罢,"她补说。

我打开信,认得潘新可夫的笔迹。

"亲爱的马叉!"(他用大而且清楚的字写着)"昨天你将你的头靠着我的,我问你做什么,你说——'我想听听你在想什么。'我现在要把我想的什么告诉你,我想若使马叉能够学会认字写信那是多么好!她就能知道我这信……"

马叉望了我一眼。

"这是在诺夫哥乐写给我的,"她讲,"他正要教我念书的时候。看别的信罢。这里有一封从西比利亚寄来的。这里念这封罢。"

我读信。信都是很亲爱,很深情的。在一封从西比利亚寄来的第一封信里潘新可夫称马叉做他最好的朋友,应承寄钱给她做盘费到西比利亚去,结尾有着几句话——"我吻你那美丽的小手;这里的女子没有你那样的手;她们的头也及不上你的,她们的心亦不及……好好念我给你的那些书,常常想我,我也不会忘记你的。你是个唯一关心我的女子;所以我也只是属于你的……"

"我看他对你很有情,"我一面还她的信,说道。

"他很爱我,"马叉回答,把信好好地收入袋里,眼泪慢慢地顺着她的颊边流下。"我总是相信他;若使上帝给他长命,他决不会抛弃我。愿上帝给他天上的安乐!"……

她用绢角一擦眼睛。

"你现在住在那里?"我问。

"我现在住在莫思科;我是同我的女主人同来的,但是我现在没有了地方。我找过耶可夫·伊凡里取的姨妈,可是她自己也很穷,耶可夫·伊凡里取常谈到你,"她补说道,站起来点头;"他常是爱你思量你。我前天碰着爱利赛·提摸非取,我不知道你肯不肯帮助我,因为我现在没有职业……"

"这是我最愿意的,马利亚……让我替你问问罢,你父亲姓什么?"

"彼士乐夫那,"她答着,垂下眼睛。

"我总尽力帮你忙,马利亚·彼士乐夫那,"我继续说;"可惜我在这儿也是客,认识不多体面的人家。"

马羲叹了一口气。

"若使我能够得个职业……我不能裁,却能缝,所以我常是缝点东西……我还能够看顾小孩子。"

"给她钱罢,"我想:"可是如何给法呢?"

"听,马利亚·彼士乐夫那,"我讲,免不了一点踌躇;"请你宽恕我,但你在潘新可夫处当知道我是他怎样的一个朋友……你可不可以让我送你——为目前用——一点钱?"……

马沙看我一下。

"什么?"她问。

"你是不是没有钱用?"我说。

马沙全脸飞红,垂下头来。

"我干嘛要钱?"她轻轻地讲;"你还是替我找个位置好。"

"我可以想法替你找位置,但是我不能担保成功;你不要迟疑,真的……你知道我同你不是陌生人……接了我这个吧,做我们友谊的一点纪念……"

我转过头,很快的由小簿里拿出几张钞票,交给她。

马沙站着不动,她的头垂下来。

"拿着罢,"我坚持地说。

她慢慢的抬起眼睛来,悲惨的直视着我,慢慢的将她那灰白的手由头帕下,向我伸出。

我将钞票放在她那冰冷的手上。她一句话不讲又将她的手放在头帕下面,眼睛又垂下了。

"以后,马利亚·彼士乐夫那,"我又说,"你若缺少什么东西,请你直接向我讲。我来将我的住址给你。"

"我十分谢谢你,"她讲,停了一会她又说:"他会同你讲到我没有?"

"我只在他死的前一天碰到他的,马利亚·彼士乐夫那。但是我也不敢说定……我相信他曾讲过一点关于你的事情。"

马叉用手摸了头发,轻轻按着她的脸颊,想了一会,说,"再会,"就走出了房去。

我坐在桌旁,起了好多愁思,这个马叉,她同潘新可夫的关系,他的信,苏菲亚·力可利夫那的姐姐对他的秘密的爱情……"可怜的人!可怜的人!"我颤声说。我想起潘新可夫的一生,他的童年时代,他的青年时代,费得利小姐……"好,"

我想,"你遭了这些运命!你却有很多快乐!"

第二天我又去看苏菲亚·力可利夫那。我在前室等好久,当我进去的时候,梨笛亚已坐在她母亲的身旁了。我明白苏菲亚·力可利夫那不爱再提起昨天的谈话。

我们开始谈天——我记不起谈的是什么——无非谈些城里的新闻,公众的事情……梨笛亚常插进她的小话,乖巧地望着我。在她那活动的小脸孔上忽然有一种像煞有介事的神情……这聪明的小女孩一定是猜中了她母亲特意使她留在她身旁的。

我起身告别。苏菲亚·力可利夫那引我到门口。

"我昨天没有回信,"她站在门口说;"真的!我怎么能答你?我们的生活不是我们能够做主的;我们都有个锚,谁若是不用他的意志是不能离开这个锚的——这锚就是我们的义务观念。"

我一句话也没有讲,只点头表示赞成,就离开了这年轻的清教徒。

我整晚都留在房里,但是我并不想她;我不停地想我亲爱的忘不了的潘新可夫——最后的一个理想主义者;那悲惨仁慈的感情带着甜甜的苦味穿入我的心,在我这还未全老的心弦上引起回声来……不讲实际的心地单纯的理想主义者,愿上帝给你的余骸以安宁!希望上帝给一切重实际的人——这种人对你是不能了解的,他们现在或者还笑在墓中的你哩——望上帝给他们百分之一那种纯净快乐的经验,虽然命运同人们对你很不好,这种纯净快乐是你那可怜的平淡无奇的一生中却充满着的。

(一八五五作)

The Red Flower
红　　花
（英汉对照）

V. M. Garshin　著

梁遇春　译注

"英文小丛书"之一，上海北新书局，1930年9月付排，1930年10月初版

Vsevolod Mikhaylovich Garshin
（1855—1888）

他的著作完全是短篇小说，情绪紧张，使人们读起来会色变。至于能够真挚地描写出素朴的人生，这是他和俄国一切大文豪共有的本领。在俄土战争时候，他当一名志愿兵，他有好几篇小说都是叙述他在前线的经验。晚年他染上疯疾，这篇小说大概带了自传的色彩。

这篇小说里的疯子可说是一个舍身的理想主义者，为着拯救人类，自愿走上毁灭之途的人，也就是替人类背十字架的好汉。这种脚色本来被世上聪明的人们当做疯子看待，因为他的行为是那班专顾私人利害，自命清醒的人们所无法了解的。Garshin在这篇小说前面有"为纪念屠格涅夫而作"几个字，也许他觉得屠格涅夫也是这么一个疯子罢。他和许多俄国文学家一样自杀死了，不知道他有没有带什么战利品到坟墓里去！

The Red Flower

I

"In the name of[1] His Imperial Majesty[2] the Emperor Peter the First, I order an inspection of this madhouse!"

These words were uttered in a loud, sharp, resonant voice. The clerk of the hospital, who was registering the new patient in a large, ragged book on an inkstained table, could not retrain a smile. But the two young men who had accompanied the patient did not smile. They could scarcely stand on their legs after two days and two nights passed, without sleep, alone with the madman whom they had

---

1　in the name of：name 作"名义"解。所以 in the name of 是"以某人的名义",也就"代表某人"（as representing）的意思。若使意译起来,可译做"奉某人的命"。

红　花

一

"用当今皇上彼得第一的名义,我要视察这所疯人院。"

这几个字是用一种洪亮的,尖利的,同响彻的声调说出。医院的书记正把这个新病人登记到沾着墨水的桌上的一大本破旧的簿子里,听着不禁微笑一下。但是和这个病人一道来的那两个年青的人们并不笑。他们几乎站不稳他们的脚,因为已经有两天两晚没有睡觉地独自守着这个疯人了;他们坐火车刚才把他带到医院来。离目的地还有两站远的地方,那疯疾变得更

2　His Imperial Majesty:对于皇帝的尊称。

just brought by train to the hospital. At the last station but one[1] the fit of madness had become worse; they had mananged to obtain a strait-jacket[2], and with the aid of the guard and a gendarme, had put it on[3] the patient. In this way[4] they had been able to bring him to the town and the hospital.

He looked terrible. Over his grey suit, which he had torn into tatters[5] in his fits of madness, was a coarse sail-cloth jacket, with a wide opening at the neck, fitting close to his figure: the long sleeves pressed his arms crosswise to his breast and were tied at the back. His bloodshot eyes stared wildly (he had not slept for more than forty-eight hours) and shone with a restless, fiery brightness; a nervous movement twitched his lower lip; his matted curly hair fell on his forehead like a mane; with rapid heavy steps he paced from one corner of the office to the other, examining with curiosity the old cupboards full of papers and the oilcloth-covered chairs, and now and then[6] glancing at his travelling companions.

"Take him into the ward on the right."

"I know, I know! I was here with you before, a year ago. We

---

1 the last but one: 末了第二。
2 strait-jacket: 一种材料坚固的紧身短衣，专用于拘束蛮野的疯人。
3 to put it on: to clothe the person with it 使某人穿这件衣服。
4 in this way: thus 若是；这样子。
5 tatters: 破布，这字常用复数，因为既是烂碎的布，当然不是整块厉害了;他们设法找到一件拘束疯人的紧身短衣,靠着车里警备队和一个宪兵的帮助,使这病人穿上那件衣服。这样子,他们办到将他带到城里医院。

他脸上现出可怕的神气。他穿着一套灰色的衣服,当疯病发作时已经扯得褴褛不堪了,外面盖上一件粗帆布的短衣,颈项上开一个大口,紧紧地贴着他身上;短衣的长袖将他的双手交叉地压在他胸前,袖子就在他背后打一个结。他那充血的眼睛激昂地凝视着(他已经有四十八个多钟头没有睡觉了),射出不安的,凶猛的光辉;一种神经衰弱的筋肉跳动老是拉扯他的下唇;他那纠结的,波纹般的头发像鬃毛一样遮盖他的前额;他的脚步急促而沉重,他从办公室的一个角落到另一角落踏来踏去,好奇地观察满着纸张的旧柜子,油布罩着的椅子,有时瞧一下他的旅伴。

"送他到右边的病室去。"

"我知道,我知道!去年,我曾经到这里过,同你们一起。

的,已经化成无数碎片了。

6　now and then: at intervals 间或;时常。

went over the hospital. I know all about it, and it will be difficult to deceive me, " said the patient.

He turned to the door, which the warder opened for him. With the same rapid, heavy, and resolute step, lifting his insane head high, he went out of the office and almost running turned to the right into the insanity ward. Those who accompanied him could hardly keep pace with[1] him.

"Ring! I cannot—you have tied my arms."

The hall-porter opened the door and the travellers entered the hospital.

The house was an old brick, building constructed like all old-fashioned government offices. Two large rooms, one the dining-room and the other the common living-room[2] for the quieter patients, a broad passage with a glass door at the end that looked out[3] on a flower garden, and about twenty bedrooms, occupied the ground-floor. There were two other rooms: one with padded walls and the other only boarded, in which the violent patients could be confined, and likewise a huge, vaulted, half-dark room which served as a bathroom. The upper story was occupied by the women. From it came a confused noise broken by howls and lamentations. The hospi-

---

1 to keep pace with: to go at equal speed with 同速度前进。
2 living-room: sitting room 居室，起坐室，是人们白天休息的地方。
3 to look out: to have a view; afford a view 可以望见。

我们那时走遍全医院。我全知道里面的一切情形,想骗我是不容易的。"病人说道。

他转过身来向着门,那扇门看守者替他开了。用同样急促,沉重同坚决的脚步,高抬着他那疯狂的头,他走出办公室,差不多是快跑,转进疯人院的右边。跟着他走的人们几乎赶不上他。

"按门铃!我不能按——你们已经把我的两臂捆起了。"

内院看门的人开了大门,这几个旅客就走进医院。

那屋子是一座旧的砖屋,建筑得像一切老式的衙门。底下那一层一共有两间大房子,一间是食堂,一间是给比较安静的病人们住的公共房子,一条宽阔的走道,道口有一扇玻璃门,正望着一所花园,走道的两旁有二十间左右的寝室。此外还有两间房子:一间的墙壁里装填有软的东西,一间房里的四壁只镶了木板,凶猛的病人可以闭在里面,还有一间高大的,拱形圆顶,半黑暗的房子,那是当作浴室用的。上层是疯女人们所住。从那里来了嘈杂的吵闹声音,有时被哀号和悲啼所打断。

tal had been built for eighty patients, but as it was the only one in that part of the country and was used by several neighbouring provinces, there were often as many as three hundred patients confined in it. In each of the small rooms there were from four to five beds. In winter when the patients were not allowed to go into the garden, and the iron-barred windows were kept closed, the air became unbearably suffocating.

The new patient was taken into the bathroom. The impression which this room produced even on a healthy person was depressing, and it acted even worse on[1] a deranged and excited imagination. It was a vast, vaulted room with a slippery stone floor, lighted but dimly by a single window in the far corner. The walls and vaults were painted dark red. Two stone baths, which looked like two oval holes filled with water, were on a level with[2] the black and dirty floor. The large copper stove with a cylindrical boiler, that served to heat the water, and a whole system of copper pipes and taps, occupied the corner oppsite the window. All this had a strangely fantastic and gloomy effect on a disordered mind, and the man who had charge of the bathroom, a stout, silent Little Russian[3], only added to this impression by his sombre visage.

---

1 to act on: to exert influence 影响；感动。
2 on a level with: at same height 在同一平面上。
3 Little Russia: 是乌克兰 Ukraine，波兰的东南部同捷克斯拉夫这所医院盖时只预备给八十个病人住，但是因为它是这带地方唯一的疯人院，邻近好几省也都用它，所以常常有不下三百个病人关在它里面。每个小房间安有四五架床铺。冬天时候，当病人们不许到花园去；铁窗又紧紧地闭着，那里面的空气变得不能忍受地闷人。

新病人被引到浴室里面去。就说是一个健康的人，这间房子在他身上所生的印象也是抑郁的；对于一个错乱的同奋激的心灵，它的影响甚至于更坏。那是一间广大，有拱形圆顶的房子，铺着滑脚的石板，只从远远角落的一只窗口得到些朦胧的光线。墙壁和拱形圆顶是涂上深红的颜色。二个石澡盆，看起来好像满着水的两个椭圆形的洼处，是和龌龊的黑石板居于同一平面上。那个大铜火炉同圆柱状的汽锅，那是烧水用的，和整套铜管同龙头占住窗口正对面的那个角落。这一切布置对于一个神经错乱的人会生出一种奇怪地荒诞的同愁闷的印象；管浴室的人，一个强壮的，缄默的小俄罗斯人，他那惨淡的脸孔只是增浓了这个印象。

Czechoslovakia 的东部那一带地方的别名。

When the patient was brought into this room to be given a bath and, according to the invariable system of the chief doctor, to have a blister applied to the nape of his neck, he became terrified and grew violent. Absurd thoughts, each more monstrous than the other, crowded into his brain. What was this? The Inquisition[1]? The place of secret execution, where his enemies had decided to do away with[2] him? Perhaps even Hell? At last the idea entered his mind that it was a place of torture. He was undressed, despite all his resistance. His malady doubling his strength he was easily able to tear himself out of the grasp of several keepers, so that they fell on the floor. At last four of them threw him down, and each taking him by a leg or an arm plunged him in the warm water. It appeared to him to be boiling, and all sorts of disconnected, broken thoughts of tortures by boiling water and red-hot irons passed through his disordered brain. Choking with the water he swallowed, and convulsively jerking his legs and arms by which the keepers held him tightly, he gasped for breath and shouted such incoherent speeches that it would be impossible even to imagine what they were like without actually hearing them. They were a mixture of prayers and curses. He screamed as long as[3] he had any strength left; at last he became quiet, and shed-

---

1 Inquisition：中古时代天主教对于异教徒常用酷刑审问，然后把他放在柴堆上烧死，或者用滚汤烫死，那种残忍的地方是不堪想的。

2 to do away with：to abolish；to get rid of 铲除；毁灭；弄死。

当这个病人被带进这间房里去洗澡,照院长永不改变的规矩,人们拿一块发泡膏贴到他颈背上时候,他害怕起来,变凶猛了。荒唐的念头,越来越荒诞,涌到他头上。这是什么?天主教裁判所吗?私自行刑的地方,他的敌人们决定在这里把他了结吗?也许,就是地狱吗?最后他想起这是一个施行酷刑的场所。他被人家脱下衣服了,尽管他怎样拼命抵抗。他的病使他的力气加一倍大,他很容易从那几个看守者的紧握里把自己扯出,因此他们都摔倒石板上。最后,四个人把他摔倒,每人抓着一只腿或者一只臂,将他投进温水里。在他看起来,这正是沸腾着;关于滚水同红热的铁各样极刑的种种纷乱不相连的想头走过他那糊涂的脑子。他所吞下的水壅塞了他的气息,他痉挛地突然伸出他的手脚,看守者就靠抓住这手脚才能够把他紧紧地拘住,他这时喘气,喊出这么不连贯的话,假使没有亲耳听到,真不能想像这些话是什么样子。这些话是祈祷同咒诅混在一团。他高声叫嚷,当他还有力气剩下的时候;最后,他

---

3 as long as: whilst; provided that 当;假使。

ding hot tears, uttered words that had not the slightest reference to what had gone before.

"—Great martyr Saint George! Into your hands I commit my body—my soul—no—oh no—!"

The keepers still held him although he was now quite quiet. The warm bath and the bag of ice that had been put on his head had done their work. But when they took him almost senseless out of the bath and placed him on a stool to apply the blister, the remains of his strength and his deranged thoughts seemed again to revive.

"Why do you do this? Oh why?" he cried. "I do not want to harm a soul! Why do you want to kill me? Oh, oh oh! Oh, good Lord! Oh, you who have been martyred before me! I beseech you, save me!..."

The burning of the blister on his neck made him struggle desperately. The attendants could not master him and did not know what to do. "There's nothing for it,"[1] said the soldier who had applied the blister, "we must wipe it off."

These simple words made the patient shiver. Wipe what? Wipe what off? Wipe whom off? Wipe me off? Thought he, and in mortal terror[2] he closed his eyes. The soldier took a coarse linen cloth in

---

1 there is nothing for it but to: we can only 我们只能够。这句话就是套这个公式来，不过将 but to 改做 we must 了。

2 in mortal terror: in great terror 大惧。

变安静了，流下热泪，说出跟刚才的狂号绝不相关的话来。

"——伟大的殉道者圣乔治！我交给你我的肉体——我的灵魂——不——啊，不——！"

看守者还抓住他，虽然他现在已经十分安静了。温水的洗澡同搁在他头上的冰袋产生了效力。但是当他们把他差不多无意识了从浴盆抬出，放在一张凳子上，来贴起泡膏药，他剩下的力气和他乱七八糟的思想仿佛又复活了。

"你们为什么干这件事？啊，为什么？"他大嚷。"我并不想伤害人！你们为什么要杀死我？啊，啊；啊！啊，仁慈的上帝呀！啊，你们殉道在我之前的人们呀！我恳求你们，救我！……"

药膏在他颈上的发烧使他不愿生死地挣扎。和他一起的人们不能压住他，他们不知道怎么办好。"没有办法，"贴上膏药的那个兵士说道，"我们非把它擦去不可。"

这句普通的话使那病人发抖。擦什么？把什么擦去？把谁擦去？把我擦去吗？他想着，害怕得要命，他闭起他的眼睛。

both hands and pressing heavily passed it rapidly over the patient's neck, tearing away the blister and with it the upper skin, leaving a bare, raw wound. The pain of this operation, which would have been undearable to a calm and healthy man, seemed to the patient like the end of all things. He tore himself desperately out of the hands of the attendants, and his naked body fell on the stone floor. He thought they had chopped off his head. He wanted to cry out but was not able to. He was carried unconscious to his bed and passed after a time into a long and profound sleep.

II

He awoke in the night. All was quiet. He could hear the regular breathing of the sleepers in the larger room next door. From somewhere in the distance came the strange, monotonous voice of a patient confined for the night in the padded room, who was talking to himself, and above, in the woman's ward, a hoarse contralto[1] was singing a wild song. He felt an awful weakness, as if all his bones were broken; his neck ached horribly.

"Where am I? What has happened to me?" passed through his mind. Then with wonderful clearness he remembered the last month of his life, and he understood that he was ill, he understood his

---

1 contralto：女人所唱的最低的音，介于tenor男高音和soprano女高音之间。

那个兵士双手捧一块粗麻布，用力地压着，很快地擦过病人的颈项，扯去那张膏药，以及一片外皮，剩下一个暴露的擦伤的伤口。这一下手术所给的苦痛是一个心平气和，身体健康的人所受不了的，由这个病人看来，真好像是一切生命的终止。他拼命把自己从这一班照呼他的人们手里扯出，他那赤条条的身体直躺在石板上面。他想他们砍下他的头了。他要喊出声来，但是做不到。他无意识地被抬到他的床上，过一会儿沉到一阵长久的浓睡里去了。

二

夜里他醒来。四围是静悄悄的。他能听出隔壁大房子里睡着的人们的通常呼吸的声音。从远处某地方来了一个病人奇怪的，单调的声音，这个人那晚上是关在墙壁填有软东西的房子里，他正在对着自己说话；楼上，在妇女病室里，一个粗厉的女性最低音正唱着一首狂歌。他觉到一种可怕的孱弱，好似他所有的骨头都断了；他的颈项可怖地疼痛。

"我在什么地方呢？我碰到了什么事情呢？"这些疑问经过他心里。然后，心里明澈得奇怪地他记起他最近一月内的生活，

malady. He remembered a number of absurd thoughts, words, and actions, and these recollections made his whole body tremble. "That is all over[1], thank God that is all over!" he murmured, and fell asleep again.

An open window with an iron grating looked into a sort of blind alley[2] between high houses and stone walls. Nobody ever went into this part of the grounds, and it was thickly overgrown with all sorts of wild bushes and lilacs, which were in full bloom at this season of the year. Beyond these bushes, just opposite the window, was a high wall over which the tops of the trees in the large garden could be seen brilliantly illuminated by the moon. To the right rose the white walls of the hospital with its iron-grated windows lit up from within. To the left the walls of the mortuary also shone white in the bright moonbeams. The rays of the moon fell through the grated window on the floor and shone on part of the patient's bed, his pale, worn face, and closed eyes. He exhibited no signs of madness now.

He was sleeping the deep, heavy sleep of an exhausted man, without dreams, without the slightest motion, almost without breathing. For a few moments he awoke in his full senses[3], as if quite well —only to arise the next morning as mad as ever.

---

1 over: at an end 结束了，过去了。
2 blind alley: an alley having but one opening 只有一头可通的小巷；绝道。
3 in full senses: in wholly sane state 在神经十分健全状态之下。

他知道他病了，他知道他患了什么病。他忆起许多荒诞的思想，言语，同行为，这些回忆使他浑身发抖。"那全过去了，谢谢上帝，那全过去了！"他喃喃地自语，又睡了。

一个打开的窗子，窗外有铁的格子，望着介于高屋子同石墙之中的一种死胡同。从来没有人到过这地方，地面密密地丛生有种种野的矮树同紫丁香花，这季里正盛开。这群矮树之外，刚对着这个窗子，是一片高墙，墙外大花园里的树梢给月亮清朗地照着，隔墙可以望见。胡同的右边高耸起医院的白墙，许多铁窗现于房里面的灯光之中。胡同的左边，坟地的围墙也是在光明的月光中显出白色。月光穿过这铁窗，射到地板上，照见病人床铺的一部分，他惨白憔悴的脸孔，同紧闭的眼睛。他现在没有露出一丝疯狂的状态。

他像一个疲倦无力的人深沉地熟睡了，没有梦，没有一点儿的转动，几乎是没有呼吸。有一会儿，他神识十分清爽地醒来，仿佛什么毛病都没有了——只是第二天早上起来还是和从前一样地疯狂。

III

"How do you feel this morning? " asked the doctor the following day.

The patient, who was only just awake, was still lying under his bedclothes.

"Very well, " he answered; he jumped up, put on his slippers, and seized his dressing-gown[1], "Splendid! There's only one thing: here! " And he pointed to the back of his neck. "I can't turn my head without pain. But that's nothing. All is well if only one understands, and I do understand. "

"Do you know where you are? "

"Certainly, doctor! I am in a madhouse. If only you understand, it is all quite the same[2]. It does not matter[3] at all! "

The doctor looked earnestly in his eyes. His handsome, delicate face, with its well-brushed, golden beard and quiet, blue eyes that looked through gold-rimmed spectacles, was immovable and unfathomable. He was observing.

"Why are you looking so attentively at me? You will never read what I have on my soul, " continued the patient, "but I see quite

---

1 dressing-gown:早上梳头洗脸时所穿的便衣,有点像中国的长衫。

2 it is all the same:it makes no difference 不会生出什么不同。

3 matter:make a difference 有关重要,大都加上有一个否定字,以表示"无关紧要"。

三

"今天早上你觉得怎么样？"第二天医生问道。

这个病人刚才醒来，还躺在他被窝底下。

"很好，"他答道；他跳起来，穿上他的拖鞋，抓住他的便衣。"好极了！只是有一点：这里！"他指着他的颈背。"我头一转动总免不了痛。但是这算不得什么。要一切都是对的，只要一个人能够了解，我是能了解的。"

"你知道你此刻在什么地方吗？"

"知道之至，医生！我是在疯人院里。只要一个人能够了解，这是绝不碍事的。这是绝对无关紧要的！"

医生用心地瞧他的眼睛。医生漂亮文雅的脸孔，以及它那刷得很整齐的金黄色须子，同从金边眼镜望外看的沉静的蓝眼睛，是丝毫不动的，神秘不可测的。他正在观察这个疯人。

"你为什么这样注意地瞧我？你永不能看透我心中的思想，"疯人继续说道，"但是我十分明白地看出你心上写了什么。你为

clearly what is written on yours. Why do you commit evil? Why do you collect such numbers of unhappy people and keep them here? For me it is all the same—I understand it all and am calm; but for them? Why this suffering? When a man has reached the point of having a great thought in his soul—the common thought—it is all the same to him where he lives—what he feels. Even to live—or not to live...is it not so? "

"Perhaps, " answered the doctor; he sat down on a chair in the corner of the room, so as to be able to watch the patient, who was now pacing the room with rapid steps from corner to corner, shuffling along in his large horse-leather slippers and flapping his dressing-gown of cotton material with broad red stripes and large flowers. The orderly and inspector who had accompanied the doctor stood at attention[1] near the door.

"And I have got it! " cried the patient. "When I found it, I felt as if I were born again. My feelings grew more acute, my brain worked as it had never done before. What was formerly attained only by a long process of speculation and conjecture I now know by intuition. I have, in fact, reached the point that has been worked out[2] by philosophy. I am experiencing in myself the great idea that space

---

1 to stand at attention：to stand in a military attitude of readiness 立正。
2 to be worked out：to be effected by labor and exertion 努力而后得到的。

什么干这件坏事？你为什么搜集了这么多不幸的人们，把他们监禁在这里？对于我，这是绝不碍事的——我完全能够了解，我心境是安宁的，但对于他们？为什么叫他们这样受苦？当一个人达到他灵魂里怀有一个伟大的思想——一个普遍的思想——那么随便在那里住——随便有什么感觉——对于他都是一样的。甚至于活着——或者不活着……对不对？"

"也许是对的，"医生答道；他就坐在房里角落上一张椅子上，为的是能够窥察这个病人的举动，他现在正是急步地从一个角落到另一角落走来走去，拖着他那马皮大拖鞋，让他那宽红条同大花的棉布便衣随意摆动。跟医生来的助手同监督立正地站在门边。

"我获到那伟大的思想了！"病人喊道。"当我发现它时候，我觉得好像我重新生到世界上。我的感觉变得更锐敏，我的脑子从来没有这么活动过。以前专靠思索同推测的一阵悠长的程序得到的结论，我现在凭着直觉一下子就明白了。实在说起来，我已抓到哲学所推求出的结论了。我自己心里体验出这个伟大

and time are fictions[1]—I am living in all centuries—I am living without space—everywhere or nowhere, just as you like. I am therefore quite indifferent whether you keep me here or let me go away—whether I am free or bound. I have noticed that there are here some others like me, but for the rest of the crowd it is awful. Why do you not set them at liberty? Who requires—"

"You said, " interrupted the doctor, "that you live outside space and time. On the other hand it is impossible not to agree that we, you and I, are in this room, and that it is now" —the doctor pulled his watch out of his pocket—"half-past ten on the sixth day of May of the year 18—What do you think about that? "

"Nothing. It's all the same to me where I am or when I live. If it is all the same to me, does it not mean that I am everywhere and always? "

The doctor smiled.

"Strange logic," he said, getting up; "perhaps you are right. Good morning. Would you like a cigar? "

"Thank you;" he stopped in his walk, took a cigar, and with a nervous movement bit off the end.[2] "This helps me to think," he

---

1 德国哲学家康德就把时空认为没有真实的存在，不过是我们思想时的一种形式。

2 雪茄烟放在嘴里的那一头总是用烟叶封住，所以在开始抽之前，要把它咬去一点。

的观念：空间和时间是虚幻的东西——我是活在一切世纪里面——我是住在空间之外——我是无所不在，我是无所在，随你说罢。所以，我绝不关心，你们把我〈关〉在这儿，或者放我走——给我自由，或者监禁起来。我看出这里有几个像我这样的，但是对于这群里其它的人们，这种拘留是可怕的事。你为什么不放他们走？谁要——"

"你说，"医生打断他的说话道，"你是活在时空之外的。然而，你不能不承认，我们，你同我，是在这间房子里面，现在是"——医生从他衣袋里掏出他的表——"一八——年五月六日十时半钟。你以为何？"

"不相干的。对于我都是一样的，无论我活在什么地方，什么时候，若使这对于我既然都是一样的，那么这岂不是对于说我是无处不存在同无时不存在的。"

医生微笑了。

"奇怪的逻辑，"他说，站起来；"也许是不错的。祝你早安。你想抽一根雪茄烟吗？"

"谢谢你"，他停下不走，拿一根雪茄，现出神经衰弱的样子，咬去烟的末端。"这可以助我去默想，"他说，"这也是宇宙

said; "this is the universe—microcosm. At one end alkalis, at the other acids: that is the equilibrium of the universe by which the elements are neutralized. —Good-bye, doctor! "

The doctor proceeded on this round[1]. Most of the patients were awaiting him, standing drawn up[2] near their beds. No authorities are treated with such respect as the doctors in charge of a madhouse are treated by their patients.

The patient, when he was left alone, continued to pace the room in fits and starts[3] from corner to corner. They brought him some tea. Without sitting down he swallowed in two gulps the contents of a large mug and in an instant devoured a large piece of white bread. Then he went out of the room and for several hours walked without once stopping from end to end[4] of the building with his rapid, heavy gait. It was a rainy day and the patients were not allowed to go into the garden. When the orderly looked for the new patient he was directed to the end of the passage, where he found him with his face pressed to the glass door earnestly looking out at the flower-garden. His attention was attracted by an unusually bright red flower belonging to the poppy family[5].

---

1 round: a course ending where it began; a circuit 循环走一遍。
2 to draw up: to form in regular order 排队。
3 in fits and starts: spasmodically 旋作旋辍地。

——小天地。一头是碱质,一头是酸性;这是宇宙的平衡,一切的原素因此都得到中和。——再见,医生!"

医生继续他的巡视。大多数病人都正等候他,成排地站在他们各自的床铺旁边。任何权威者的受人们尊敬,都不如疯人院里担任诊务的医生那样受病人们的尊敬。

这个病人,当剩下一个人独自在房里时候,忽作忽辍地继续向房里几个角落踏来踏去。他们拿茶进来给他。也没有坐下,他两口气就喝干一大杯茶,一下子食尽一大块白面包。然后他走出房子,一连好几个钟头,未曾停足一下,用他那急促同沉重的脚步,从屋里的这头到那头来回地走动。这是一个雨天,医院不许病人们到花园去。当助手寻找这个新病人时候,人们告诉他到走道的尽头,他看见他在那里脸压着玻璃门,用心地望那花园。这个病人的注意力是给一朵非常鲜明的红花,属于罂粟科的,吸引住。

---

4 from end to end:from one extremity to the other 自此端至彼端。
5 family:按植物分类法,凡是性质根本相近者就同属一科,叫做某某科?

"Please come and be weighed!" said the orderly, touching his shoulder. When the patient turned to him he almost reeled back with alarm; there was such a wild look of wickedness and hate shining from those senseless eyes. When he saw it was the orderly, he at once altered the expression of his face and obediently followed him without saying a word, as if plunged in deep thought. They went into the doctor's receiving room; the patient got on[1] the small, decimal weighing-machine without help; the orderly weighed him and registered "109 pounds" opposite his name in a book. The next day his weight was 107, the third day 106.

"If it goes on[2] like this he will not live long," said the doctor, and ordered the patient to be fed as well as possible.

Notwithstanding all their efforts and the unusual appetite of the patient, he got thinner every day, and every day the orderly entered in the book a smaller and smaller number of pounds. The patient scarcely slept at all and passed his days in uninterrupted movement.

IV

He was conscious that he was in a madhouse, he was even conscious that he was ill. Sometimes, as on the first night, he awoke in the stillness, after a whole day of violent movement, feeling pains in

---

1 to get on: to mount 登。
2 to go on: to continue 继续；老是。

"请来称一下！"助手说道，推一下他的肩膀。当病人转身来朝着他时候，他差不多恐吓得蹒跚走开；因为从两个无意义的眼睛里发出一种这么野蛮的凶恶的神情。当他看见助手叫他，他立刻变换他脸上的表情，规矩地跟着他走，一个字也没有说，好像沉于深思里去了。他们走进医生的私人诊室；这个病人踏上小架的十进的秤〔称〕重机，并没有人扶他上去；助手称了他，就在一本簿子里他名字的对面记下"一百零九磅"。第二天他的重量是一百零八，第三天是一百零七。

"假使老是这么下去，他活不得多久了，"医生说，命令尽力拿好的东西给他吃。

不管他们费了这么多的力气，同病人的食欲多么强，他却是一天一天地瘦下去了，每天助手记下更少数目的磅数。病人几乎完全没有睡，白天总在不断的走动里过去。

四

他自知他是在一所疯人院里，他甚至于自知他病了。有时，像第一晚上那样，他在寂静中醒来，于整天剧烈活动之后，觉

all his limbs and a terrible heaviness in his head, but in a complete state of consciousness. Perhaps it was owing to the absence of all outer impressions in the stillness and the semi-darkness of the night, or perhaps it was the weak working of the brain of a man only just awake, that caused him at such moments fully to understand his position, and he seemed for the time[1] to be quite well; but with the return of day, with the return of light and the awaking of life in the hospital, he was seized by waves of impressions which his diseased brain could not control, and once more he was a madman. His condition was a strange mixture of correct judgement and utter absurdity. He knew that he was surrounded by mental invalids, but at the same time he thought that each one was some person he had formerly know, or read of in books, or heard about, who was trying secretly to conceal himself or was being concealed. The hospital was inhabited by men of all countries and all times. Here he found both the living and the dead. Here were all the celebrated and also the soldiers who had fallen in the last war and risen again. He imagined himself in some magic, enchanted circle, having collected in himself all the strength of the world, and in a haughty exaltation he considered himself the centre of this circle. They, his companions in the hospital, had all assembled here with the intention of performing a great

---

1 for the time: for the time being 当时。

得他的四肢都疼痛，头里有一种可怕的沉重，但是心里十分明白。也许是因为寂静中，同夜的半黑暗里，外面一切印象都消失了，也许是因为一个才醒过来的人脑筋不大活动，使他在这种时候完全了解他的地位，当时他好像什么病也没有了；但是当白天回来，光明回来，同医院里的一切生命觉醒了的时候，他被许多印象的波涛抓住，那是他这有病的脑子所管束不住的，他又变成为一个疯人了。他的情形是正确的判断同极端的荒谬的奇怪混合。他知道他四围都是神经不健全的病人，但是同时他因为个个人是他曾经认识过的，或者在书里念过的，或者听别人说过的某人，这些人暗地里设法将自己隐藏，或者是别人将这些人隐起。他以为这医院住有各国同各时候的人们。在这里他碰到活着的同已死的人。住在这里有地上一切享盛名，有权力的人们，以及前次战争里死去又回生的兵士。他认为他自己是在一种神秘的，具有魔力的一团人里面，世界的力量都聚于他的一身，得意扬扬地自命为这团人群的中心。他们，他医院里的同伴，集在这里为着干一件大事业，他模糊地觉得那是

work, which dimly appeared to him as a gigantic undertaking for the destruction of evil on the earth. He did not know how it would have to be done but he felt that he possessed sufficient strenght to accomplish it. He could read the thoughts of other men, saw in each thing its whole history. The great elms of the hospital garden told him old legends of the past; the buildings, that had really been built a fairly long time, he imagined to have been constructed by Peter the Great, and he imagined that the Tsar[1] had resided there at the time of the battle of Poltava. He could read it on the walls and on the crumbling plaster, on pieces of brick or tile which he found in the garden: the whole history of the house and garden were written on them. He peopled[2] the small building that served as a mortuary with tens and hundreds of people who had long been dead, and he gazed fixedly at a little window that opened from its basement into a corner of the garden, seeing in the uneven and rainbow-coloured reflections of the old and dirty glass familiar faces he had once met in life, or whose portraits he had seen.

Fine bright weather set in[3] and the patients spent the whole day[4] in the open air in the garden. The not very large part of the garden

---

1 Tsar: 有时拼作 Czar，是俄国皇帝的称呼，好像日本人叫日皇做 Mikado.

2 to people: to fill with people 移殖人民到某地方。

毁灭地上的罪恶这么一个伟业。他不知道这件事是怎么样办去，但是他觉得他具有充足的力量，可以成就这件大事。他能够看透别人的思想，在一切东西里瞧出它全部的经过。医院花园的大榆树告诉他过去的旧传说；这座屋子，那的确是已经盖了许久了，他臆测是彼得第一建筑的，他臆测俄皇在这里住过，当布多洼战争时候。他能够从墙壁上，将崩坏的灰泥上，同他在花园看见的雾砖飘瓦，得到这个消息：屋子同花园的全部历史都写在它们上面。他心中认为这所小墓园里住有成千成百久已死去的人们，他直着眼睛注视花园一角落里墓园地下室的窗子，从那块污垢陈旧的玻璃的不平的和虹彩色的映照看出他曾经碰过的，或者在像片上见过的许多熟识的脸孔来。

晴朗光明的天气来了，病人们整天都在花园里露天中过活。划出给他们的那块不很大部分的花园是密密地栽了树木，有空隙的地方，就锄作花床。督察使能够做一点事的病人们都在园

---

3 to set in: to begin 开始；来了。
4 to spend day: to pass day in some place 过日子。

allotted to them was thickly planted with trees, and where it was possible there were beds of flowers. The overseer made all who were capable of doing any work occupy themselves in the garden. All day long they swept the paths or strewed sand on them, weeded and watered the beds of flowers, cucumbers, melons, and water-melons that had been dug up and planted by their hands. One corner of the garden was overgrown by cherry-trees and bordered by an avenue of elms; in the middle of it, on an artificial mound, were the most beautiful flower-beds of the whole garden: bright flowers formed the borders of the highest parts of this mound and in the centre was a large and rare red and yellow dahlia. This dahlia formed the centre of the whole garden and also marked its highest point, and it was observed that many of the patients attributed to it some mysterious power. To the new patient, too, it seemed to be something uncommon, a sort of Chief of the garden and the buildings. Along all the paths were flowerbeds also planted with flowers by the patients. Here grew every sort of flower that can be found in the gardens of Little Russia—standard roses, brilliant petunias, tall tobacco-plants with small pink blossoms, mint, marigolds, nasturtiums and poppies. Here too, not far from the porch, grew three plants of a particular species of poppy, much smaller than the usual poppy and differing from it by the unusual brightness of its brilliant blood-red colour. It was this flower that had so impressed the patient when, on his first morning

里作工。整天里，他们打扫园地的道路，或者撒上黄沙，除去野草，灌水给花床，胡瓜，甜瓜同西瓜，这些地是他们亲手掘的，栽上了种子。花园的一个角落满种了樱桃树，有一条夹道都是榆树的小路从旁边经过；花园在中心，在一堆人做的土山之上，有几片全园里最娇艳的花床：这堆土山的最高处四面有明媚的鲜花绿着，中心点是一丛高大罕见的，杂开红黄两颜色花的天竺牡丹。这丛天竺牡丹做了全园的中心点，也标明出它的最高峰，人们看出许多疯人把这丛花视为具有一种神秘的力量。这位新病人也觉得这是与众不同的，仿佛是这座花园同这所屋子的领袖。园里的道旁也都是花床，也是病人们栽种的。在这里生长了在小俄罗斯任何花园里所能找到的一切鲜花——直杆的蔷薇，灿烂的撞羽朝颜，带有小红花的高大的烟草，薄荷，金盏草，荷叶莲，同罂粟花。在这里，离走廊不远的地方，生长有三株特种的罂粟，比通常的小得多，和通常不同的地方最显明的是它那明眼的血红颜色的特别鲜明。也就是这种花那么感动了这位病人，当他在医院的第一个早晨，他从玻璃门望

in the hospital, he had looked through the glass door into the garden.

The first time he went into the garden he stopped to look at these bright red flowers before he went down the steps. There were only two flowers out[1], and they grew as if by chance[2] on a spot that had not been weeded and were surrounded by orach and some sort of steppe grass.

The patients passed out of the door one by one and each received from the warder who stood there a thick knitted white cap with a red cross on the forehead. These caps had been used during the war and bought at an auction by the hospital. But the patient naturally attached a special and mysterious significance to this red cross. He took his cap off, and looked at the cross and then at the poppies. The flowers were brighter.

"They conquer, " said the patient—"but we shall see."

He went down the steps that led from the porch, looked round, and not noticing the warder who was standing behind him stepped over a flower-bed and stretched his hand towards the flower, but could not make up his mind[3] to pluck it. He had a sensation of heat and a feeling of pricking, first in his outstretched hand and then in his whole body, as if some strong current of an unknown power

---

1 out: open 花开。
2 by chance: casually; accidently 偶然; 意外。

着花园时候。

第一回他走进花园，他停步来瞧这些鲜红的花朵，在他走下台阶之前。只有两朵开着，它们好象偶然生在一块未曾除过野草的地方，四围是滨藜和草原上它种的野草。

病人们一个一个走出门去，每人从站在那里的看守者领了一顶厚厚的线织白色小帽，额前有一个红十字。这些帽子是战争时候用的，医院在拍卖场买到的。但是这病人自然加一个特别的，神秘的意义在这个红十字上面。他脱下他的帽子，看一看那红十字，然后又瞧那罂粟花。那丛花更见鲜明了。

"现在是它们胜利，"这病人说道——"但是我们要看一看将来如何。"

他走下走廊的台阶，向四面望一下，没有注意到站在他背后的看守者，踏过一片花床，伸出手向那朵花，但是不能下个决心把它摘下。他感到一种热同刺痛，起先在他那伸出去的手，后来全身都如此，仿佛一个莫名其妙的力量的强烈潮流从那红

---

3 to make up one's mind: to form resolution; to resolve to do 决心。

were emitted from the red petals, and were penetrating into his whole system. He got nearer and stretched his hand quite close to the flower, but it seemed to him to defend itself by breathing out a deadly poisonous breath. He became giddy; he made a last desperate effort and had already seized hold of the stem when suddenly a heavy hand was laid on his shoulder. It was the warder who had caught hold of[1] him.

"You must not pluck the flowers, " said the old Little Russian, "and you mustn't walk on the flower-beds. There are many of you madmen here; if each of you takes only one flower, the whole garden will be stripped, " he said in a persuasive tone, still holding his shoulder.

The patient looked at him, silently released himself from his grasp, and in great agitation went along the path. "Oh, unfortunate men! " he thought. "You do not see, you are blinded to such an extent that you even defend it. But whatever it may cost me I will destroy it. If not today, then tomorrow we will measure our strength[2]. And if I perish—will it not be all the same? "

He walked about the garden until late in the evening, making acquaintance with other patients and entering into strange conversations with them, in which each only heard answers to his own insane

---

1 to catch hold of: to grasp 抓住。

花瓣发出，现在穿入他的全身。他走得更近，伸出他的手很近那朵花，但是由他看来这朵花好象吐出一阵致人死命的毒气，来保卫自己。他变晕眩了；他拼命使一下最后的劲，已经抓住它的茎了，忽然间有一只沉重的手放在他肩膀上。这是看守者抓他。

"你不应该摘花，"这个小俄罗斯老人说道，"你也不该在花床上走。这里有许多你们这种疯人；假使你们每人只采一朵花，全园立刻会摘空了，"他用劝告的口吻说，还拿着他的肩膀。

这个病人望他一下，悄悄地将自己从他的紧握里解开，很震动地沿着道儿走去。"啊，不幸的人们！"他想。"你们看不见，你们是盲目得以至于居然去保护它。但是不管我会吃什么大亏，我总要毁灭它。若使不是今天，那么明日我们一较量我们的力气罢。就说我死去——那还不是一样的吗？"

他在花园里散步，一直到黄昏，和别个病人结识，跟他们谈奇怪的话，这些谈话里他们只听到用神秘的，荒谬的言语说

---

2 to measure strength: to test ability by contest 比较气力，一决胜负。

thoughts expressed in mysterious and absurd words. The patient walked about first with one companion and then with another, and by the end of the day he was still more convinced that "all was ready, " as he said to himself. "Soon, soon these iron bars will fall in ruins[1] and these prisoners will be let out and hurry away to all the corners of the earth, and the whole world will shake, and throw off its worn-out coating, and appear in a new and splendid beauty." He had almost forgotten the flowers; but when he left the garden and was going up[2] the steps, he again perceived them in the darkening, dewy grass, looking like two burning red coals. Then the patient lagged behind, and getting where the warder could not see him, waited for a favourable moment. Nobody saw him jump over the flower-bed, pluck one of the flowers, and hastily put it in his bosom under his shirt. When the cool, dew-covered petals touched his body, he got as pale as death and his eyes opened wide with terror. A cold sweat came out in beads on his forehead.

Lamps were lighted in the hospital. While waiting for their supper most of the patients lay down[3] on their beds; only a few restless ones hurriedly walked about the rooms and passages. The patient with the flower in his breast was among them. He walked about, his

---

1 in ruins: 荒废；颓废。ruins作废墟解释时，常居复数。
2 to go up: to ascend 走上去。
3 to lie down: to assume lying position 躺下。

出的答辞,回答他们自己疯狂的思想。这个病人起先和一个伴侣同散步,然后又跟另一个,当那天终止时候,他更相信"一切都准备好了",他对着自己就是这样说。"很快,很快。这许多铁杆会倒下,化为废物,这班囚人会被释放出去,赶紧跑到世界上的各处,一直到海角天涯,全世界会震动了,弃掉它破损的旧衣,涌现在灿烂光明的美丽之中。"他差不多忘记那丛花儿了;但是当他离开花园,走上台阶时,他又瞧见它们在阴沉转黑的,露湿的草里,看起来很像两块烧得通红的煤球。于是这个病人故意落后,走到看守者瞧不见他的地方,等候一个良好的机会。谁也没有看见他,他跳过花床,摘下那丛红花的一朵,匆忙地把它藏在胸前,衬衣底下。当那些清凉的,沾着夕露的花瓣触他的身体时候,他变得脸色惨白如死人,他的眼睛吓得睁开很大。一阵冰冷的汗珠来到他的额上。

医院里面点起灯了。等候着他们的晚餐,一大半病人躺在他们自己床上;只有几个不安静的匆促地在房里同走道里走动,胸前藏有红花的那个病人也在内。他四处乱走,他的双臂痉挛

arms convulsively crossed over his breast; it seemed as if he wanted to crush, to shatter the plant he carried there. When he met anyone he got as far as[1] he could out of their way[2], seeming to fear even to touch them with his clothes. "Don't come near me, don't come near me! " he cried. In the hospital little attention was paid to such exclamations. He continued to walk faster and faster, taking larger and larger steps; he walked about hour after hour[3] with a sort of exasperation.

"I will tire you out[4]. I will suffocate you! " he said fiercely and hoarsely. Sometimes he ground[5] his teeth.

Supper was served in the dining-room. Several large gilded and painted wooden bowls containing a sort of thin millet gruel were placed on each of the long tables, which were without table-cloths; the patients sat round the tables on benches and each received a hunch of rye bread. About eight men ate with wooden spoons out of the same bowl. A few who were ordered better food were served separately. Our patient quickly swallowed his portion, which had been brought by the attendant to his room, and not being satisfied with what he had received went into the general dining-room.

"May I sit down here? " he asked the inspector.

---

1 as far as: to the extent to which 达到；一直到。
2 out of the way: at a distance from 远避；躲开。
3 hour after hour: for many hours 多几个钟头。

地叉在胸前；好像他要压坏，要弄碎他搁在那里的花朵。当他遇到任何人时候，他尽力远避他们，仿佛甚至于怕将他的衣服蹭他们。"不要走近我！不要走近我！"他喊道。在医院里这类狂呼是没有什么人去注意。他继续越走越快，愈是大步地踏来踏去；他带着愤怒地一连走好几个钟头。

"我必定要叫你累死。我要使你闷死！"他凶猛地，声音沙哑地说道。有时他切齿咬牙。

晚餐开在食堂里。几只金边画花的大号木碗盛有一种小米稀饭放在每个长桌子上面，那是没有桌布的；病人们围着桌子坐在凳子上，每人领一块黑面包。差不多有八个人用木匙从同一只碗里食稀饭。我们这位病人很快地吞下他那份的东西，那是招呼他的听差拿到他房里的；觉得没有吃够，他走进公共食堂来。

"我可以坐在这里吗？"他问监督。

---

4 to tire out：to weary to the point of exhaustion 使之力竭。

5 ground 是 grind 的过去格，它的意思是咬牙切齿，发出摩擦的声音（to rub together with a grating noise）。

"Have you not had your supper?" inquired the inspector as he poured further portions of gruel into the bowls.

"I am very hungry, and I must get as much strength as I can. Food is my only support; you know that I do not sleep at all."

"Eat, my good fellow, and may it do you good! Tarass, give him a spoon and some bread."

He sat down before one of the bowls and ate an enormous portion of gruel.

"Now that's enough, that's enough!" said the inspector at last, when all the others had finshed and our patient still continued to sit at the bowl scooping up the gruel with one hand and firmly holding his breast with the other. "You will over-eat yourself."

"Ah, if you only knew how much strength I require, how much strength! Good-bye, Nikolai Nikolaevich," said the patient, getting up from table and pressing the inspector's hand with all his strength.

"Good-bye!"

"Where are you going?" asked the inspector, smiling.

"I? Nowhere. I am remaining here. But perhaps tomorrow we shall not see one another. Thank you for all your kindness," and he once more pressed the inspector's hand. His voice shook and there were tears in his eyes.

"Calm yourself, my dear fellow, calm yourself," answered the inspector. "Why do you have such dark thoughts? Go to bed and get

"你不是已经食过晚餐吗?"监督问道,当他再倒些稀饭到碗里时候。

"我饿得很,我又是非好好地培养我的精力不可。食品是我惟一的援助;你知道我简直没有睡觉。"

"食罢,我的可爱朋友,我真希望它能给你好处!达拉斯,给他一个匙子和几块面包。"

他坐在一只碗子之前,吃下非常多的稀饭。

"现在,够了,够了!"监督最后说道,那时别人都吃完了,我们这位病人还是坐在碗旁,一边手拿匙挖起稀饭,一边手坚决地按在胸前。"你将吃得太多了。"

"啊,你不晓得,我需要多少力气,多少力气!再见,力古尼·力古利维支,"病人说道,从桌边站起,用尽他所有的力气和监督握手。

"再见!"

"你要到那里去?"监督微笑地问道。

"我?什么地方也不去。我还是滞在这儿。但是也许明天我们彼此不能再见面了。谢谢你一向对我的好意,"他又握一下监督的手。他的声调颤动,他眼里有泪。

"你自己宽心罢,我亲爱的朋友,你自己宽心罢,"监督答道。"你为什么有这悲愁的念头?到床上去,快点睡觉罢。你需

to sleep quickly. You require more sleep; when once you sleep properly you will soon get better."

The patient began to sob. The inspector turned away to order the attendants to be quicker clearing away the supper things. In half an hour all were asleep in the hospital with the exception of[1] one man, who lay in his clothes on his bed in the corner room. He was shaking as if with ague, and convulsively he held his hands to his breast, which he imagined was impregnated with some unknown deadly poison.

V

He did not sleep all night. He had plucked that flower because he felt that it was a deed he had been destined to do. When he had first looked out of the glass door the brilliant red petals had attracted his attention, and it appeared to him that at that moment he fully understood what he was bound to perform on this earth. In this blood-red flower was concentrated all the evil of the world. He knew that opium was made of poppy-seed. Perhaps this thought had grown and attained gigantic dimensions in his mind, developing into a horrible and grotesque phantom. The flower in his eyes concentrated in itself all evils, it drew into its petals all the innocent blood that had ever been shed, and it was this caused their deep red colour, it absorbed

---

1 with the exception of: except 除开。

要更多的睡眠；当你一好好地睡觉，你就快好了。"

这个病人开始呜咽。监督转过身来叫听差们赶快将饭具收拾起来。过了半个钟头，医院里所有病人都睡着了，除开一个人，他和衣睡在角落里一个小房间的床上。他浑身发抖，好像发了疟病，痉挛地他双手按着胸前，他以为那里沾染了一种莫名其妙的，致死命的毒质。

五

他整晚没有睡觉。他摘下那朵花，因为他觉得这是注定他干的事情。当他第一次从玻璃窗向外望时候，那些灿烂的红花瓣引起他的注意，他看出那时他完全明白他在世上应当做的是什么事。世界上一切的罪恶都集中于这朵血红的鲜花里。他知道鸦片是用罂粟种子制的。也许这个观念在他心里长大而占有极大的范围，化为一个怪诞可怕的幽灵。在他眼里这朵花集中有一切的罪恶到它自己身上，它将世界里一向无辜的人们所流的血都注到它的花瓣里，所以她的花瓣有那种深红的颜色，它又吸收有人类一切的眼泪同一切的苦痛辛酸。这朵花是和上帝

all the tears and all the gall and bitterness of humanity. This was a mysterious and terrible being in opposition to God-Satan¹, who had taken a humble and innocent form. It was necessary to pluck and kill it. But even this was not enough—it was necessary to prevent it in dying from flooding the whole world with its poison. That is why he had hidden it away in his bosom. He hoped that by morning the flower would have lost all its strenght. Its evil would be transferred to his breast, to his soul, and there it would be conquered; or perhaps it would conquer, and then he would perish—die, but die like an honourable wrestler, like manking's chief wrestler, for never yet had anyone dared to fight against all the evil of the world at once.

"They did not see it. I saw it. Could I allow it to live? Death is better!"

With failing strength he lay in this imaginary, unreal struggle, but was exhausted by it all the same². The next morning the doctor's assistant found him almost dead. After a few hours, however, he revived, jumped out of bed, and began running about the hospital as usual, talking to the patients and to himself louder and more disconnectedly than ever. He was not allowed to go into the garden; the

---

1 Satan: 撒但, 就是魔鬼, 人们的最大敌人; 据说他本来也是天使, 因为违背上帝的旨意, 从天堂开除出来。Milton 在《失乐园》里也采取这种说法。

2 all the same: just the same 还是一样的。

做对头的一个神秘可怖的东西——可说是采取一种低微的，天真的外形的撒但，真是非把它摘下杀死不可。但是甚至于这样还是不够的——一定要阻止它在毁灭时将它的毒质流遍全世界。所以他把它藏在胸前。他希望明天早上这朵花会失掉它所有的力气。它的毒质会转移到他胸里，他灵魂里，在那里它就被征服了；或者它战胜了，那么他就毁灭了——死了，但是死得像一个光荣的角力者，为人类而角力的一个大人物，因为从来没有人胆敢一下子向世界一切的罪恶宣战。

"他们没有看见它。我看见了。我能够让它活下去吗？宁可我自己死罢！"

力气渐渐地销沉了，他躺着做这种幻想的，没有实在的根据的奋斗，但是仍然弄得累极了。第二〈天〉早上医生的助手看见他几乎死去了。然而，过了几个钟头，他精神又恢复，跳下床来，开始在医院里跑来跑去像往常那样，比以前更大声地，更不连贯地向病人们，向自己说话。医院不准他到花园里；医生看到他的体重一天一天地减少，又不能睡着，整天老是不停地走动，

doctor, seeing that his weight decreased every day, that he could not sleep, and that all day long[1] he never ceased his wanderings, ordered that a large dose of morphia should be injected under his skin. He did not resist; fortunately his insane ideas seemed at that moment to coincide with this operation. He soon fell asleep; his wild movements ceased, and the loud melody, caused by his own irregular footsteps, that had rung all the time in his ears died away too. He became unconscious and ceased to think of anything, even of the second red flower that it was necessary for him to pluck.

Three days later however, he was able to pluck it, before the very[2] eyes of the warder, who was not in time[3] to prevent him. The warder ran after him. With loud cries of triumph, with sobs and lamentations, the patient ran into the house, rushed into his bedroom, and hastily hid the plant under his shirt.

"How dare you pick the flowers? " demanded the warder who had followed him. The patient, who was already lying on his bed in his accustomed position—with his arms crossed over his breast—began to talk such nonsense that the warder only removed silently from his head the cap with the red cross, which in his hurry he had forgotten to take off, and left him alone. The imaginary struggle

---

1 all day long: through the whole day 整天里。
2 very: 这个字本身没有什么意义，不过用来加重语气，和 even,

叫人将一大剂吗啡打到他皮肤底下。他并不抵抗；侥幸得很，他疯狂的想头当时仿佛和这种手术一致。他很快睡着了；他那胡乱的行动停了，他自己不规则的脚步所产生出的响亮音节，那老是回旋在他耳朵里的，也消失了。他变得失掉了意识，什么也不想了，甚至于他应当摘的第二朵红花。

可是三天之后，他能够把它摘下，就当着看守者的眼前，他来不及阻止他。看守者追他。发出得意的狂喊，又呜咽着，哀哭着，病人跑到屋里去，奔进他的卧室，匆忙地把这朵花隐藏在他衬衫底下。

"你怎么敢摘花？"跟他跑的看守者诘问他。这个病人已经躺在他床上了，照着他通常那种姿势——双手按着胸前——开始说出这么无意义的话，看守者只好悄悄地从他头上解下那红十字的帽子，病人在匆忙里忘记脱下，让他一个人在那里。那种幻想的奋斗又开始了。这个病人觉得红花发出悠长的，蛇也

---

even the 差不多，所以这一句也可以改做 even before the eyes of the warder。
   3 in time：sufficiently early 来得及。

began again. The patient felt that currents of evil issued from the flower in long, serpent-like coils, which wound themselves round him, pressed and crushed his limbs, and imbued his whole body with their poisonous effluvia. He wept and, at intervals[1], when he was not heaping curses on his enemy, prayed to God. The flower was faded by the evening. The patient trod under his feet the blackened plant and then, carefully collecting all the remains from the floor, carried them into the bathroom, where he threw the formless little mass of vegetation into the stove amongst red-hot, burning coals, and watched for a long time how his enemy fizzled and shrivelled up and at last turned into[2] a soft, snowwhite heap of ashes. He blew upon it and it disappeared.

The next day the patient was worse. Deadly pale, with hollow cheeks and deeply-sunken, glowing eyes, he now went about with tottering steps, often stumbling in his insane wanderings, and talked and talked unceasingly.

"I should not like to have to use force, " said the chief doctor to his assistant.

"But it is imperative to stop this exertion. Today his weight was only 93 pounds. If it goes on like this, he will be dead in two days."

---

1 at intervals: occasionally 间或; 有时。

似地卷曲着的毒流，这个毒流自己围绕他，迫压他的肢体，将它的流质染上他全身。他哭泣，有时当他没有咒诅他仇敌时候，就向上帝祷告。黄昏时花枯萎了。这个病人用脚践踏这变黑的花朵，然后，小心地从地板上捡起残瓣，带到浴室去，在那里他扔这小堆不成形的花瓣到火炉里，在红热的，正燃烧的煤球之中，有很久的工夫注视着他的敌人怎样发出嘶嘶的声音，皱缩了，最后化为一堆雪白的软灰。他用口吹这堆灰，它就无影无踪了。

第二天这个病人情形更坏了。脸色惨白得像死人，双颊凹进去，眼睛深陷而灼灼发光，他现在脚步蹒跚地走着，在他这疯狂的游行中常常失脚，不停地说话。

"我不愿迫得非用武力不可，"院长对助手说道。

"但是这种费力的确有阻止的必要。今天他的体重只九十三磅。若使这样下去，两天之内他就会死去。"

---

2 to turn into：to change into 变为。

The chief doctor reflected. "Morphia? Chloral [1]?" he said, half questioningly.

"Only yesterday, morphia had no effect. Order him to be tied to his bed. I doubt whether he will live long."

VI

The patient was bound. He lay in a strait-jacket on his bed firmly tied with broad bands of linen to the bars of his iron bedstead; but his wild movements did not decrease, they rather became greater. For many hours he never stopped trying to free himself from his fetters. At last by a strong effort he succeeded in tearing one of the bands and released his legs, and thus managed to slip out of the other bandages. Then he began to walk about the room with bound hands, shouting out all sorts of wild, unintelligible speeches.

"Oh, what's the matter with you?[2]" cried the warder. "What devil has helped you? Grisha, Ivan, come here. The patient has got loose."

Then all three fell upon[3] him and a long struggle began, which was tiring to the keepers, but was torture for the patient, who was defending himself and using up[4] the remainder of his almost

---

1 Chloral: 是一种化合物CCl₃CHO, 为安眠之用。

2 what is the matter with you?: what has gone wrong with you? 你有什么意外的事故?

3 to fall upon: to assault 攻击。

4 to use up: to consume the whole of 消耗尽。

院长沉思一下。"吗啡？水化绿醇？"他说道，一半怀疑的样子。

"单是昨天，吗啡已不生效力了。叫人把他缚在床上罢。我怀疑他还会活多久。"

六

这个病人是缚住了。他穿了紧身短衣躺在床上，宽条的布带将他缚在他铁床的栏上；但是他那蛮野的挣扎并没有减少，到〔倒〕是更加剧烈了。有好几个钟头，他老是不断地想摆脱这个桎梏。最后靠一阵蛮劲，他做到扯破一个布条，解放出他的双腿，于是设法从其它束缚里滑出。然后他开始在房里走动，双手还是捆着，喊出各种胡乱的，无人能懂的话。

"啊，你到底怎么一回事？"看守者大声说道。"那个魔鬼帮了你？格力沙，伊凡，来这里。那个病人又随意走动了。"

然后三个人向他进攻，一场长久的格斗开始了，这使看守者感到疲倦，但是对于病人简直是虐刑，他现在自卫着，用尽他几乎已竭的力量的剩余。最后他们做到将他摔在床上，他们

exhausted strength. At last they were able to throw him on the bed, where they fastened him even tighter than before.

"You do not understand what you are doing!" cried the patient, quite out of breath. "You will all perish! I saw a third which was hardly open. Now it will be quite ready. Let me finish this work. It must be killed, killed, killed! Then all will be ended, all will be saved. I would send you, but it is only I who can do it. You would die if you even touched it!"

"Be quiet, sir, be quiet," said the old warder, who had been left on duty near the bed.

Suddenly the patient became quiet. He had decided to trick the warder. All day he was kept bound to his bed, and he was left in the same position for the night. After giving the patient his supper the warder spread a rug on the floor and lay down on it. In a minute he was fast asleep and the patient began his work.

He turned his body in such a way as to be able to touch the iron bar of the bed and feel it with his wrists through the long sleeves of the strait-jacket, and then began quickly and violently rubbing the coarse sailcloth against the bar. After a time the thick material gave way[1] and he was able to release his fore finger. Then the work went more rapidly. With an adroitness and suppleness which would be

---

1 to give way: to fail to resist; to break down 不能抵抗了；破了。

甚至于比以前更紧地把他缚在那里。

"你们不明白你们干什么!"这个病人喊道,完全喘不过气。"你们都快灭亡了!我从前看见一个第三朵红花,那时几乎还没有开。现在已经十分预备好快开了。让我完成这工作。那是一定要杀死的,杀死,杀死!然后一切都结束了,一切都得救了。我想派你们去干,但是只有我才能做这件事。你们会死去,甚至于假使你们只碰它一下!'

"安静,先生,安静,"老看守者说道,医院派他在床边看护他。

忽然间这个病人安静了。他决定好用诡计骗看守者。整天他始终扎在那里,晚上还是处于同样的姿势。拿晚餐给这病人后,看守者铺一块毯子在地板上,躺下来睡。一会儿他就睡熟了,这病人也开始他的工作。

他这样子转过身去,使他能够和床铺的铁栏接触,用紧身短衣长袖子里面的他的手腕摸着,然后开始急促地,凶猛地将这粗帆布和铁栏相擦。过了不久,这粗厚的衣料生了裂口,他能够解放出他的食指。此后就进行得更快了。具有一种矫捷同

inconceivable in a sane man, he managed to untie the knot that attached the sleeves at his back, unlaced the strait-jacket, and then sat listening for a long time to the snores of the warder. The old man was sleeping soundly. The patient took off the jacket and released himself from the bed. He was free. He tried the door. It was locked from the inside, and the key was probably in the warder's pocket. He was afraid of waking the old man if he began to search in his pockets, so he decided to leave the room by the window.

It was a calm, warm, dark night; the window was open; the stars shone in the black sky. He looked at the stars, recognised familiar constellations, and was delighted that they, as he thought, understood him and had sympathy with him. With blinking eyes he saw the endless rays that they sent him and his insane determination increased. It was necessary to bend the thick bar of the iron grating in order to squeeze through the narrow opening into the blind alley which was overgrown with bushes and climb over the high stone wall. There the last struggle would begin, and after wards—perhaps even death.

He tried to bend the thick iron bar with his naked hands, but the bar did not yield. Then he twisted the strong sleeves of the strait-jacket into a cord, fixed it to a forged iron spike at the end of a bar, and hung with his whole weight upon it. After desperate efforts that

轻柔,那在一个精神健全的人已是神妙不可测了,他设法解开双袖在他背后所打的结子,松开紧身短衣,然后坐下听了许久看守者的鼾声。老人睡的顶熟。这病人脱下紧身短衣,把自己从床上释放出。他得到自由了。他试去开门。门已经有人从里面锁了,钥匙或者在看守者袋里。他怕一搜他衣袋就惊醒他,所以他决定从窗子离开这房子。

这是一个恬静温暖的黑夜;窗子开着:星群在黑暗的天上发光。他望着星群,认出熟识的星座,很高兴他们,他以为,了解了他,对他生了同情。霎眼着,他看见它们送给他的无终极的长光,他那疯狂的决心也更加厉害了。那是必需的,将铁栅栏的厚格子弄湾〔弯〕,为的是才可以从这狭窄的开口挤出,到丛生有矮树的死胡同,再爬过高石墙。在那里最后的奋斗将开始了,此后——也许甚至于难免一死。

他试用他的赤手去弄湾〔弯〕那厚铁条,但是铁条不屈服。然后他把紧身短衣的坚固袖子绞成一根绳子,挂在一个铁条末端的一粒铸铁的长钉子上面,使他全身的力来捶下。经过了一

almost exhausted his strength the spike bent: a narrow passage was opened. He squeezed himself through it, and grazing his shoulders, elbows, and bare knees, managed to get through[1] the bushes and found himself near the wall. All was quiet, the flickering night-lights shone but dimly through the windows of the large building; nobody could be seen in the rooms. Nobody saw him; the old man who was on duty at his bedside was probably sound asleep. The stars blinked caressingly at him, and their rays penetrated to his very heart.

"I am coming to you, " he whispered, looking up to the sky.

All in tatters after his first efforts, with bleeding knees and arms and broken nails, he began to look for a convenient place to climb the wall. He noticed that some bricks were missing where the stone wall joined the mortuary. Feeling[2] for these spaces, and making full use of[3] them, he managed to scale the wall, and catching hold of the branches of the elm-trees that grew on the other side was able with their aid to let himself quietly down[4] to the ground.

He ran to the familiar place near the porch. The flower with its partly-opened petals looked dark, but showed clearly above the dewy grass.

"The last one! " whispered the patient, "the last one! Today it

---

1 to get through: to pass 走过。
2 feeling: examining by touching 摸索。
3 to make full use of: to make the best use of 尽量利用。

阵几乎用竭他的力量的拼命使劲,那长钉子湾〔弯〕下了:开一个狭窄的过道。他挤过去,擦伤了他的肩膀,肘节,同露出的膝盖,设法穿过矮树,最终看见自己走到墙边。一切都是安静的,闪动的灯光只是朦胧地从大屋子的窗子发出;看不见房子里面的任何人。谁也没有看见他;在他床旁看守他的那个老人也许睡得正浓。星群慈爱地向他霎眼,他们的光线贯穿了他的心窍。

"我就要到你们那里去了,"他低声说,眼望着天。

第一下努力之后,全身褴褛,膝臂流血,指甲也破了,他开始找一个方便地方来爬墙。他看出石墙和墓地毗连的地方少了几块砖。摸寻这几个空洞,好好地利用它们,他设法跳上墙,抓到墙外生的榆树的树枝,藉着它们,居然无声地让自己落到地面。

他跑到廊边熟识的地方。含着半开花瓣的花朵现出暗淡颜色,但是明白地显在沾露的野草之上。

"最后一个!"这病人低声说道,"最后一个!今天不是胜利

---

4 to let down: to set down 放下。

is victory or death! It is all the same to me now. Wait, " he said, looking up to the sky: "I will be with you soon."

He pulled up the plant, tore it to pieces, crushed it, and holding it firmly in his hands, returned to his room by the way he had come.

The old man was still fast asleep. The patient had hardly reached his bed when he fell unconscious upon it.

In the morning he was found dead. His face looked calm and bright, the emaciated features with their thin lips and deeply sunken eyes wore an expression of proud happiness. When they put him on the stretcher they tried to open his hand and take out the red flower, but his muscles were rigid, and he carried his trophy with him to the grave.

就是死！现在对于我都是一样的。等一会儿，"他仰视天空说道："我快同你们在一块儿了。"

他拔起这朵红花，扯成散片，压碎，紧握在他手里，从他来的那条路回到他房里。

老人还是熟睡着。这病人仅仅走近床边，就失掉意识地倒在上面。

早上人家看见他已死了。他的脸孔现出恬静同欣欢，那个憔悴的面貌以及薄嘴唇同深陷的眼睛露出胜利的快乐。当他们将他搁担架上面时候，他们试去张开他的手，拿出那朵红花，但是他的筋肉硬化了，那就带他的战利品到坟墓里去了。

Esther

厄斯忒哀史

（英汉对照）

W. H. White 著

梁遇春 译注

"英文小丛书"之一，上海北新书局，1930年10月付排，1930年12月初版

William Hale White
（1831—1913）

他的父亲是一家书铺的老板，一个有幽默趣味同卓然自立的性格的人，又是一个不服从英国国教的人，他的童年是在恬静的乡下里过去，后来到大学攻神学，因为他具有怀疑精神被开除了。此后的生涯就平淡地过去，在政府各机关里做事。他喜欢研究天文学，自己盖两个观象台，他觉得天文学是我们精确智识的象征，借此我们可以扩张我们的心境，对于人生得到一种合理的自信态度。这方面和那爱星空的歌德很有些相似。

他译了斯宾罗萨（Spinoza）的伦理学，著有几本长篇小说（都不是很长的）：*The Autobiography*，*The Deliverance*，*The Revolution in Tanner's Lane*，*Miliams' Schooling*，*Catharine Furze*，*Clara Hopgood*。第一本和第二本是带了自传性质，是极诚恳动人的自剖文字。此外还有几篇短篇小说和讨论宗教、文学、哲学种种问题的文章。

他的创造的主要情调是悲哀，一种默默的惆怅。他既不赞颂人生，也不咒诅人生，只是怀个凄然的心境来观察人生，描写人生。这大概是因为他的本质是 melancholy 罢。他和其他具有哀怨情怀的作家一样，写出极恬静清晰的散文，是近代一位散文名家。

William Hale White
(Mark Rutherford)
(1831—1913)

Esther

Blackdeep Fen, 24 Nov. 1838.

My dear Esther, —This is your birthday and your wedding-day, and I have sent you a cake and a knitted cross-over[1], both of which I have made myself. I can still knit although my eyes fail a bit[2]. I hope the cross-over will be useful during the winter. Tell me, my dear, how you are. Twenty-eight years ago it is since you came into the world. It was a dark day with a cold drizzling rain, but at eleven o'clock at night you were born, and the next morning was bright with beautiful sunshine. Some people think that Blackdeep must always be dreary at this time of year, but they are wrong. I love the Fen

---

1 cross-over: a kind of woman's wrap that crosses in front 胸前没有开口的女衣。

厄斯忒哀史

布拉克第普·樊,二十四日,十一月,一八三八年。

我亲爱的厄斯忒,——今天是你的生日,也是你结婚的纪念日,我寄给你一块饼,一件毛织的背心,这两件东西都是我自己制的。我还能够编织,虽然我的眼力比以前弱些了。我希望这件背心冬天里于你有用。我亲爱的,告诉我你的近况罢。你来到世界已经二十八年了。那是一个阴天,下着凄冷的微雨,夜里十一点钟你生下来,第二早却有美丽的阳光照耀着。有些人以为布拉克第普在这季里一定老是阴郁的,但是他们错了。

---

2 a bit:a little 有些;稍微。

country. It is my own country. This house, as you know, has belonged to your father's forefathers for two hundred years or more, and my father's old house has been in our family nearly as long. I could not live in London; but I ought not to talk in this way, for I hold it to be wrong to set anybody against what he has to do[1]. Your brother Jim[2] is the best of sons. He sits with me in the evening and reads the paper to me. He gose over to Ely market every week. He has his dinner at the ordinary[3], where many of the company drink more than is good for them[4], but never once has he come home the worse for liquor[5]. I had a rare[6] fright a little while ago. I thought there was something[7] between him and one of those Stanton girls at Ely. I saw she was trying to catch him. It is all off[8] now. She is a town girl, stuck-up[9], spends a lot of money on her clothes, and would have been no wife for Jim. She would not have been able to put her hand to[10] anything here. She might have broken my heart, for

---

1 这里所说的"无法避免的事情"是指厄斯忒不能不住在伦敦，因为她的丈夫是在那里干事情。

2 Jim：外国人叫亲热的人时候，常将名字缩短。Jim 这个字就是 James 的简称，此外也有把它减做 Jem，Jemmy，Jimmy 等等。其它的例子如 John 只喊做 Jack；Thomas 喊做 Tom；Elizabeth 喊做 Bessy 等等皆是。

3 ordinary：这字本来的意义是人们，在旅馆里或者其它公共食堂里所用的通常的、有定价的餐膳。后来贩卖常餐的馆子也叫做 ordinary 了。

4 to drink more than is good for them：喝了超过于他们有益的分量的酒；就是喝得太多了的意思。

我爱樊这个地方。它是我的家乡。这座屋子,你知道,属于你父亲的祖宗已经有二百年了,或者还不止;我父亲的老屋在我们家里几乎也有这么悠久的历史。我在伦敦住不下去,但是我不该这样说,因为我认为那是错的,使人不满于他所无法避免的事情。你的兄弟小杰是一个再好不过的儿子。他晚上陪我坐,念报纸给我听。他每星期到伊里市场一次。他就在那里饭店用餐,同座的人们有许多喝酒太多,但是他从来没有一次回家时现出醉酒的神气。不久以前,我有一个大恐慌。我那时猜他同伊里地方斯坦吞家里一位姑娘有些关系。我看出她想抓到他。这场风波现在完全过去了。她是一位城里姑娘,爱摆架子的,花费许多钱在她衣服上面,绝不能做小杰的一个良妻。她来这里一定是什么事也不能做。她也许会使我心碎,因为她一定设

---

5 the worse for liquor:因为酒而失却常态;醉了。
6 rare:great 大。
7 something:有些事情,不能看清,所以只是这么模糊地说着。
8 off:discontinued 过去了。
9 stuck-up:arrogant, conceited 骄傲;摆架子。
10 to put one's hand to:to assist with; to lend a hand to 帮助;协理。

she would have tried to draw Jim away from me. I don't believe, my dearest child, in¹ wedded love which lessens the love for father and mother. When you were going to be married what agony I went through! It was so wicked of me, for it was jealousy with no cause. I thank God you love me as much as ever. I wish I could see you again at Homerton, but the journey made me so ill last winter that I dare not venture just yet. —Your loving mother,

Rachel Sutton.

Homerton, 27 Nov. 1838.

My dearest Mother, —The cake was delicious: it tasted of Blackdeep, and the cross-over will be most useful. It will keep me warm on cold days, and the love that came with it will thicken the wool. But, mother, it is not a month ago since you sent me the stockings. You are always at work² for me. You are just like father. He gave us things not only on birthdays, but when we never looked out for them. Do you remember that week when wheat dropped three shillings a quarter? He had two hundred quarters which he might have sold ten days earlier. He was obliged to sell them at the next

---

1 to believe in: to have faith in the existence or efficacy, advisability of 相信……的存在，有用，或者有益。
2 at work: working 工作。

法离间小杰同我的感情。我最亲爱的孩子,我不相信天下有一种减少了对于父母孺慕之情的结婚爱情。当你从前快出嫁时候,我尝过多么难受的苦痛呀!那是我万分的不对,因为那是无端的妒忌。现在我谢谢上帝,你正像往常那么爱我。我希望能够再到荷马敦看你们,但是前一次旅行使我去年冬天身体那么不舒服,我此刻不敢冒险了。

——你亲爱的母亲,累折尔·萨吞。

荷马墩,二十七日,十一月,一八三八年。

我最亲爱的母亲,——那块饼很可口,吃起来有布拉克第普风味,那件背心将是极有用的。它在冷天里会使我感到温暖,它所带来的爱情会加厚羊毛。但是,母亲,那也是这一月内的事情,你送那些褥子给我。你总是为我工作着。你正同父亲一样。他不单是在我们生日里给我们东西,并且在我们绝没有预料得到东西的时候。你记得那个星期吗,当每一吨四分之一的麦落价三先令?他有五十吨麦,那可以在十天之前卖去。他只

market and lost thirty pounds, but he had seen at Ely that day a little desk, and he knew I wanted a desk, and he bought it for me with a fishing-rod and landing-net[1] for Jim.

My husband said he could not think of anything I needed and wrote me a cheque for two pounds.

O! that you could come here, and yet I am certain you must not. My heart aches to have you. In my daydreams I go over the long miles to Blackdeep, through Ware, through Royston, through Cambridge, through every village, and then I feel how far away you are. I turned out[2] of the room the other day[3] the chair in which you always sat. I could not bear to see it empty. Charles noticed it had gone and ordered it to be brought back. He may have suspected the reason why I put it upstairs. My dearest, dearest mother, never fear that my affection for you can become less. Sometimes after marriage a woman loves her mother more than she ever loved her before.

It is a black fog here and not a breath of air is stirring. How different are our fogs at Blackdeep! They may be thick, but they are white and do not make us miserable. I never shall forget when I was last in Fortyacres and saw the mist lying near the river, and the

---

1 landing-net: net for landing large fish when hooked 一种袋网用以取已经钓好的大鱼上陆。

2 to turn out: to expel from place 赶出一个地方。

3 the other day: a few days ago 几天之前。

好在第二次市集时出售，因此失丢了三十镑钱，但是那天他在伊里看见一张小书桌，他知道我要一张小书桌，他就买来给我，还带一条钓鱼竿同袋网给小杰。

我丈夫说他想不起我正需要什么东西，寄一张两镑支票给我。

啊！我多么希望你能够来这里，然而我十分知道你是不该来的。我的心疼痛，因为想同你在一块儿。在我睁着眼睛做的梦里，我默想从这里到布拉克第普的长途，经过威耳，经过罗益斯顿，经过剑桥，经过个个乡村，然后我觉得你是在多么远的地方呀。前几天我将你常坐的那张椅子从房里撑出。我不忍看它空旷地站在那里。查理斯发觉那张椅搬走了，叫人把它搬回。他也许猜出我把它弄到楼上去的理由。我最亲爱的，最亲爱的母亲，绝用不着害怕我对于你的感情会减少。有时，出嫁后一个女人爱她的母亲更甚于她一向的那样爱她。

这里是一片黑雾，一丝的空气也不通。我们布拉克第普的雾是多么不同呀！它们也有浓密的时候，但是它们是白色，不使我们愁闷。我绝不会忘记我前一次在福提亚克斯的情形，那

church spire bright in the sunlight. The churchyard and the lower part of the church were quite hidden.

What a mercy[1] Jim was not trapped by Dolly, for I suppose it was she. Jim is not the first she has tried to get. You are quite right. She might have broken your heart, and I am sure she would have broken Jim's, for she is as hard as a millstone[2].—Your loving child,

Esther.

Blackdeep Fen, 3 Dec. 1838.

Your letter made me feel unhappy. I am afraid something is on your mind. What is the matter? I was not well before I went to Homerton the last time, but maybe it was not London that upset me. If you cannot leave, I shall come. Let me hear by the next post.

Homerton, 5 Dec. 1838.

I told Charles I was expecting you. He said that your sudden determination seemed odd. "Your mother," he added, "is a woman

---

1 What a mercy: What a piece of good fortune attributable to a special providence 多么好的一场好运气，那是特别蒙天之庥的。

2 millstone: either of two circular stones for grinding grain or other substance; also, the kind of stone of which they are composed 磨谷或其他东西用的那种圆石；或者可以做这种磨石的石头。

时我看见雾低布河旁，礼拜堂的尖塔却在阳光里发亮。教堂坟地同教堂下部完全隐起来了。

多么侥幸呀，小杰没有上多丽的圈套，我想你说的是她。小杰不是她所想抓到的第一个人。你是很对的。她也许会使你心碎，我敢说她会叫小杰心碎，因为她的心是同磨坊石头一样硬。

——你亲爱的女儿，厄斯忒。

布拉克第普·樊，三日，十二月，一八三八。

你的信使我感到不安。我怕你心里有什么事情搁住。什么事呢？前次到荷马墩之前，我已经是不舒服了，所以也许不是伦敦搅乱了我的健康。若使你不能离开，我就来到你那里罢。下次邮车来的时候，请给我一封覆信。

荷马墩，五日，十二月，一八三八。

我告诉查理斯我现在等着你。他说你这突然的决定好像有些奇怪。"你的母亲，"他还说，"是一个凭着冲动行事的女人。

who acts upon impulses[1]. She ought always to take time for consideration. This is hardly the proper season for travelling." I asked him if he would let me go to Blackdeep. He replied that, unless there was some particular[2] reason for it, my propsal was as unwise as yours. What am I to do? A particular reason! It is a particular reason that I pine for my mother. Can there be any reason more particular than a longing for the sight of a dear face, for kisses and embraces? You must counsel me.

Blackdeep, 15 Dec. 1838.

As Charles imagines I am carried away[3] by what he calls impulses, I did not answer your letter at once, and I have been thinking as much as I can. I am not a good hand at it[4]. Your dear father had a joke against me. "Rachel, you can't think; but never mind, you can do much better without thinking than other people can with it." I wish I had gone straight to you at once, and yet it was better I did not. It would have put Charles out[5] and this would not have been pleasant for either you or me. I would not have you at Blackdeep

---

1 impulses: sudden tendency to act without reflection 不加思索的突然行动的趋向；冲动。
2 particular: special 特别的。
3 to be carried away: to be transported, or inspired 被……所感动。

她应当事事都慢慢考虑一下，这季是不大宜于旅行的。"我问他肯让我到布拉克第普吗。他答道，除非有什么重要的理由，否则我的提议正像你的一样不智。我要怎么办呢？一个重要的理由！我渴想一见我的母亲，这岂不是一个重要的理由吗！世界里还有别的什么理由更重要过渴望见到一个亲爱的脸孔，渴望得到接吻同拥抱呢？你得告诉我应当怎么办。

布拉克第普，十五日，十二月，一八三八。

查理斯既然认为我是受他所说的冲动所支配，所以我不立刻覆你的信，却尽我的能力去思索一番。我在这方面不是个好脚色。你亲爱的父亲对于我有一句笑话。"累折尔，你不能思想；但是，不要紧，你不思想地行事比别人思想后行事还强得多。"我希望我立刻一直到了你那里，然而我还是不去好些。那会使查理斯不高兴，这是你我所不愿意的。现在无论如何我绝

---

4 a good hand at：skillful at 善于；精于。
5 to put one out：to irritate on 激怒。

now for worlds[1]. The low fever[2] has broken out, and today there were two funerals. Parson preached a sermon about it; it was a judgement from God. Perhaps it is, but why did it take[3] your father three years ago? It is all a mystery, and it looks to me somethimes as if here on earth there were nothing but mystery. I have just heard that parson is down with[4] the fever himself.

Do let me have a long letter at once.

Homerton, 20 Dec. 1838.

A Mrs. Perkins has been here. She sat with me for an hour. She spends her afternoons in going her rounds[5] among her friends, as she calls them, but she does not care for them, nor do they care for her. She looks and speaks like a woman who could not care for anybody, and yet perhaps there may be somewhere a person who could move her.

I am so weary of the talk of my neighbours. It is so different from what we used to[6] have at Blackdeep. Oh me! those evenings

---

1 for worlds: on any account; even if you give me worlds 无论如何；即使你拿大千世界来相酬。

2 low fever: a fever marked by a feeble pulse, clammy skin, and nervous depression 一种热病，它的征候是脉搏低微，皮肤湿寒同精神郁结。这里译做"低热病"是照字面译，因为译者没有进解剖室操刀过，不知道中国通用的专门医学名词。

3 to take: to remove from life 弄死。

不肯让你来布拉克第普。微热病现在又流行了，今天有两家人安葬。牧师关于这事有一篇诲言，说是上帝的责罚。也许是罢，但是为什么这个病三年前把你父亲带到坟墓里？这完全是一个神秘，有时我觉得世上没有别的东西，只是神秘。我刚才听说牧师自己也害了微热病。

你千万得立刻写一封长信给我。

荷马墩，二十日，十二月，一八三八。

一位柏琴兹太太刚才在这里。她和我坐谈一个钟头。她把她的下午都用在循环地找她的朋友，她是这样称呼她们的，但是她对于她们并不关切，她们也不欢喜她。她的神气同谈话好像一个不会爱任何人的女人，然而也许世上某处有一个人能够打动她的心。

我是这么厌倦于我邻居们的谈话。那和我们在布拉克第普所常听到的是如是不同。啊！那是多么快乐的晚上！当父亲夜

---

4 down with fever：prostrate with fever 发热躺下来了。
5 rounds：circuits 循环游行。作此解时常居复数。
6 used to：accustomed to 常常惯于。

when father came in at dark, and Mr. and Mrs. Thornley came afterwards and we had supper at eight, and father and Mr. Thornley smoked their pipes and drank our home-brewed ale and we had all the news—how much Mr. Thornley had got for his malt, how that pig-headed[1] old Stubbs wouldn't sell his corn, and how when he began to thresh it and the ferrets[2] were brought, a hundred rats were killed and bushels of wheat had been eaten.

You ask me what is the matter. I do not deny I am not quite happy, but it would be worse than useless to dwell upon[3] my unhappiness and try to give you reasons for it. London, in the winter, most likely does not suit me. I shall certainly see you in the spring, and then I hope I shall be better.

Blackdeep Fen, Christmas Day, 1838.

As a rule it is right to hide our troubles, but it is not right that you should hide yours from me. You are my firstborn[4] child and my only daughter. There are girls who are very good, but between their mothers and them there is a wall. They do what they are bid; they are kind, but that is all. They live apart from those that bore them. I

---

1 pig-headed: obstinate 固执。
2 ferret: kind of pole-cat used in catching rats 捕鼠用的臭猫。
3 to dwell upon: to write or speak at length 详论。
4 firstborn: eldest 顶大的女儿。

里回来，托尼先生同太太跟着也来，我们八点钟用晚餐，父亲同托尼先生抽他们底烟斗，喝我们家酿的麦酒，我们听到一切新闻——托尼先生的麦芽卖了多少钱，固执得同猪一样的老头子士达布斯怎样不肯卖他的谷，以及当他开始打谷，把捕鼠的猫带来时候，杀死了一百个耗子，有不少的麦给它们吃去了。

你问我什么事使我不乐。我并不否认我是不十分高兴，但是去细论我的忧郁，想向你说出那理由，这不单是无补于事，而且还有别的坏影响。伦敦，冬天里，大概和我不相宜罢。春天里我一定会看见你，我希望那时我会好些。

布拉克第普·樊，圣诞日，一八三八。

照例我们应当隐藏起我们的烦恼，但是你不该把你的向我隐藏。你是我头胎生下的孩子，又是唯一的女儿。有些女儿性格很好，但是在她们母亲同她们之间有一片墙。她们照她们母亲所吩咐的话做去；她们也是温厚殷勤，但是只是这么多了。她们的生活和生她们的人们是隔膜的。这种的孝顺同感情我看

would not give a straw for such duty and love. I gathered one of our Christmas roses this morning. We have taken great care to keep them from being splashed and spoilt. There was not a speck on it. I put it in water and could not take my eyes off it. Its white flower lay spread open and I could look right down into it. I thought of you. When you were a little one—ay, and after you were out of short-frocks[1]—you never feared to show me every thought in your mind, you always declared that if you had wished to hide anything from me, it would have been of no use to try. What a blessing that was to me! How dreadful it would be if, now that you are married, you were to change! I am sure you will not and cannot.

Homerton, 1 Jan. 1839.

The New Year! What will happen before the end of it? I feel as if it must be something strange. I have just read your last letter again, and I cannot hold myself in[2]. My dearest mother, I confess I am wretched. It might be supposed that misery like mine would express itself with no effort[3], but it is not so: it would be far easier to describe ordinary things. I am afraid also to talk about it, lest that which is dim and shapeless should become more real.

---

1 short-frock: 小孩穿的外衣，所以 out of short-frocks 是指已经成年了。
2 to hold in: to keep in check 制止住。
3 with no efforts: not forcibly 不是有力地。

的不值一根草。今天早上我摘了一朵我们的圣诞节玫瑰。我们一向很小心不让它们沾污了，弄坏了。它上面一个污点也没有。我将它放在水里，我的眼睛不能离开它。它的白花展开着，我能够一直看下去。我想起你了。当你是个小姑娘——不，甚至于当你已经不穿短袍子的时候——你绝没有怕将你心里个个的想头拿给我看，你常常说若使你想把什么想头藏起不让我看，那是白费了功夫。这对于我是多么大的幸福呀！那是多么可怕，若使现在嫁人后，你却变了！我相信你不会变，而且不能够变。

荷马墩，一日，一月，一八三九。

新年！在这年底之前会有什么事发生呢？我觉得好像一定有些奇事。我刚才又念一遍你最近这封信，我不能自制了。我最亲爱的母亲，我承认我是愁闷得很。也许人们以为像我这样的悲哀不会有力地说出，其实不然，因为描状通常的事情是很容易的。我又不敢谈这件事，怕的是本来是模糊未成形的惆怅会变为更真实的。

Since the day we were married Charles and I have never openly quarrelled. He is really good: he spends his evenings at home and does not seem to desire entertainment elsewhere. He likes to see me well dressed and does not stint in house expenditure, although he examines it carefully and pays a good many of the bills himself by cheque. He has been promoted to be manager of the bank, and takes up[1] his new duties today. Mrs. Perkins, whose husband is one of the partners, told me that he had said that there is nobody in the bank equal to Charles for sound sense and business ability; that everything with which he has to do goes right[2]; he is always calm, never in a hurry[3], and never betrayed into imprudence. This I can well believe. As you know, Jim asked him a month ago in much excitement for advice about Fordham, who owed him £200. Jim had heard there was something wrong. Charles put the letter in the desk and did not mention it to me again till a week afterwards, when he asked me to tell Jim the next time I wrote to Blackdeep that he need not worry himself, as Fordham was quite safe. It is certainly a comfort to a woman that her husband is a strong[4] man and that he is much respected by his employers. Of what have I to complain? O mother, life here is so

---

1 to take up: to enter upon 开始执行。
2 to go right: to take a good course 走一条顺利的道；成功。
3 in a hurry: in undue hestiness 在无谓的匆忙里。

自从我们结婚那天起，查理斯同我素来没有公然吵架过。他的确是好丈夫；他晚上都花在家里，不像想到别地方去寻乐。他喜欢看我穿着好衣服，家中用费并不吝惜，虽然他仔细考察一切款项的用途，许多帐都是他自己用支票付的。他升到做银行的总经理，今天开始执行他的新职务。柏琴兹太太，她的丈夫是一个股东，告诉我他丈夫说银行里没有一个人在正确的眼光同办事能力这两方面赶得上查理斯；凡是他经手过的事情都是成功的；他永远是冷静，绝没有感到匆忙，绝不会弄糊涂了。这是我很能相信的。你也知道，小杰前月很张皇地问他福特汉姆的情形，这个人欠他二百金镑。小杰听说这个人的情形不妙。查理斯把信放到书桌里，不向我再提起这件事了，等到过了一个星期，他吩咐我下次写信到布拉克第普时候告诉小杰，他用不着白担心，因为福特汉姆的经济情形是十分安全的。这对于女人的确是个安慰，她的丈夫是一位精明强干的人，很受他的东家们的尊敬。我所要埋怨的是什么呢？啊，母亲，这里的生

---

4 strong: having intellectual power, endurance, etc 有识见、毅力等等。

dull! This is not the right word; it is common, but if you can fill it up with my meaning, there is no better. It will then be terrible. There is hardly a flower in the garden, although not a weed is permitted. The sooty laurels unchanging through winter and summer I hate. Some flowers I am sure would grow, but Charles does not care for them. Neatness is what he likes, and if the beds are raked quite smooth, if the grass is closely shaven and trimmed and not a grain of gravel in the path is loose, he is content. He cannot endure the least untidiness in the house. If papers are left lying loosely about, he silently puts them evenly together. He brings all his office ways into the dining-room; the pens must never be put aside unwiped and the ink-bottles must be kept filled to a certain height. We do not get much sun at any time of day in Homerton, and we face the west. Charles wishes the blinds to be drawn when it shines, so that it may not fade the curtains. We have few books excepting Rees's cyclopaedia, and they are kept in a glazed case. If I look at one I have to[1] put it back directly I have done with it. I saw this place before I was married, but it did not look then as it looks now, and I did not comprehend how much

---

1 to have to: to be obliged to 不得不。

活是这么无聊！"无聊"不是合式的字；这字太普通了，但是你若使能够填进我的意思，那么这是个再凑巧不过的字了。那么，这将成为一个可怕的字了。这里花园几乎没有一朵花，虽然一根野草也不许长在里面。我厌恶那历冬夏而不变的，煤黑色的桂树。我相信有些花在这个园里可以生长，但是查理斯不喜欢它们。他所高兴的是洁净；若使花坛是耙得很平的，若使草地是修剪得整整齐齐，园里马路上没有一粒小石子松了，那么他就满意了。他不能忍受屋里有一丝丝的不洁。若使纸张随便散在桌上，他一声不则地把它们整齐地归在一处。他将他办公室的一切习惯带进食堂；笔绝不应当没有揩干放在桌上，墨水瓶一定要盛有相当分量的墨水。在荷马墩，一天里任何时候，我们都见不到许多的太阳光，然而，我们却是朝西的。查理斯要把遮阳帘放下，当阳光照耀时候，为的是要保着挂幕不落色。我们没有什么书，除开了一部李氏百科全书，那又是放在玻璃柜子里面。若使我拿出一本，看完就得立刻归还原处。在他结婚之前，我看见这个地方，但是那时的印象和现在的印象不同，

Blackdeep was a part of me[1]. The front door always open in daytime, the hollyhocks down to the gate, the strawberry beds, the currant and gooseberry bushes, the lilacs, roses, the ragged orchard at the back, the going in and out without "getting ready", our living-room[2] with Jim's pipes and tobacco on the mantel-shelf, his gun over it, his fishing-tackle in the corner—I little understood that such things and the ease which is felt when our surroundings grow to[3] us make a good part of[4] the joy of life. When I came to Blackdeep for my holiday and lifted the latch, it was just as if a stiff, tight band round my chest dropped from me. I have nothing to do here. We keep three servants indoors. I would much rather have but two and help a little myself. They are good servants, and the work seems to go by mechanism without my interference. I suggested to Charles that, as they were not fully employed, we should get rid of one, but he would not consent. He preferred, he said, paid service. To me the dusting of my room, paring apples, or the cooking of any little delicacy, is not service. The cook asks for orders in the morning; the various dishes are properly prepared; but if I were Charles, and my wife understood her business, I should like to taste her hand[5] in them. I never venture

---

1 a part of me：同她个人的精神有密切的关系，几乎是分不开的，所以说变成她的一部分了。
2 living-room：sitting-room 闲坐的房子，和卧室相反。
3 to grow to：to coalesce 合成一体。
4 a good part：a great part 一大部分。
5 hand：skill 技能。

那时我也不晓得布拉克第普在我心里占多么重要的部分。白天里总是开着的大门，一直到大门口的蜀葵，草莓的花坛，覆盆子同醋栗的小树林，紫丁香花，玫瑰花，后面那片杂乱的花园，"没有预备"的随意出入，我们闲坐的房子，火炉架上有小杰的烟斗同烟，上面挂着他的枪，角落上放有他的钓鱼具——我那时不大知道这些东西当我们的环境跟我们溶在一起时所感到的快感是构成了人生快乐的大部分。当我来到布拉克第普过放假的日子，拿起门闩时候，真好像一条紧束着我胸口的硬带离我而去。在这里我无事可干。我们家里用三个仆人。我倒很愿意只用两个，我自己从旁帮助一点儿。她们是好仆人，家里事情同机械一般地天天干下去，用不着我的干涉。我向查理斯提议，她们既然不很忙，我们还是减少一个罢，但是他不答应。他高兴，他说，用钱买来的服役。由我看起来，拂拭我自己的房子，削苹果，或者煮些好吃的小东西，并不算服役。早上厨子问我吃什么菜；种种各盘的菜好好地预备了；但是假设我是查理斯，我妻子懂得她做的事情，我倒喜欢有时尝一尝她亲手烹饪的菜。我现在绝没有冒险到

into the kitchen. "The advantage of paid service", added Charles, "is that if it is inefficient you can reprimand or dismiss." Nothing in me finds exercise. I want to work, to laugh, to expect. There was always something going on[1] at Blackdeep, no two days alike. I never got up in the morning knowing what was before me till bedtime. That outlook too from my window, how I miss it! —the miles and miles of distance, the rainbow arch in summer complete to the ground, the sunlight, the stormy wind, the stars from the point overhead to the horizon far away—I hardly ever see them here.

You will exclaim "Is this all?" If you were here you would think it enough, but it—. The clock is striking one. Charles is to be at home to lunch. He is going to buy the house and is to meet the owner this afternoon, an old man who lives about ten minutes' walk[2] from us. Charles thinks the purchase will be a good investment and that another house might be built on part of the garden.

Blackdeep, 15 Jan. 1839.

I am not surprised you find London dull, but I grieve that it has taken such an effect on you. I hoped that, as you are young, you would get used[3] to the bricks and mortar and the smoke.

---

1 going on: getting on 进行着。
2 ten minutes' walk: 走路要花十分钟时间的距离。
3 to get used: to become accustomed 惯于。

厨房去过。"用钱买来的服役的好处,"查理斯还说,"是在乎若使不行,你能够责备或者开除。"我身里没有一种力气有使用的机会。我要工作,大笑,期望。在布拉克第普时总是有些事情,没有两天是同样的。每天从起身一直到就寝我不知道这天里会有什么事发生。从我房里窗子望见的光景,我多么思念呀!——几十里辽远的平原,夏天两头连到地的虹弧,阳光,暴风,从头顶一直到远处水平线的星群——我在这儿几乎没有看到它们。

你会惊奇地喊道"就是这些理由吗?"假设你自己在这里,你会以为很够了,但是那——。钟打一点了。查理斯快回来用午餐了。他将去买那座屋子,今天下午去会那卖主,一个老头子,他的家和我们这里相隔一段,走十分钟的路。查理斯以为这下购置将成很好的投资,在那花园上可以另盖一座屋子。

布拉克第普,十五日,一月,一八三九。
我并不惊奇你觉得伦敦无聊,但是我很伤心它于你有这么大的影响。我希望,你既是还年青,你将惯于砖头灰泥和烟雾的环境。

Jim came in and I had to stop. The Lynn coach is set fast in the snow near the turnpike at the top of our lane, and he is going to help dig it out. I will take up my pen again. You are no worse off than thousands of country girls who are obliged to live in streets narrower than those in Homerton. I cannot help boding you are not quite free[1] with me. I do beseech you to hide nothing. There must even now be something the matter[2] beyond what I have heard. I cannot say any more at present. My head is in a whirl. May be you will have a child. That will make all the difference to you.

Homerton, 20 Jan. 1839.

How shall I begin? I must tell the whole truth. Mother, mother, I have made a great mistake, the one great mistake of life. I have mistaken the man with whom I am to live. Charles and I were engaged for two years. I have discovered nothing new in him. I was familiar with all his ways and thought them all good. I compared him with other men who were extravagant and who had vices, and I considered myself fortunate. He was cool, but how much better it was to be so than to have a temper, for I should never hear angry words from him which cannot be forgotten? I remembered how measured

---

1 free: frank; unreserved 坦白。
2 something the matter: something wrong 有些意外的事故。

小杰进来了，我得停笔。林赤公共马车陷在我们巷口栅栏旁边的雪里，他现在去帮人家把它掘出。我要再拿起笔来。你的情形并不比成千成万的乡下姑娘更坏，她们也是〈被〉迫得住在比荷马墩区里街道更窄的小街上。我免不了觉得你对于我不十分坦白。我求你什么也不要遮瞒。必定还有些我所未听到的重要事情。此刻我不能再说什么。我的思想是纷至沓来。也许你将有一个小孩。那会把你的环境完全变更了。

荷马墩，二十日，一月，一八三九。

我怎么开头呢？我得说出全部的真情。母亲，母亲，我铸成了一个大错，一生里唯一的大错。我看错做我终身伴侣的男人。查理斯同我结婚两年了。我没有发现出他的什么新的性质。我早已熟悉他的一切习惯，认为都是好的。我把他拿来同其他胡闹的和有嗜好的人们相比，我觉得自己有幸。他是冷淡的，但是这比起坏脾气好了许多了，因为我绝不会从他听到永不能忘记的怒话？我记起我的叔叔罗伯的说话是多么有分寸，他是

my uncle Robert's speech was, how quiet he was, and yet no two human beings could have been more devoted to one another than uncle and aunt. Charles's quietude seemed so like uncle's. Charles was very methodical. He always came to see me on the same days, at the same hours, and stayed the same time. It provoked me at first, but I said to myself that he was not a creature of fits and starts[1] and that I could always depend on him. He always kissed me when we met and when we parted. I do not remember that he ever had me in his arms, and I never felt he was warm and eager when we were alone together; but I had heard of men and women who married for what they called love, and in a twelvemonth it had vanished and there was nothing left. Of many small particulars I took but[2] little notice. When we chose the furniture I wanted bright-coloured curtains, but he did not like them and bought dark red, gloomy stuff. I tried to think they were the best because they would not show the London dirt. I had a bonnet with scarlet trimmings which suited my black hair, but he asked me to change them for something more sober, because they made me conspicuous. Again I thought he was right, and that what might do[3] for the country might not be proper in town. Trifles! And yet to me now what a meaning they have! Two years—and everything

---

1 fits and starts: capricious impulses and movements 作辍无常。
2 but: only 只是。

多么安详，然而天下人不能够比叔叔婶婶更彼此相亲爱了！查理斯的安详看起来这么像我叔叔的。查理斯是很严正的。他总是在一定的日子，一定的时候来望我，他滞留的时间也是一定的。这起先使我生气，但是我对自己说他不是个任性的人，我可以永远知道他是靠得住的。他总是在我们相会同分手时候和我接吻。我记不起来他曾拥抱我过，我绝没有感到他是热烈的，兴奋的，当我俩独自一起时候；但是我曾听到男人同女人为着他们所谓爱情而结婚，一年内爱情消减了，没有别的任何东西剩下。还有许多零星细节，我都不大去注意。当我拣选家具时候，我要颜色鲜明的挂幕，但是他不喜欢它们，购买深红色，阴森森的料子。我特意去想这些是最相宜的，因为不会现出伦敦尘土的痕迹。我有一顶镶红花边的帽子，那和我的黑发很相称，但是他叫我换上一些颜色暗淡的花边，因为那使我太惹人注目了。我又想他是对的，在乡下可以的，在城里也许不行。零星小事！然而对于我它们现在含有多么大的意义呀！两年——什么都变了，虽然，像我刚才

---

3 to do：to serve 适用。

is changed, although, as I have just said, I have found nothing new! The quietude is absence of emotion, different in its root from uncle Robert's serenity. It is the deadly sameness of a soul[1] to which nothing is strange and wonderful and a woman's heart is not so interesting as an advertisement column in the newspaper. He never cares to look into mine. I do not pretend that there is anything remarkable in it, but if he were to open it he would find something worth having. This absence of curiosity to explore what is in me kills me. What must the bliss of a wife be when her husband searches her to her inmost depths, when she sees tender questions in his eyes, when he asks her *do you really feel so*? and she looks at him and replies *and you*? I could endure the uneventfulness of outward life if anything not unpleasant happened between me and Charles. Nothing happens. Something happens in my relationship to my dog. I pat him and he is pleased; he barks for joy when I go out. I cannot live with anybody with whom I am always on exactly the same even terms—no rising, no falling, mere stagnation. I am dead, but it is death without its sleep and peace. Fool, fool that I was! I cannot go on[2]. What shall I

---

1 to deadly sameness of a soul 灵魂可怕的单调。
2 to go on: to continue, to persever 继续；支持下去。

所说的，我并没有发现什么新性质！他的安详是感情的缺乏，根本上同我们叔叔罗伯的恬静不同。那是一个灵魂的死一般的单调，由它看起来，世上没有一件东西是奇怪的，一个女人的心还不如报纸里的广告栏那么有趣。他绝不去观察我的心。我并不是说我的心里有什么奇特的东西，但是若使他来打开它，他会发现值得占有的东西。这种好奇心的缺乏，不想去探讨我心里的情调，真是致我的死命。那必定是一个妻子多么大的幸福呀，当她的丈夫搜寻到她心里的最深一层，当她在他眼睛里看到殷勤的疑问，当他问她，"你真觉得这样吗？"她也望着他，答道"你呢？"我能够忍受外生活的平淡，若使我同查理斯之间常有什么不是不快意的事情发生。然而，我们之间是什么事情也不发生的。我跟狗的关系里有些事情发生。我抚着它，它高兴了，当我出去时候，它喜欢得狂吠。我不能同任何人同居，当我跟他始终居于那个平淡无谓的情形里——既不升高，也不降落，单单是呆滞着。我算是死了，但是这是一种没有得到长眠同安宁的死。傻子，我从前真是一个傻子！我不能再往下写了。我有什么可干呢？若使查理斯贪

do? If Charles drank I might cure or tolerate him; if he went after[1] another woman I might win him back. I can lay hold of nothing.

A child? Ah no! I have longed unspeakably for a child sometimes, but not for one fathered[2] by him.

Blackdeep, 24 Jan. 1839.

I knew it all, but I dared not speak till you had spoken. Your letter came when we were at breakfast. I could not open it, for my heart told me what was in it. Jim wondered why I let it lie on the table, and I made some excuse. After breakfast I took it upstairs into my own room and sat down by the bed, your father's bed, and cried and prayed. If he were alive, he would have helped me, or if no help could have been found, he would have shared my sorrow. It is dreadful that, no matter[3] what my distress may be, he cannot speak. What counsel can I send you? I have had much to do with[4] affliction, but not such as yours. My love for you is of no use. I will be still. I have always found, when I am in great straits and my head is confused, I

---

1 to go after: to visit as a wooer 当个情人去追求。
2 to be fathered: to be begotten 生下的。
3 no matter: it makes no diffirence 不管；无论。
4 to do with: to get on with 对付。

酒，我可以医好他，或者容忍他；若使他去追求另一个女人，我也许可以把他弄得回心转意。现在我却不能抓到任何东西。

生一个小孩？啊，不！有时我说不出地渴望得到一个小孩，但是叫他做父亲的小孩我却不想要。

布拉克第普，二十四日，一月，一八三九。

我早已明白一切了，但是在你说出之前，我不敢道破。你的信来时，我们正用早餐。我不能打开它，因为我的心已预料到里面说的是什么话。小杰纳罕为什么我让它躺在桌上，我就随便托辞一下。早餐后，我带它到楼上，我自己房里，坐在床旁，你父亲的床，我哭泣祈祷着。若使他还活着，他会帮助我；假使是无能为力的，他也会分了我的忧愁。这真是可怕，无论我的苦痛是怎么样子，他总不能说话。我能给你什么劝告呢？我对付过许多烦恼，但是未曾碰到像你这样的。我对于你的爱情是无用的。我决定现在不则一声。我一向老觉得，当我在很大困难里，我的头是胡涂了的时候，我必得噤口，什么举动都

must hold my tongue[1] and do nothing. If I do not move, a way may open out to me. Meantime, live in the thought of Blackdeep and of me. It will do you no harm and may keep you from sinking.

Homerton, 30 Jan. 1839.

No complaint, no reproof. You might have told me it was perhaps my fault.

I always have to reflect on what I am about to say to him. I go through my sentences to the end before I open my lips. He dislikes exaggeration, and checks me if I use a strong word; but surely life sometimes needs strong words, and those which are tame may be further from the truth than those which burn. When he first began to think about buying the house, I was surprised and talked with less restraint than is usual with me. After a little while he said that I had not contributed anything definite to a settlement of the question. I dare say I had not, but it is natural to me to speak even when I do not pretend to settle questions. He seems to think that speech is useless for a distinct, practical purpose. At Blackdeep almost everything that comes into my head finds its way to my tongue.[2] The repression here is unbearable.

---

1 to hold one's tongue: to keep silent 静默，缄口不言。
2 就是想到那里，说到那里，毫无顾忌同迟疑的意思。

没有。若使我毫无活动，也许会有一条路子呈现我的面前。现在，你就在怀念着布拉克第普同我里面过日子罢。这于你不会是有害的，也许还使你免得意志完全沉没了。

荷马墩，三十日，一月，一八三九。

来信没有埋怨的话，没有责备的话。你很可以对我说也许那都是我的错。

我总得把我要对他说的话先思量一下。我将我说的整句话在心想好，然后再开口。他不喜欢过实失真的话，总是止着我，当我用一个强烈的字眼；但是人生的确有时需要强烈的字眼，雅驯的辞句也许会比烈火般的言语跟真相离得更远。当他第一次谈到购买那座屋子，我很惊奇，说话时不像通常那么有节制。过了一会儿，他说我并没有贡献什么意见，关于解决这个问题。我敢说我没有，但是我自然会说许多话，甚至于当我并不企图解决什么问题时候。他好像以为说话是无谓的，除非有一定实用的目的。在布拉克第普，几乎凡是我想起来的都到我舌头上。在这里，那抑制是不可忍的。

Last night it rained, and Charles's overcoat was a little wet at the bottom. He asked that it might be put to the fire. Directly he came down in the morning he felt his coat and at breakfast said in his slow way, "My coat has not been dried." I replied that I was very sorry, that I had quite forgotten it, and that it should be dried before he was ready to start. I jumped up, brought it into the room and hung it on a chair on the hearth-rug. He did not thank me and appeared to take no notice. "I am indeed very sorry," I repeated. He then spoke. "I do not care about the damp; it is the principle involved. I have observed that you do not endeavour systematically to impress my requests on your mind. If you were to take due note of them at the time they are made, and say them aloud two or three times to yourself, they would not escape your memory. Forgetfulness is never an excuse in business, and I do not see why it should be at home." "O Charles!" I cried, "do not talk about principles in such a trifle; I simply forgot. I should be more likely to forget my cloak than your coat." He did not answer me, but opened a couple of letters, finished his breakfast, and then began to write at the desk. I went upstairs, and when I returned to the breakfast room he had gone. In the evening, he behaved as if nothing had passed between us. He would have thought it ridiculous if such a reproof had

昨晚下雨，查理斯的外套下缘有些潮湿。他说可以拿去烘一下。今早他一下来，就摸一摸他的外套，早餐的时候用他那从容不迫的态度说道，"我的外套没有烘过。"我答道我很觉得难过，我完全忘却了；我现在要把它烘干，在他预备出去之前。我跳起来，拿它到房里，挂在炉边地毡上的椅子上面。他也不谢我，好像不去理会。"我的确很觉得难过，"我又说。他于是说话了。"我并不在乎那潮湿；我所不满意的是这里面所含的意义。我看出你不努力去有系统地把我的请求设法记在心里。若使当我说出时候，你就注意着，大声地对自己重复说两三遍，这些话绝不能逃出你的记忆。在公务方面，忘却绝不能成为一个借口，我看不出为什么在家里这可以。""啊，查理斯！"我喊道，"这些小事里你不要谈什么意义；我只是忘却了。比起你的外套，我更容易忘了我自己的大衣。"他没有答我，却扯开两封信，吃完他的早餐，然后开始在他桌上写字。我上楼去，当我回到用早餐的房子，他已出门了。晚间他照常行事，好像我们里面并没有发生什么事情。他会以为那是很滑稽的，若使这么一

unsettled[1] a clerk at the bank, and why should it unsettle me? The clerk expects to be taught his lesson daily. So does every rational being.

Nothing! Nothing! I can imagine Mrs. Perkins' contempt, if I were to confide in her. "As good a husband as ever lived. What do you want, you silly creature? I suppose it's what they call passion. You should have married a poet. You have made an uncommonly good match and ought to be thankful." A poet! I know nothing of poets, but I do know that if marriage for passion be folly, there is no true marriage without it.

Blackdeep, 7 Feb. 1839.

I am no clearer now than I was a fortnight ago. I wish I could talk to somebody, and then perhaps my thoughts would settle themselves. Last Sunday I made up my mind[2] I would come to you at all costs; then I doubted, and this morning again I was going to start at once. Now my doubts have returned. Jim notices how worried I am, and I make excuses.

I cannot rest while I am not able to do more than put you off[3]

---

1 unsettled: unfixed; disordered 心乱。
2 to make up one's mind: to determine 决定。
3 to put off: to turn aside from a purpose 敷衍。

个责备会使银行里一个书记精神不安,那么为什么会使我不安呢?书记预料出天天会得到教训。每个有理性的人也都该这样了。

算不得什么!算不得什么!我可以想像出柏金兹太太的轻蔑,若使我把心里话对她说出。"世上找不出再好的丈夫。你所要的是什么,你这傻家伙?我想是人们所谓的热情罢。那么你应当嫁给一个诗人。你结了一个非常好的婚姻,该感谢上帝!"一个诗人!我并不晓得诗人是什么样子,但是我知道若使为热情而结婚是件愚蠢的事,恐怕天下一切真正的婚姻都带有愚蠢的意味罢。

布拉克第普,七日,二月,一八三九。

我现在正同两星期前那么糊涂。我希望我能对谁说出这事,那时也许我的思想会变有头绪些。前星期日我下个决心不顾一切到你那里去;然后我又踌躇,今早我又快立刻出发。现在我的踌躇又回来了。小杰看出我是多么烦恼,我对他说出其他的托辞。

我总觉得不安,当我只能够拿请你耐心地忍受你的运命这

by praying you to bear your lot patiently. It is so hard to stand helpless and counsel patience. Could you give him up[1] and live here? I am held back, though, from this at present. I am not sure what might happen if you were to leave him. Perhaps he would be able to force you to return. You have no charge to make against him which anybody but myself would understand.

I must still wait for the light which I trust will be given me. It is wonderful how sometimes it strikes down on me suddenly and sometimes grows by degrees like the day over Ingleby Fen. I lay in bed late this morning, for I hadn't slept much, and watched it as it spread, and I thought of my Esther in London who never sees the sunrise.

Homerton, 14 Feb. 1839.

There is hardly anything to record—no event, that is to say—and yet I have been swept on at a pace which frightens me. The least word or act urges me more than a blow. Yesterday I made up my accounts and was ten shillings short[2]. I went over[3] them again and again and could not get them right. I was going to put into the cash box ten shillings of my own money, but I thought there might be

---

1 to give up: to abandon; to cease to have to do with (a person) 离开; 同某人脱离关系。
2 ten shillings short: 短了十先令; 差了十先令。
3 to go over: to examine 研究。

类话来敷衍你。这是很苦痛的事情，无能为力地站住，劝人忍耐。你能够丢开他，来这里住吗？然而我现在又不敢讲这话。也许他能够强迫你回去。除开我以外，没有别人能够了解你所能举出的他的错处。

我只得仍然等候那忽然来的灼见，我相信我可以得到。那是奇怪的，有时它忽然降临到我头上，有时渐渐地显明像伊格涅背·樊的曙光。今早我在床上躺到很迟，因为我晚上没有睡多少，我看见曙光的慢慢开展，我就想起在伦敦永远不能看见日出的我的厄斯忒。

荷马墩，十四日，二月，一八三九。

几乎没有什么值得记载的——就是说，没有事情发生——然而我是这么迅速地被冲去，真叫我害怕。仅仅一句话或者一些举动感动着我比一拳还厉害。昨天我结账，短了十个先令。我算了又重算几遍，无法纠正好。我打算把我自己的钱十先令放进现银匣子里，但是我想也许里面有些错误，查理斯总是细

some mistake and that Charles, who always examines my books, would find it out, and that it would be worse for me if he had discovered what I had done than if I had let them tell their own tale[1]. After dinner he asked for them, counted my balance, and at once found out there was ten shillings too little. I said I knew it and supposed I had forgotten to put down[2] something I had spent. "Forgotten again?" he replied, "it is unsatisfactory. There is evident want of method." He locked the box and book in the desk and read the newspaper while I sat and worked. Next day I remembered the servant had half-a-sovereign to pay the greengrocer, and I had not seen her since I gave it to her. When Charles returned from the bank my first words were, "O Charles, I know all about the half sovereign; I am so glad. Would not you have acknowledged you were glad too?" He looked at me just as he did the night before. I believe he would rather I had lost the money. "Your explanation," was his response, "makes no difference, in fact[3] it confirms my charge of lack of system. I have brought you some tablets which I wish you to keep in your pocket, and you must note in them every outgoing at the time it is made. These items are then to be regularly adjusted, and transferred afterwards." I could not restrain myself.

"Charles, Charles," I cried, "do not charge me, as if I had com-

---

1 to tell their own tale: to reveal themselves 自己漏泄出里面的毛病。
2 to put down: to set down 记录下来。

查我的账簿的，或者会看出；那是于我更不利的，若使他发现我私自放进十先令，比起我让账簿自己说出里面的错误。用餐后，叫我拿账簿来，把出入算一下，立刻发现少了十先令。我说我知道，我想大概我忘记将我用了的一笔款记下。"又是忘却？"他答道，"这叫人不满意，分明缺乏方法。"他将匣子同账簿锁在书桌里，读报纸，我坐在一旁工作。第二天我记起来女仆拿了十先令给鲜果商，我后来没有见到她，因此忘却了。当查理斯从银行回来，我第一句话是，"查理斯，我知道那十先令的下落了。我多么欢喜。你也承认你也高兴吗？"他看着我正像前晚一样。我相信他到〔倒〕愿意我完全失掉那钱了。"你的解释，"这是他的答话，"是无关紧要的，那实在更证明了我所说的缺乏方法。我带几张小表给你，我希望你把它们放在你衣袋里，每次付钱时候你得立即记在上面。这些小账后来再好好地算一下，转记到大簿子上面。"我不能自制了。

"查理斯，查理斯，"我喊，"不要定我的罪状，好像我犯了

---

3 in fact: really 其实。

mitted a crime. For mercy's sake[1], soften! I have confessed I was careless; can you not forgive?" "It is much easier," was the answer, "to confess and regret than to amend. I am not offended, and as to forgiveness I do not quite comprehend the term. It is one I do not often use. What is done cannot be undone. If you will alter your present habit, forgiveness, whatever you may mean by it, becomes superfluous." His lips shut into their usual rigidity. Not a muscle in them would have stirred if I had kissed them with tears. No tears rose; I was struck into hardness equal to his own, and with something added. I hated him. "Henceforward," I said to myself, "I will not submit or apologise; there shall be war."

16 Feb. 1839.

I left my letter unfinished. War? ... How can I make war or continue at war? I could not keep up[2] the struggle for a week. I am so framed that I must make peace with those with whom I have disagreed or I must fly. I would take nine steps out of the ten—nay, the whole ten which divide me from dear friends; I would say that this or that was not my meaning. I would abandon all arguing and wash

---

1 for mercy's sake: 乞怜的惊叹词，可以译做"体上天慈悲"之意。
2 to keep up: to continue 维持下去。

一种罪了。为着慈悲的缘故,温和些罢!我自认我是不小心;你不能原谅吗?""自认同追悔,"他的答话是,"比起改过是容易得多了。我并没有生气,至于'原谅'我不大了解那个字的意义。那是一个我不常用的字。已经做过的事情是无法更改了。若使你能够革去你现在的习惯,原谅,不管你认为这字含有什么意思,变成无用了。"他的嘴唇闭成它们常具的严厉神气。它们上面的筋一条也不会动,假使我和泪吻它们。我也没有眼泪起来;我弄得同他一样的冷心,还加上别的分子。我"恨"他。"从此后,"我对自己说,"我既不屈服,也不道歉;我们开战罢。"

十六日,二月,一八三九。

我的信没有写完就搁下。战争?我怎么能够同人开战或继续在战争状态里呢?我不能支持那种奋斗到一星期。我的性格是这样,我必定跟同我吵架的人们讲和,否则我必定逃走。我走开十步后会退回九步——不,我会退回我同我亲爱朋友相隔的十步;我会解释道这句话或者那句话他误解了。我一定会抛

away differences¹ with sheer affection. Toward Charles I cannot stir. Sometimes, although but seldom, my brother Jim and I have quarrelled. Five minutes afterwards we have been in one another's arms and the angry words were as though they had never been spoken. Forgiveness is not a remission of consequences on repentance. It is simply love, a love so strong that in its heat the offence vanishes. Without love—and so far Charles is right—forgiveness even of the smallest mistake is impossible.

It is a thick, dark fog again this morning. At Blackdeep most likely it is bright sunlight.

Charles does not seem to suspect that his indifference has any effect on me. I suppose he is unable to conceive my world or any world but his own. If he were at Blackdeep now and the sun were shining, would it be to him a glowing, blessed ball of fire?

He may have just as much right to complain of me as I have to complain of him. He sets store on² the qualities necessary for his business and he knows what store the partners set on those qualities in him. No doubt they are of great importance to everybody. It must be hard³ for him to live with a woman who takes so little interest in

---

1 differences: disagreement in opinion 争执；意见的不同。
2 to set store on: to value highly 看重；重视。
3 hard: unpleasant 苦痛；不悦。

弃一切的辩论，用纯净的感情来洗掉一切不和。但是对于查理斯，我不能让步。有时，虽然很稀少，我的兄弟小杰同我吵架。五分钟后我们两人彼此拥抱着，愤怒的话好像根本没有说过一样的。原谅并不是忏悔后责任的豁免。那完全是爱，一种这么强烈的爱，在它的热度里那些过失烟消云散了。没有爱——在这方面查理斯是对的——就是对于最微末过失的原谅也是办不到的。

今早又是一片浓密的黑雾。在布拉克第普大概全是明亮的阳光罢。

查理斯好像没有猜出他的冷淡于我有什么影响。我想他在他自己的世界外不能了解尚有我的世界或者其他的世界。若使他此刻在布拉克第普，太阳正照耀着，他会觉得那是一个光亮的，可感谢的火球吗？

他可以有同样多的权利来埋怨我，正如我有权利埋怨他。他很看重他职务所必须的那副本领，他也知道东家们对于他这副本领是多么重视。无疑地那些本领对于个个人都是很重要的。这于他一定是很苦痛的，和一个女人同居，她这么不关心城里

city affairs and makes so much of [1] what to him is of no importance. He looks down upon[2] me as though I were not able to talk on any subject which, for its comprehension, requires intelligence. If he had married Miss Stagg, who has doubled the drapery business at Ely, they might have agreed together very well.

  This is true, but I come back to myself. The virtues are not enough for me. Life with them alone is not worth the trouble of getting up in the morning. I thirst for you: I shall come, whatever may happen.

Blackdeep, 20 Feb. 1839.

  I cannot write an answer to your letter. You must come. I could not make up my mind last night, but this morning the light, the direction, as my mother used to say, was like a star. How you remind me of her! Not in your lot but in your ways, and she had your black hair. She was a stranger to these parts. Where your grandfather first saw her I do not know, but she was from the hill country in the far south-west. She never would hear anything against our flats. When folk asked her if she did not miss the hills, she turned on[3] them as if she had been born in the Fens and said she had found something in

---

 1 to make much of: to pet; to treat as weighty 喜欢；认为重要。
 2 to look down on: to despise 轻蔑。
 3 to turn on: to retort 反唇相稽。

的事情，却非常留神他所认为不重要的事情。他瞧不起我，好像我不能谈到需要理智去了解的题目。若使他娶了在伊里把成衣铺扩张成一倍大的斯达格姑娘，他们可以很和谐。

这些话都是对的，但是我要回头来说到我的本身了。这些美德于我是不够的。单同着这些美德一起过日子是不值得我们早上起来。我渴望见你：我将到你那里去，无论会有什么事情发生。

布拉克第普，二十日，二月，一八三九。

我不能够回你的信。你一定得来这里。昨晚我不能决定，但是今晨光线，指示出方向，我母亲常说，正如一颗指迷的明星。你多么使我忆她！不是你们命运相类，却是你们态度，她也有你那种黑发。她不是生长在这里的。你的父亲〔外祖父〕第一次在什么地方看见她，我不知道，但是她是来自西南远方，群山起伏的地方。她绝不肯听人们毁骂我们的平原。当人们问她有没有怀念家乡的青山，她拦住他们好像她是在泽地生长大的，说道她觉

them better than hills. But how I do wander on! That has nothing to do with you now, although I could tell you, if it were worth while[1], how it came into my head. I shall look out for you this week.

Lombard Street, 14 Mar. 1839.

Dear Esther, —You have now been away three weeks and I shall be glad to hear when you intend to return. Your mother I hope is better,[2] and if she is not, I trust you will see that your absence cannot be indefinitely prolonged. I am writing at the Bank, and your reply marked "Private" should be addressed here. Some changes, now almost completed, are being made in the lower rooms at Homerton which will give me one for any business of my own. —Your affectionate husband,

Charles Craggs.

Blackdeep, 17 Mar. 1839.

Dear Charles, —My mother is not well, and I shall be grateful to you if you will give me another week. I am sorry you have made alterations in the house without saying anything to me. It will be

---

1 worth while: worth the time which it requires; worth the pains and expense 值得费那么多时间；值得花那么多的麻烦。

2 厄斯忒离开她的丈夫时一定托辩她母亲身体不舒服，所以这里她丈夫说希望她母亲好些了。

得泽地有强过青山的地方。但是我说得离题太远了！这些话现在同你都是不相干的，虽然我能够告诉你，若使这是值得说的，这些事是多么有力地回到我的记忆里。这星期里我等候着你。

郎巴街，十四月，三月，一八三九。

亲爱的厄斯忒，——你现在已经离家三个月了，我很想知道你打算在什么时候回来。我希望你母亲的健康进步了，若使她并没有好些，我相信你也会看到你的远离不能够无限度地延期。我此刻在银行里写这封信，你的覆信，外面注明"私函"可以寄到这里。荷马墩底下一层的房子有些改造进行着，现在快完成了，将来我可以独自有一间房子，随便做我的事情。

——你亲爱的丈夫，查理斯·克剌格斯。

布拉克第普，十七日，三月，一八三九。

亲爱的查理斯，——我母亲还没有好，我会很感谢你，若使你让我再滞一星期。我觉得难过你把屋子里面改造一番，却

better now that I should not come back till they are finished. —Your affectionate wife,

Esther Craggs.

Homerton, 19 Mar. 1839.

The paperhangers and painters have left; the carpets will be laid and the furniture arranged today. I trust to see you when I come home on the 22nd instant. This will nearly give you the week you desired. I shall be late at the Bank[1] on the 22nd, but if you are fatigued with your journey there is no reason why you should not retire to rest, and we will meet in the morning.

Blackdeep, 21 Mar. 1839.

I had hoped for a little delay, for I shrank from the necessity of announcing my resolve, although it has for some time been fixed. I shall not return. The reason for my refusal shall be given with perfect sincerity. I do not love you, and you do not love me. I ought not to have married you, and I can but plead the blindness of youth, which for you is a poor excuse. I shall be punished for the remainder of my days, and not the least[2] part of the punishment will be that I have done you a grievous injury. Worse, however—ten thousand

---

1 I shall be late at the Bank 我在银行里会滞到比通常更迟的时候。
2 not the least: the greatest 最大的。

没有先向我提过。现在还是等完全修改成功,我再回去好些。

——你亲爱的妻子,厄斯忒·克剌格斯。

荷马墩,十九日,三月,一八三九。

裱糊匠同油漆匠都已走了;今天要铺上地毡,把家具排好。我相信本月二十二日我回家时候会看见你。这差不多给了你所要求的一星期时光了。二十二日我在银行会滞迟些,但是若使你因为旅行疲倦了,你当然尽可以去休息,我们就在第二早见面。

布拉克第普,二十一日,三月,一八三九。

我希望多耽搁一会儿,因为我一想起宣布我的决心的必要就有些害怕,虽然那决心已打好一些时候了。我不回家了。我拒绝回家的理由将十分诚恳地说出。我没有爱你,你没有爱我。我不应该嫁你,我只能归诿于青春的盲目,那由你看起来是个无聊的辩解。我的余生将受这场过失的责罚,这责罚里最大部分是我觉得对不住你,给你一个甚可悲伤的损害。

times worse—would it be for both of us if we were to continue chained together in apathy or hatred. I would die for you this moment to make good[1] what you have lost through me, but to live with you as your wife would be a crime of which I dare not be guilty. This is all, and this is enough.

Homerton, 24 Mar. 1839.

Madam, —I am not surprised at the contents of your letter of the 21st instant, nor am I surprised that your determination should have been made known to me from your mother's house. I have no doubt that she has done her best[2] to inflame you against me. How she contrives to reconcile with her religion her advice to her daughter to break a divine law[3] I will not inquire. I am not going to remonstrate with you; I will not humiliate myself by asking you to reconsider your resolution. I will, however, remind you of one or two facts, and point out to you the consequences of your action, so that hereafter you may be unable to plead you were not forewarned.

You will please bear in mind that you have abandoned me; I have not abandoned you. You disappointed me: my house was not

---

1 to make good: to compensate 补偿。
2 to do one's best: to do all one can 尽力；竭力。
3 a divine law 基督教徒认为婚约是种神圣的契约，不能随便取消的。

然而，那是更坏——更坏得一万倍——对于我们，若使我们继续练〔链〕在一起，在无情或厌恶之中。我愿意此刻为你死去，来报偿你因我而受的损失；但是同你住一起，做你的妻子，这么大的罪是我所不敢犯的。就是这些话了，这些话已经够了。

荷马墩，二十四日，三月，一八三九。

太太，——我并不纳罕你二十一日发的信的内容，我也不觉奇怪，你会从你母亲家里让我知道你的决心。我深信她一定是尽力煽动你来反对我。她怎样设法调和她的信仰同她叫她女孩去破坏一个神圣法律的劝告，我是不想探询的。我现在不去规劝你，也绝对不去弄低我自己的身份，请你重新考虑你的决议。然而，我要向你提醒一两件事，指出给你看这举动的结果，为的是此后你不能说你没有受过警告。

请你记在心里，是"你"弃了"我"；我并没有弃你。你使我失望：我的家庭没有照我的希望管理着，但是我预备好忍受

managed in accordance with[1] my wishes, but I was prepared to accept the consequences of what I did deliberately and I desired to avoid open rupture. I hoped that in time[2] you would learn by experience that the maxims which control my conduct rest on a solid basis; that I was at least to be esteemed, and that we might live together in harmony. I repeat, you have cast me off, though I was willing you should stay.

You confess you have done me a wrong, but have you reflected how great that wrong is? I have no legal grounds for divorce, and you therefore prevent me from marrying again. You have damaged my position in the Bank. Many of my colleagues, envious of my success, will naturally seize their opportunity and propagate false reports, and I therefore inform you that I shall require of you a document which my solicitor will prepare, completely exonerating me. This will be necessary for my protection. A Bank manager's reputation is extremely sensitive, and a notorious infringement of any article of the moral code would in many quarters cause his commercial honesty to be suspected.

You allege that you are sincere, but I can hardly acquit you of hypocrisy. Your sentimental excuse for deserting me is suspicious.[3]

---

1 in accordance with: in harmony with 和谐；相合。
2 in time: finally 终必。

我审量再三后干出的事情的结果,我总是想避免公开的破裂。我从前还希望你终久会从经验里看出管理着我的行动的那些格言是站在坚固的基础上面;我最少是值得敬重的,我们可以和谐地一同过活。我还要说一遍,你弃掉了我,虽然我是愿意你还滞下去的。

你自认你给我一个损害,但是你有没有想过那损害是多么大的?我没有法律上的理由可以离婚,所以你阻止了我的再去结婚。你也破坏了我在银行的地位。许多同事,嫉妒我的成功,当然会抓着他们的机会,宣传假造的谣言,所以我通知你我要你签一张我律师预备好的文件,完全表白我的无罪。这对于我的自保是必须的。一个银行经理的名誉是极易动摇的,道德律里任一条的众目昭彰的干犯会在许多地方引起他商业上的诚实也受人怀疑。

你申明你是诚恳的,但是我几乎不能说你没有虚伪。你弃我的理由——没有感情——是令我生疑窦的。

---

3 他不相信她单是因为不爱他而离开他,总以为一定是因为她爱上了另一个男子,所以这里冷讽一句。

When the document just mentioned has been signed, I shall send a copy of it to the rector of your parish. Without it he will know nothing but what you and your mother tell him, and he will be in a false position[1].

I hereby caution you that I shall not lose sight of you, and if at anytime proof of improper relationship should be obtained, I shall take advantage of it.

Charles Craggs.

Blackdeep, 26 Mar. 1839.

Dearest Mother,—This letter came this morning, and I send it at once to you at Ely. Am I to answer it? When I read some parts I wished he had been near me that I might have caught him by the throat. I should have exulted that for once[2] I could move him, although it should be by terror. It is strange that not until now did I know he was so brutal. Notice that, according to him, if a wife leaves her husband it must be for a rival. He does not understand how much she can hate him, body and soul, and with no thought of a lover; that her loathing needs no other passion to inflame it, and that the touch

---

1 false position: a position that makes one acts against one's principles 当一个人受人蒙蔽了，不知不觉间干出跟自己的主张相违的事情时，我们说他处于一个"错误的地位"。

2 for once: one time at least 至少一次。

当刚才说的那个文件签好字了,我将送一副本给你教区里的牧师。没有看到这个文件,他除开你和你母亲告诉他的话外是一无所知的,他将处于干出和他素来的主张相冲突的事情的地位了。

我还要警告你,我将永远留神你,若使在任何时候我得到你不合法的关系的证据,我将利用那证据。

查理斯·克刺格斯。

布拉克第普,二十六日,三月,一八三九。

最亲爱的母亲,——附上一封信是今早收到的,我立刻转到伊里给你看。我回他的信吗?当我念到信里面有些地方,我真希望他在我身旁,为的是我可以抓住他的咽喉。我将觉得高兴,因为总有一回我能感动他,虽然是用恐怖的手段。这真奇怪,一直到现在,我才晓得他是这么兽性十足的。请你注意,照他说的,若使一个妻子离开她的丈夫,那么一定是为着另一个爱人的缘故。他不能了解她是多么恨他,身体同灵魂两方面都在内,而且绝没有想到另一个爱人;她的厌恶用不着别个热

of his clean finger may be worse to her than a leper's embrace.

When I had written so far I was afraid. I knelt down and cried to our Father who is in Heaven. —Your loving daughter,

Esther.

Ely, 28 Mar. 1839.

You must not reply. I have always tried not to answer back[1] if it will do no good. In a way[2] I am not sorry he has written in this style to you. It proves that the leading[3] I had was true. I feared cruel claws ever since I first set eyes on him notwithstanding he was so even-tempered; and I am glad he has not shown them till you are safe in Blackdeep. I know what you will have to go through[4] in time to come[5], but for all that[6] I am sure I am right and that you are right. I am more sure than ever. I am sorry for him, but he will soon settle down[7] and rejoice that you have gone. That spiteful word about my religion does not disturb me. I have my own religion. I have brought up my children in it. I have taught them to fear God and to love the

---

1 to answer back: to rebuke sancily 刻薄地回骂。
2 in a way: in a certain sense 在某种意义之下。
3 leading: guidance 指导。
4 to go through: to suffer 遭受。
5 in time to come: in the future time 将来。
6 for all that: in spite of that; nevertheless 虽然;无论。
7 to settle down: to become quiet after agitation 纷扰后归于平静。

情来煽动,他那洁净的手指的接触由她看来比一个麻疯人的拥抱更可怕。

当我写了这么多,我觉得恐惧。我跪下,哭求在天的上帝。

——你亲爱的女儿,厄斯忒。

伊里,二十八日,三月,一八三九。

你千万不要复他的信。我素来不去反唇相稽,若使那是无补于事了。我也不很觉难过,他用这样口气写信给你。那证明了我的向导是正确的。自从我第一次见到他,我就怕他具有可怕的利爪,不管他好像是多么没有脾气;我很高兴,你已安全地在布拉克第普之后,他才露出利爪。我知道你将来会经历多少苦痛,但是虽然有那么多苦痛,我十分相信这一回举动里我是对的,你是对的。我比以前更相信了。我为他难过,但是很快他将把一切安排好,心里高兴你已离他了。他那句关于我的信仰的轻蔑的话没有搅乱我。我有我自己的信仰。我用这信仰教育我的儿女。我教他们敬畏上帝,爱我们的救主耶稣基督,

Lord Jesus Christ, who has stood by[1] me in all my troubles and guided me in all my straits whenever I have been willing to wait His time. I bless God, my dear child, that you have not gone away from your mother's faith—ay, and your father's too—and that you can still pray to your Heavenly Father in your distress. Be thankful you have been spared the worst, that you have not grown hard.

I shall come back this week; your aunt wants you here, and a change will do you good.

Blackdeep, 10 Apr. 1839.

I am glad you went to Ely, for yesterday the parson called to see you. He had received a letter from Mr. Graggs, and considered it his duty as a Christian minister to endeavour to bring about a reconciliation. I told him at once he might spare himself the pains, for they would be useless. He replied that I ought to think of the example. Well, at that I broke out[2]. I asked him whether that slut of a Quimby girl wasn't a worse example, who at five-and-twenty had married Horrocks, the hoary old wretch, for his money, and leads

---

1 to stand by: to show oneself faithful to; to help 现出忠于；帮助。
2 to break out: to throw off restraint; to exclaim suddenly 扔开拘束；忽然大喊出来。

在我一切苦难之中他总是援助我,在我一切窘迫里他总是指导我,只要我愿意等候他的启示。我亲爱的孩子,我感谢上帝,你没有失却你母亲的信仰——而且,也是你父亲的——和你在你的烦恼里还能够向你的天父祈祷。你当感谢,你避免了那最可怕的情形,那是说你没有弄得麻木心死了。

这星期里我将回来;你的姨母希望你能到这里来,变更一下环境于你将有好处。

布拉克第普,十日,四月,一八三九。

我觉得高兴,你到伊里去了,因为昨天牧师来拜望你。他接一封克刺格斯先生给他的信,认为那是一个基督教牧师的责任,去努力做成个和好如初。我立刻对他说他可省去这番辛苦,因为一切调停都是无用的。他答道我应当想这是多么坏的一个例子。听了这句话,我大怒了。我问他那个乱七八糟的金拜姑娘是不是一个更坏的例子,她二十五岁时候贪荷洛克斯,那个白发萧萧的可怜的老头子的钱,嫁给他,使他过一种狗的生活。

him a dog's life¹. Had he ever warned either of them? They go to church regular. I was very free², and I said I thought it was a bright example that a woman should have given up a fine house and money in London because there was no love with them, and should have come back to her mother at Blackdeep. Besides, I added, why should my Esther suffer a living death for years for the sake of the folk hereabouts? They weren't worth it. She was too precious for that. "Oh!" but he want on again, "they have souls to be saved. Husbands and wives may be led to imagine there is no harm in separating, and may yield to the temptations of unlawful love." This made me very hot, and I gave it him back sharp³ that a sinner could find in the Bible itself an excuse for his sin.

He said no more except that it would be a nice scandal for the Dissenters, and that he trusted God would bring me into a better frame of mind. He then went away. His reasoning went in at one ear and out at the other. Parsons are bound to preach by rule. It is all general; it doesn't fit the ins and outs⁴.

---

1 to lead one a dog's life: to worry or persecute him 跟他捣乱，使度个苦痛的生活。
2 free: outspoken 畅言无隐。
3 to give it him back sharp: to reprimand him sharply 痛骂。
4 the ins and outs: all the details of the matter 详细情形。

他向他们两人曾经给过警告没有？他们现在也是和别人一样到礼拜堂去。我直接痛快地说一大篇话，我说我想这是个光明的例子，一个女人会因为夫妇中没有爱情，就弃却伦敦城里的好住宅和财富，回到布拉克第普她母亲的家里。而且，我还说，为什么我的厄斯忒要为着这里人们的缘故去忍受几十年虽生犹死的生活？他们是不值得她的牺牲。她太可宝贵了。"啊！"他却说道，"他们有该受救的灵魂。丈夫们和妻子们也许因此会认为离居没有什么害处，会接受非法恋爱的引诱。"这句话使我很生气，我深刻地驳他道一个想犯罪的人甚至于能够从《圣经》里找到他的犯罪的借口。

他不讲什么，只说这将给非国教徒一个很妙的诽谤机会，同他相信上帝将叫我怀个更高明的意见。他于是走去了。他的理论这边耳朵进来，从那边耳朵出去。牧师不得不照例说教。说的全是空泛的话，不宜于解决人生里个个复杂的问题。

Blackdeep, 1 May. 1839.

You had better stop at Ely as long as you can. Everybody is gossiping, for parson has told the story as he heard it from your husband. It is worse for Jim than for me, as he goes about among people here, and although they daren't say anything to him about you, there is no mistake as to what they think. Mrs. Horrocks inquired after me, and said she was sorry to hear of my trouble. Jim told her I was quite well, and that the two cows were now all right. He wouldn't let her see he knew what she meant.

Last night, Jim, who has been talking for a twelve-month past about going to his cousin in America, asked me whether I would not be willing to leave. I have always set my face against[1] it. To turn my back on[2] the old house and the Fen, to begin again at my time of life in a new strange world would be the death of me. More than ever now am I determined to end my days here. They'd say at once we had fled. No, here we'll bide and face it out[3].

They did not fly. Years went on, and to the astonishment of their neighbours — perhaps they were a little sorry — there was no sigh

---

1 to set one's face against: to oppose 反对。
2 to turn one's back on: to leave 离开。
3 to face it out: not be cowed by it 不给它所威吓住。

布拉克第普，一日，五月，一八三九。

你能在伊里住多久，就住多久罢。这里个个人都拿你这件事做谈话的题材，因为牧师照他从你丈夫所听来的向人说出这事的始末。小杰比我更苦，因为他在这里跟人们来往；虽然他们不敢向他提起你的什么事情，他明白地看出他们心里想的是什么。荷洛克斯太太询我的近况，说她觉得难过，听到我在烦恼里。小杰告诉她我身体很健康，我们那两匹牛也很好。他不让她看出他知道她所指的是什么。

小杰这一年来老是谈着到美洲找他的表兄弟，昨晚问我愿意不愿意出国。我素来是反对他这个计划。转过身来离开这所老屋子同樊，在我这样年纪再到一个生疏的新世界里开始另一幕的生活，这对于我几乎是等于死。比以前更坚决，我打定主意在这里度过我的余生。否则，他们一定立刻说我们逃了。不，我们将滞在这里，抵抗这些评论到底。

她们并没有逃走。一年一年地过去了，她们的邻居真觉得

that Esther had a lover. Mrs. Horrocks's eyes were feline, but she was obliged to admit she was at fault. Jim married, and an agreeable opportunity was presented for the expression of amazement that his wife's father and mother felt safe in allowing their child to enter such a family—but then she come from Norwich.[1] The majority of the poor in Blackdeep Fen sided with the Suttons[2], and here and there a pagan farmer boldly declared that old Mrs. Sutton and her daughter were of a right good sort, and that there was not a straight forrarder[3] man than Jim in Ely market. But to respectable Blackdeep society the Suttons remained a vexatious knot which it could not unpick and lay straight. Nobody, as Mrs. Horrock observed, knew how to take them. Mrs. Graggs wore her wedding-ring, and when she was in Mrs. Jarvis's shop looked her straight in the face[4] and asked for what she wanted as if she were the parson's wife.[5] But that, according to Mrs. Horrocks, just showed her impudence. "What a time that poor Craggs in London must have had of it!" (Mr. Horrocks was not pres-

---

1 他们只好说因为小杰妻子的家族是外乡人，不知道他姐姐的浪漫行为，所以肯把女孩嫁到这样人的家里。

2 the Suttons：当提到一家里好几个人时候，就将这家的姓加上 s，上面再用 the 字。

3 straight forrarder：more straightforward 乡下人的口音同文法总是奇怪一点。

4 to look one in the face：to regard one firmly or boldly 坚决地或者勇敢地看着他。

奇怪——也许她们有些失望——并没有看出什么可以证明厄斯忒有一个爱人。荷洛克斯太太的眼睛是不断地四面观察,像个猫的眼睛,但是她也迫得只好承认她错了。小杰结婚了,这是一个很好的机会给他们去表示惊奇,他妻子的父母居然放心让他们的孩子进到这么一个家庭——但是她是来自瑙威池,所以又作别论了。布拉克第普·樊大多数的穷人是站在萨吞母女这边的,在一些地方有一两个具有异教徒精神的农夫大胆地宣言萨吞老夫人同她的女儿是好人,同伊里市场里没有一个比小杰再正直坦白的人了。但是在布拉克第普上等社会里,萨吞家仍然是一根无法解松同拉直的麻烦结子。荷洛克斯太太就说,没有人知道怎样去了解她们。克刺格斯太太还戴着她的结婚戒指,当她在查维思太太铺子里,她睁着眼睛望她,叫拿她所需要的东西,好像她是牧师太太。但是照荷洛克斯太太的意见,这正表现出她的厚颜无耻。"可怜的克刺格斯从前在伦敦过的是多么

---

5 牧师在小乡村里几乎是全村最尊敬的人,他的太太当然配得睥睨一世了。

ent.) "Lord! how I do pity the man." "And yet," added Mrs. Jarvis, "and yet, you might eat your dinner[1] off Mrs. Craggs's floor. I call it hers, for she cleans it."[2] Clearly the living-room ought to have been a pigsty. It was particularly annoying that, although Mrs. Sutton and her family by absence from church had become infidels, they did not go to the devil openly as they ought to do, and thereby relieve Blackdeep of that pain and even hatred which are begotten by an obstinate exception to what would otherwise be a general law. Parson often preached that everybody was either a sheep or a goat[3]. The Suttons were not sheep—that was certain; and yet it was difficult to classify them as ordinary Blackdeep goats, creatures with horns. Mrs. Jarvis had heard that there was a peculiar breed of goats with sheep's wool and without horns. "Esther Graggs," she maintained, "will one day show us what she's after[4]; mark my word, you'll see. If that brazen face means nothing, then I'm stone-blind."

---

1 to eat one's dinner: to be studying for the bar 用功预备当律师。

2 这里是讥笑厄斯忒现在要干许多粗事情, 如擦地板之类。

3 a sheep or a goat: 见《新约·马太福音》中。"当人子在他荣耀里, 同着众天使降临的时候, 要坐在他荣耀的宝座上, 万君都要聚集在他面前。他要把他们分别出来, 好像牧羊的分别绵羊山羊一般。把绵羊安置在右边, 山羊在左边。于是王向那右边的说, 你们这蒙我父赐福的, 可来承受那创世以来为你们所预备的国。"所以后来就拿绵羊山羊来比喻善人恶人。

4 after: in pursuit or quest of 寻求的。

苦的日子呀！"（荷洛克斯先生当时不在场。）"天呀！我多么哀怜他。""然而，"查维思太太说道，"然而，你可以站在克剌格斯太太的地板上学当个辩护士。我叫做克剌格斯太太的，因为那些地板是她洗扫的。"分明的，她们闲坐的房子应当变得不净像个猪圈。这真是特别恼人，虽然萨吞太太同她女儿因为不到礼拜堂已经变为异教徒了，她们并没有鬼混得一塌胡涂，其实她们应当那样，而使布拉克第普的人们免受见到一个常例有一个顽梗的例外时所尝的苦痛，甚至于痛恨。牧师常常说一个人不是一只绵羊，就是一只山羊。萨吞母女不是绵羊——这是一点不错的事实；但是也不容易把她们归类于普通布拉克第普的山羊，那班头上有角的东西。查维思太太听说天下有特种的山羊，身上有绵羊的羊毛，又没有角。"厄斯忒·克剌格斯，"她坚持，"有一天会现出给我们看她所追求的是什么；记着我的话，你们将来会看见到。若使那个厚脸孔没有含有意义，那么我真是个十分的瞎子。"

After Jim's marriage Esther continued to manage the house and the dairy, leaving the cooking to her sister-in-law and the needlework to her mother. Soon after five o'clock on a bright summer morning the labourer going to his work heard the unbarring of Mrs. Sutton's shutters and the withdrawal of bolts. The casement windows and the door were then flung open, and Esther generally came into the doorway and for a few minutes faced the sun. She did not shut herself up[1]. She walked the village like a queen, and no Fen farmer or squireling[2] ventured to jest with her. Mrs. Jarvis could not be brought to admit her stone-blindness and clung to the theory of somebody in London; but as Esther never went to London, and nobody from London came to her, and the postmistress swore no letters passed between London and the Sutton family, Mrs. Jarvis became a little distrusted, although some of her acquaintances believed her predictions with greater firmness as they remained unfulfilled. "I don't care what you may say; don't tell me," was her reply to sceptical objections, and it carried great weight.

Esther died of the Blackdeep fever in the fifth year after she came home. As soon as he received the news of her death Mr. Graggs married Mrs. Perkins, who had been twelve months a widow, was admitted into partnership, and is now one of the most respected men in the City.

小杰结婚后，厄斯忒继续管理家务同牛乳房，烹饪让她嫂子去干，针线让她母亲去干。夏天的清晨，五点钟打过了一会儿，工作去的工人会听到萨吞太太的户扉去闩，铁栓也拿开了。窗子同大门都打开了，厄斯忒常常走到门口，望着太阳几分钟。她并不把自己关闭起来。她在乡里走路，有如一个皇后，樊里没有一个农夫或者小地主敢向她开玩笑。查维思不肯承认她的完全盲目，紧抓着伦敦有个情人的理论；但是因为厄斯忒绝没有到伦敦去，也没有人从伦敦来找她，邮务员太太又誓言伦敦同萨吞家没有信函来往，查维思太太也变得有些怀疑了，虽然有几位朋友更坚决地相信她的预言，因为它们还没有实现。"我不管你们怎么说；你们不要告诉我，"这是她对于怀疑主义者的诘问的答辞，这句话是具有很大的效力的。

厄斯忒在她回家后五年患布拉克第普流行热病死了。他一听她死的消息，克剌格斯先生立刻娶柏金兹太太，她已当一年的寡妇了，他也被认为一个股东，现在是京城里一个受人们尊敬的人物。

---

1 to shut oneself up：to imprison oneself 把自己囚闭起来。
2 squireling：a petty squire 小地主；小乡绅。

The Poet's Portmanteau
诗人的手提包
（英汉对照）

George Gissing 著

梁遇春 译注

"英文小丛书"之一，上海北新书局，1931年3月初版

George Gissing

（1857—1903）

他的父亲是一个药剂师，他受过良好的教育，能够拿希腊诗歌做消愁解闷的东西。十九岁时候，他被一个普通的女人迷了，把她娶来，还偷一位朋友的皮夹子给她，因此下狱。二十岁时候，流落到美国去，当照相师，装置煤气灯的人，报馆访员糊口。后来从德国回英国来，专靠写稿子谋生，但是常有得不到东西吃的时候，英国博物院的盥洗所是他唯一洗澡的地方。他的妻子变成醉鬼，后来甚至于随便当人姘头。她死了，他又不能忍受寂寞的独身生活，就向随便遇到的女人求婚，把她娶来。起先他的朋友再三劝阻他，但是他天真地答道："他们同样地可以叫他不吃通常的食物，因为过几年后他能够买到精美的食品；然而他每天不能不有些滋养料；现在他到了一个时期，当他非有一个妻子伴着就不能过日子。"他还说："天下只有可怜的女子才肯嫁给我这么一个可怜的男子。"他们婚后的生活是不幸极了，终于离散。晚年他娶一个法国女人，他小说的销路也渐渐好起来了，生活也比较舒适些，然而夕阳无限好，不久就死了。

他写有许多长篇小说：*The Unclassed*（1884），*Demos*（1886），*Thyrza*（1887），*The Nether World*（1889），*New Grub Street*（1891），*Denzil Quarrier*（1892），*Born in Exile*（1892），*The Odd Women*（1893）。多半是描状伦敦贫民窟同工厂的灰色生活。他终身住在伦敦小屋的顶楼上，和下流的人们一起过活，深尝过贫穷的苦痛，所以对于下等社会特别有同情。他又是个悲观主义者，觉得世上无处不是凄凉的境地，太阳光总不会射到屋里。他极能道出失败人的心理，并且他的失望始终含有惆怅的诗意，所以他的书对于沦落的人们有极大的魔力。他晚年写有一本散文，*The Private Papers of Henry Ryecroft*，充满了恬静幽怨的情调，是散文里一部杰作。他还有几本短篇小说集，*Human Odds and Ends*，*A Victim of Circumstances*，*The House of Cobwebs*，上面这篇，《诗人的手提包》就是收在《人生的零碎》（*Human Odds and Ends*）里面。

他说："当今的艺术应当传达出'困苦'的意义，因为困苦是近代生活的基本音调（Keynote）。"这句话可说是他的艺术论。

The Poet's Portmanteau

I

The poet had been nourishing his soul down[1] in Devon. A petty windfall, a minim legacy, which plucked him from scholastic[2] bondage in a London suburb, was now all but[3] consumed. He turned his face once more to the mart of men, strong in the sanguine courage of two-and-twenty. His luggage (the sum total[4] of his personal property, except[5] twenty pounds sterling) consisted of a trunk and a portmanteau. The latter he kept beside him in the railway carriage—a small

---

1 down: adv. in a place away from capital 在都市以外的地方；乡下里。
2 scholastic: 当教师的。教书匠这一行生意本来叫做 the scholastic profession（教职，直译起来是书生职业）。
3 all but: nearly; almost 几乎；差不多。

诗人的手提包

一

诗人最近在得文乡下滋养他的灵魂。一笔意外的小款，一点儿遗产，把他从伦敦郊外教读生涯的束缚里拔出，现在这些钱几乎用尽了。他又回过脸来，向着人们的市场，满腔是二十二岁青年具有的乐天自信的勇气。他的行李（再加上二十镑现金，就是他私人财产的全部了）一共只是一个大箱子和一个手提包。在火车里他将这手提包放在身边——一个很破旧的小号

---

4 sum total：the amount，总共；合计。
5 except：“除了二十镑外，他的财产总共是……"这是等于说"他的财产是二十镑和……"。

and very shabby portmanteau, but it guarded the result of ten months' work, the manuscript volume (entitled *The Hermit of the Tor; and Other Poems*) whereon rested all his hopes. A few articles of clothing and of daily necessity were packed in the same receptacle. On reaching London he would deposit his trunk at the station, and carry the small portmanteau whilst he searched for a temporary lodging.

Green vales and bosky[1] slopes of Devon; the rolling uplands of Wiltshire; the streams and heaths and wooded hills of Surrey. It was late autumn, and the day drew to its close. Through mists of evening a red orb hung huge above the horizon; it crimsoned and grew lurid, athwart the first driftings[2] of London smoke; it disappeared amid towers and chimneys and squalor multiform. The poet grasped his portmanteau, and leapt out on to the platform of Waterloo Station.

One cheap room was all he wanted, and as he could not carry his burden very far be turned southward, guided by memory of the grey, small streets off Kennington Road. Twenty minutes' walk brought him into a by-way where every other[3] window offered its card of invitation to wanderers such as he. At this hour of gloom

---

1 bosky: having bosk or boscage 有灌木的；小林甚多。
2 driftings: drifts 飘浮物。
3 every other: each alternate 每隔一个。

手提包，但是它保护有十月辛苦工作的结果，手写的稿本（书名是《托尔的隐者；和其它》）他一切的希望都在这本书上面。几件衣服和日用必需品也装进这同一的提包里面。到伦敦时候，他将把他的大箱子存火车站里面，带着这个小手提包去找个暂时寄宿的地方。

火车经过了得文的绿色的山谷和树木丛生的斜坡；尉尔次的峰峦起伏的高原；萨立的河流，沼地和森林茂盛的小山。这是晚秋的时候，白天快结束了。隔着黄昏的雾看去，一轮红日庞大地挂在水平线之上；它变成深红的颜色，渐渐惨淡无光了，横于伦敦最外层的烟雾之后；它消失在高塔，烟囱和各样各式的龌龊东西里面了。诗人抓起他的手提包，跳到滑铁卢火车站的月台上。

一间租钱低廉的房子是他唯一的需要；他既不能带他这手提包走得很远，他就靠着他对于离肯宁顿路不远的几条灰色，小街的记忆，望〔往〕南走去。二十分钟的徒步带到一条僻路，那里每隔一家的窗子上都有招徕他这种流荡者的广告。当这个

there was little to choose between one house and another[1]. A few paces ahead of him sounded the knock of a telegraph messenger. Where telegrams were delivered there must be, he thought, some measure of[2] civilization; so he lingered till the boy had gone away, then directed his steps to that door.

His rat-tat[3] was answered by a young woman, whose personal appearance surprised him. Her features were handsome and intelligent, though scarcely amiable; her clothing indicated poverty, but was not such as would be worn by a girl of the working class; her language and manner completed the proof[4] that she was no native of this region. "Yes, " she said, speaking distantly and nervously, "a single room was to let, a room up at the top." The poet, as became a poet, observed with emotional interest this unexpected figure. Only a wretched little oil-lamp hung in the passage, and he could not see the girl's face very distinctly; perhaps the first impression of sullenness was a mistake; it might be only the shrinking self-respect of one whom circumstances had forced into a false position. He noticed that in her hand she held a telegram.

---

1 little to choose between them: one is almost as good as another 彼此差不多；用不着怎样拣选。

2 some measure of: some degree of 有一些。

3 rat-tat: 敲门的声音，这个字的声音就是模仿敲门的剥啄。

4 completed the proof: 完全证实。本来证据不够，现在再加上这点，黄昏时节,也看不出这家和那家的高下。在他前面几步的地方有一个送电报人敲门的声音。他想,有电报投递去的人家多少总有点文化;所以他停步等那送电报的小孩子走开,然后他的脚步望〔往〕那个门走去。

他的敲门有一个青年女人出来应话,她的外貌使他惊奇。她的脸孔是美丽聪明,虽然几乎可以说是并不和蔼可亲;她的衣服指出她的贫穷,然而又不是劳动阶级的一个女子所穿的;她的谈话和态度更明白无疑地证明出她不是这里本地的人。"是的,"她冷淡地,精神不安地答道,"有一间房子出租,一间在顶高那一层的房子。"诗人,的确像个诗人,感情兴奋地观察这个预料不到的人儿。只有一盏寒伧的小油灯挂在屋里的走廊,他不能很清楚地看见这个女子的脸孔;也许起初的印象:认她为孤僻的人,是一个错误;也许这只是羞怯不前的自尊心,因为环境使这个人处在和她本来身份不相称的地位。他看出她拿一张电报在她手里。

可以十分明白地证明了。

"Would you let me see the room?"

"Please wait a moment."

She went upstairs, and soon reappeared with a lighted candle. Leaving his portmauteau, he followed her through the usual stuffy atmosphere to a chamber of the usual dreariness.[1] His attendant placed her candle within the room, then drew back and waited outside on the landing.

"I think this would do[2]. What is the rent?"

There was hesitation. The poet stepped forward, and endeavoured to discern a face amid the shadows.

"Eight shillings—I think," he was at length answered.

Ah, then she was not the landlady. Perhaps the daughter of people who had come to grief[3]. He began to speak of details; she answered shortly, but to his satisfaction.

"I shall be glad to take the room[4] for a week or two. I'll go and bring up my portmanteau."

"It is usual"—he still could not see the speaker—"to pay a week's rent in advance."

---

1 Gissing 善于描摹伦敦穷困地方的情形，这里说的是郊外的公寓，家家都是那么闷人空气，房里总是那么凄清。

2 this would do: this would suffice 这已经可以了；no more is needed 用不着再好的。

3 to come to grief: to meet with disaster 遇到灾难。

"你肯让我看那房间吗？"

"请稍微等一等。"

她到楼上去，很快又出现，拿一枝点着了的洋烛。离开他的手提包，他跟她穿过照例是闷人的空气，到一间照例是凄凉的房子。和她同来的人将她的洋烛放在房里，然后退出去，在外面楼梯头候着。

"我想这可以住。租钱多少？"

她迟疑着。诗人走前一步，努力在阴影里去辨出这一个脸孔。

"八先令——我想是。"他最后得到这么一个回答。

啊，那么她不是女房东了。也许是一个碰到灾难的人的女儿。他开始谈各种细节了；她简短地答他，但是使他很满意。

"我很想租这个房间一两星期。我现在去把我的手提包拿上来。"

"照例"——他还是看不清这个说话的人——"是先交一星期的租钱。"

---

4 to take the room: to engage or bespeak the room 租房子。

"Oh, to be sure."

Determined to see her face in full light he took up the candle, and stepped with it on[1] to the landing. As if aware of his motive, the girl stood in a retiring attitude; but she met his gaze, and they looked, for an instant, steadily at each other. She was handsome, but her lips had a hard, defiant expression, and in her eyes he read[2] either the suffering of a womanly nature or the recklessness of one indifferent to[3] all good. Her speech favoured the pleasanter interpretation; yet, after all, the countenance disturbed rather than attracted him.

An old box stood by the head of the stairs; on this he placed the candle, and then drew from his pocket the sum he had to[4] pay. The girl thanked him coldly. He ran downstairs, fetched his portmanteau, and put it in a corner of the dark room. Then they again faced each other.

"By-the-bye, "[5] he said, wishing he could draw her into conversation, "what's the address? I have come here by mere chance."

She gave the information as briefly as possible.

"Thank you. Now I must go out and get something to eat."

---

1 stepped on: 踏上。
2 to read: to discern by observation of signs 观察。
3 indifferent to: careless or insensible to 不关心。
4 to have to: to be obliged to 不得不；必须。
5 by-the-bye: 却说；话说。偶然记起一件和刚才说的有些相关的事情时，就用这个字来做引子。

"啊，一定的。"

决定好要在十足光线之下看她的脸孔，他举起洋烛，拿着走到楼梯头。好像晓得他的动机，这个女子站在一种望〔往〕后退的姿势里；但是她并不避他的凝视，有一会见他们彼此直着眼睛相望。她是美丽的人，但是她的嘴唇有一种冷酷同轻蔑的表情，他从她的眼睛看出不是一个女性的受苦，就是一个不以人们好感为意的人的万事漠不关心的神情。她的谈话使人们倾向于采取前一较好的解释；然而，这个脸孔毕竟是使他心乱，而不是使他心喜的。

一个旧箱子站在楼梯头；他将洋烛放在上面，然后从他的衣袋掏出他所应缴的款。这个女人冷冷地谢他一声。他跑到楼下去，拿起他的手提包，安顿在这间黑暗房子的一个角落上。然后他们又脸向着脸。"呀"，他说，希望他能够引她谈下去，"这里地名是什么？我来到这里完全是出于偶然。"

她尽量简短地说出地名。

"谢谢你。现在我要出去，找些东西吃。"

The girl would not speak. There was nothing for it but[1] to turn and descend the stairs. She followed, and half-way down her voice stopped him.

"When shall you be back tonight?"

"Not later than eleven, I think."

And so they parted, the poet taking a last look at her as he opened the front door.

She had strongly affected his imagination. As he walked towards Westminster, new rhymes and rhythms sang within him to the roaring music[2] of the street. The Devon hermitage was a far, faint memory. London had welcomed him with so sudden a glimpse of her infinite romance that he half repented his long seclusion.

At about the hour he had mentioned he returned to seek a night's rest. Would the same face appear when the door opened? He waited anxiously, and suffered a sad disappointment, for his knock was answered by just the kind of person that might have been expected—the typical landlady of cheap lodgings, a puffy, slatternly woman chewing a mouthful of the supper from which she had risen.

"Good evening, " said the poet, as cheerfully as he could. "I am your new lodger."

---

1 There was nothing for it but: she could only 她只好……。
2 to sing to the music: to accompany the music with singing 和着音乐而唱。

这个女子不肯说话。他无奈何只得转过身走下楼梯。她跟着走，才走一半她的声音使他停足。

"今晚上你什么时候回来？"

"不会迟过十一点，我想。"

他们就这样分手了，诗人最后望她一下，当他打开大门时候。她深刻地激动了他的幻想。当他向着违斯敏斯德走去时候，新的韵脚和音律在他心里唱起来，和街上咆哮的音乐相应。得文的隐舍是一悠远模糊的记忆了。伦敦欢迎他以这么突然一瞥地见到它所蕴有的无限的浪漫，他有一半追悔他那长时期的遁世了。

差不多在他所说的那个时候，他回来找一夜的安歇。那个同一的脸孔会现出来吗，当大门打开时候？他焦急地等着，受到一个可伤的失望，因为他的打门是一个刚是可以预料得到的那种人来答应——价廉房子的女房东的结晶，一个臃肿的懒妇，嚼着满口的晚餐，她是从食桌上走来的。

"祝你晚安，"诗人极力现出高兴的神气说道。"我是你的新寄宿人。"

The woman stared, as if failing[1] to understand him.

"I took a room at the top[2], early this evening."

"You've made a mistake. It's the wrong 'ouse[3]."

"But isn't this—?" he named the address which the girl had given him.

"Yes, that's 'ere."

"I thought so. I remember the house perfectly. You were out, I suppose. I saw a—a young woman. I paid a week's rent in advance."

This circumstantial[4] story increased the listener's astonishment. She glared with protuberant eyes, breathed quickly, and gave a snort.

"Well, that's a queer thing. Wait a minute."

She went upstairs, and could be heard to tap at a door; but there followed no sound of voices. Then she came down again, and asked for a description of the young woman who had acted as her representative. The poet answered rather vaguely.

"We have somebody of that sort lodgin 'ere[5], but she's out. You say you paid eight shillin's[6]?"

"Yes. And left my portmanteau; you'll find it upstairs."

---

1 as if failing: as if she was failing。

2 at the top: at the uppermost storey 在最高那一层楼里面。

3 'ouse: house 英国没有受过教育的人们讲话常把 h 开头的字念成没有 h 的音，没有 h 的，反加上 h 音。

4 circumstantial: with many details 委委细细。

这个女人瞪着眼睛,好像不能够了解他的话。

"我在顶高的那一层定了一间房子,天刚黑的时候。"

"你弄错了。你说的不是这个屋子。"

"但是这不是——"他说出那个女子给他的地址。

"对的,这儿是。"

"我也想是对的。我十分明白地记得这个屋子。你那时出去了,我想。我看见一位——一位年青女子。我先交了一星期的房金。"

这个详细的叙述增加了听者的惊愕。她的眼睛突出地睁视着呼吸得很快,发出一声沉重的鼻息。"呀,这真是怪事。等一下。"她到楼上去,可以听得出她去敲一间房子的门;但是没有别的声音接下去。然后她又下来,请描状做她代表的这个女子的相貌。诗人有些渺茫地答应她。

"我们有一个这样的人住在这里,但是她出去了。你说你付了八先令吗?"

"是的。还留下我的手提包;你在楼上可以看见。"

---

5 lodgin 'ere:lodging here。
6 shillin's:shillings。

Again the landlady disappeared. When she returned her face exhibited a contemptuous satisfaction.

"There's no portmanty nowhere in this 'ouse.[1] I told you you'd made a mistake. Try next door!"

The poet was staggered. Mistaken he could not be; the little oil-lamp, a dirty engraving on the wall of the passage, remained so clearly in his mind. A shapeless fear took hold upon[2] him.

"Pray let me go up with you to the top room. I know this was the house. Let me see the room."

The woman was impatient and suspicious. At this moment there sounded from the back of the passage a male voice, asking, "What's up?"[3] A man came forward; the difficulty was explained. For a second time, the baffled poet essayed a description of the girl he remembered so well.

"He means Miss Rowe," said the husband. "She ain't in[4]? Then you just take a light, and 'ave a good look in her room."

They went up together to the first floor[5], and the poet, unable to

---

1 There's no portmanty nowhere in this 'ouse: There is no portmanteau anywhere in this house 粗人说话常用 double negative 传达一个 negative 的意思。

2 to take hold upon: to catch 抓着。

3 What's up?: what is going on? 有什么发生?

4 ain't in: am not; are not; is not in: at home.

5 the first floor: 第二层楼;第一层叫做 the ground floor。

女房东又不见了。当她回来时候,她的脸孔显出一种鄙视的满意。

"这个屋子里那里也找不到什么手提包。我早告诉你是弄错了。到第二家去试一试罢!"

诗人犹豫起来了。他是绝不会错的;小油灯,走廊壁上的一张不洁的印画,是这么明白地印在他心里。一个尚未成形的恐惧抓住他。

"请让我同你到顶高那层的房子。我知道是这个屋子。让我看一下那房子。"

这个女人不耐烦了,而且狐疑起来。这时候从走廊的后面发出一个男人的声音,"什么事?"一个男人走到面前;他们就将这个困难向他细说。这位弄得糊涂了的诗人第二次试来描状他记得这么清楚的女子的形容。

"他指的是骆女士,"这个丈夫说。"她不在家吗?那么你就拿一枝烛,去她房里仔细看一下。"

他们一同到二层楼去,诗人忍不住滞在底下,隔着相当距

keep still, followed them at a distance[1]. He was seriously alarmed. If his portmanteau were to be lost—heavens! His poems—his only copy! Some of the shorter ones he could rewrite from memory, but the backbone of his volume, *The Hermit of the Tor*, could not be reproduced. And how could the portmanteau have vanished? That girl —surely, surely, impossible! Much rather suspect these vulgar people, or some one else of whom he knew nothing.

Man and wife were searching within the room. He heard feminine exclamations and a masculine oath. Unable to control himself he pushed open the door.

"She's took her 'ook[2], " said the man, looking at him with a grin. "See—'ere's her tin box—empty! Nothing as belongs to her in the room."

"And owin'a week's rent! " cried his wife. "I might'a'[3] known better than to[4] trust her. There wasn't no good[5] in her face. She's sloped with your eight bob[6] and your portmanty, I'll take my hoath[7]! "

The poet seized the candle, and strode up the higher flight of

---

1 at a distance: far away 远离。
2 to take one's hook: to make off; to run away 逃走。
3 'a': have.
4 to know better than to: to be too discreet to 小心不至于。
5 There wasn't no good: there was not any good 参看218页注1。

离地跟他们走。他真是吓了。若使他的手提包不见了——天呀！他的诗——他惟一的稿本！里面有几首短的他能够靠着记忆重写下，但是他这本诗集的脊椎，《托尔的隐者》是不能重写下的。这个手提包怎么会变得无影无踪呢？那个女子——一定的，一定的，绝不至如是！还是怀疑这两个粗俗的人，或者他完全不认得的其他人们好得多罢。

夫妻在房里搜着。他听见女性的惊呼和男性的诅咒。不能自阻，他推开那房门。

"她跑掉了，"男人狞笑地望着他说道。"你看——这里是她的锡箱子——空了！这房子里没有一件她的东西了。"

"还欠一星期的房租！"妻子喊道。"我真不该傻得去相信她。她脸上的神气一点也不善良。她拐了你这八先令和你的手提包走了，这是我敢设誓的。"

诗人夺过洋烛，大步走上末了几级楼梯。不错，楼梯顶有

---

6 bob：shilling 复数也是这字。并不加 s。
7 hoath：oath.

stairs. Yes, there was the old box on the landing; yes, this was the room he had paid for. Pheu[1]! Pheu!

"Sal![2]" roared the man's voice, " 'ev a look and see if she's laid ' ands on anything[3] of ours! "

The woman yelled at the suggestion, and began a fierce rummage, high and low[4].

"I can't miss nothin'[5], " she kept shouting. And at length, "Go and fetch a p'liceman, D' y'ear[6], Matt[7]. Go and fetch a p'liceman. This 'ere young gent 'll be chargin' us with robbin' him."[8]

"Where's your receipt for the eight bob? " asked her, husband, turning angrily upon the poet.

"I took no receipt."

"That doesn't sound very likely[9]."

"Likely or not, it's true, " cried the other, exasperated by this insult added to his misfortune. "Fetch a policeman, or else I shall. We'll have this investigated."

"I'll jolly[10] soon do that, " was the man's retort. "Think you're

---

1 pheu: phew, interjection of disgust 鄙视的声音。
2 Sal: Sally 的简称。
3 Have a look and see if she has laid hands on anything.
4 high and low: everywhere 到处。
5 I can't miss nothing: I can't miss anything.
6 D' y'ear: Do you hear.

这个旧箱了;不错,这是他付钱租的房子。呸!呸!

"沙鲁!"一个男人声音怒吼着,"看一看她拿了我们什么东西没有!"

女人听到这个提醒就大喊一声,开始高处低处拼命搜查一阵。

"我不能掉了什么东西。"她老是嚷着。最后说道,"去找一个巡警来。你听到没有,马提。去找一个巡警来。这里这位年青先生将控告我们抢他了。"

"你那八先令的收条在那里?"她的丈夫怒气汹汹地转过来问诗人。

"我没有拿收条。"

"这说得不大像罢。"

"不管像不像,这是件真事,"诗人真是给他惹怒了。"找一个巡警来否则我要去找。我们要把这件事,彻底检查一下。"

"我很快就要去找他,"是那个人的反斥。"你以为你是对付

---

7 Matt:Matthew 的简称。
8 This here young gentleman will be charging us with robbing him.
9 sound likely:听起来不很像是真的。
10 jolly:very.

dealing with thieves, do you? Begin that kind o' talk, and I'll—'Ere, Sal, keep a heye[1] on him whilst I go for the copper[2]."

What ensued calls for no detailed narrative. Suffice it that[3] by midnight all had been done that could be done in the way of charges, defences, and official interrogation. Later, the poet sat talking with his rough acquaintances in their own parlour. After all[4], the people had lost nothing but a week's rent, and they were at length[5] brought to some show of sympathy with the stranger so shamefully treated under their roof. He, for his part[6], decided still to occupy the bedroom, which would be let to him, magnanimously, for seven-and-six pence; whilst the police were trying to track his plunderer he might as well remain on the spot. At one o'clock he went gloomily to bed, and in his troubled sleep dreamt that he was chasing that mysterious girl up hill and down dale amid the Devon moorland; she, always far in advance[7], held his fated manuscript above her head, and laughed maliciously.

II

On the eighth anniversary of that memorable day the poet

---

1 Here, Sal, keep an eye.

2 copper: to cop=to catch (of=fender) 捉, 所以警察叫做 copper, 就是巡逻者的意思。

3 Suffice it that: suffice it to say; I will content myself with saying that.

4 after all: everything else being considered 究之。

群小窃吗？你这样想吗？只要你一开始说那种话，我就要——。来，沙鲁，看着他，当我去找一个巡警来。"

结果如何是用不着细说。总而言之，午夜时候，控告，辩护，和警吏的诘问，这类事凡是能够做到的都做了。后来诗人坐在他们客厅里和他这粗野的朋友谈话。毕竟，这班人除开一星期房租外没有失掉了什么东西，他们最后弄得对于在他们屋里受这么可耻的待遇的生人现出一些同情。他，在他那方面，决定还是住这间卧室，房东慨然地减价每星期算七先令六便士租给他；当巡警想法去追踪抢他的人时候，他还是住在原地方好些。一点钟时候他愁闷地上床去睡，在他不安的睡眠里梦见他在得文旷野里上山下坡地追赶那神秘的女子；她总是远在前面，高举过头他那注定失掉的诗稿，恶意地大笑。

二

在这个值得记忆的日子的八周纪念日，诗人能够取一种觉

---

5 at length：at last 最后。
6 for his part：as far as he was concerned 至于他那方面。
7 in advance：in front；before 在前。

could look back upon[1] his loss with an amused indifference. He was a poet still, but no longer[2] uttered himself in verse. The success of an essay in romantic fiction had shown him how to live by his pen, and a second book made his name familiar "at all the libraries[3]." For a man of simple tastes he was in clover[4]. He dwelt among the Surrey hills, and on his occasional visits to London did not seek a lodging in the neighbourhood of Kennington Road.

As for *The Hermit of the Tor*, though often enough he wondered as to its fate, on the whole[5] he was glad it had never been published. To be sure[6], no publisher would have risked money on it. In his vague recollection, the thing seemed horribly crude; he remembered a line or two that made him shut his eyes and mutter inarticulately. The lyrics might be passable; a couple of them, preserved in his mind, had got printed in a magazine some five years ago. One of his ambitions at present was to write a poetical drama, but he merely mused over the selected theme.

He was thus occupied one winter afternoon as he strolled from the outlying cottage, which he had made his home, to the nearest

---

1 to look back upon: to recollect 回忆。

2 no longer: not any more 不复；再也不。

3 at all the libraries: 这是书店做广告常说的话，这处引用，当然含有调侃之意。

4 in clover: in ease and luxury 在舒适奢侈之中。

得好玩的冷淡态度回想到他的损失。他还是一个诗人,但是不再用诗的格式来表现自己了。浪漫小说的尝试的成功指示给他看怎样去靠着他的笔度日,第二本小说出版使他的名字"为一切图书馆"所熟悉。一个欲望简单的人,他现在是在极愉快的境遇里了。他住在萨立群山里,有时到伦敦去,也不到肯宁顿路邻近找寄宿的地方了。

至于《托尔的隐者》,虽然他都还常纳罕它的下落,但是就全部说起来,他觉得高兴那篇诗永远没有出版。一定的,没有书店肯把钱拿放在这上面去冒险。在他模糊的回忆里,那东西好像粗糙得可怕;他记得一两行,那使他闭起眼睛,说不明白地喃喃起来。抒情诗也许还过得去;有两诗保存在他心里,大约五年前居然刊登一本杂志里。他现在的野心之一是写一本诗剧,但是他单是默想着三个拣定的题目。

一个冬天的下午他正在这样默想着,当他从边僻的小屋——他把这个当做他的家了——散步到最近的乡村。坚硬路

---

5 on the whole:taking everything into account 总而言之。
6 to be sure:without doubt 一定无疑。

village. A footstep on the hard road caused him to look up, and he saw the postman drawing near. This encounter saved the humble official a half-mile walk; he delivered a letter into the poet's hands.

A letter redirected by his publishers; probably the tribute of an admiring reader, such as he had not seldom received of late. With a smile he opened it, and the contents proved to be of more interest than he had anticipated.

Sir,

I have in my possession[1] a manuscript which bears your name, as that of its author, and dates[2] from some years back. It consists of poetical compositions, the longest of them entitled *The Hermit of the Tor*. I cannot at present explain to you how these papers came into[3] my hands, but I should like to return them to their true owner, and for this purpose I should be glad if you would allow me to meet you, at your own place and time[4]. But for[5] a residence abroad, I should probably have addressed you on the subject long before this, as I find that your name is well known to English readers. Please direct your reply to Penwell's Library, Westbourne Grove, W., and believe me.

Faithfully yours,

---

1 in my possession: possessed by me 存在我处。
2 to date: to mark with date 记有某年某月某日。
3 to come into: to fall to 归于。

上的一个人脚步声音使他举头一望,他看见邮差走近前来。这个相逢省了这个低微的公仆半哩的路程;他交一封信到诗人手里。

一封从他的出版者转交的信;也是一个钦佩的读者的赞辞,像他近来常接到的。他含着微笑打开,内容却是比他所预料的更有趣得多。

先生,

我存有一本稿子,上面写了你的名字,算做它的作者,日期是好几年之前。里面都是诗歌,最长的一首叫做《托尔的隐者》。我现在不能向你解说这些稿子怎么会流落到我手里,但是我很想将它们归还它们的原主,因此若使你肯让我,我很高兴和你相会,地点同时间随你选定。假使我一向不在外国住,也许我早就为这事情写信给你了,我看出你的名字是英国读者所周知的。覆信请寄西城卫斯特勃伦·格罗夫,平威尔图书馆,请相信我是

诚恳地你的,

---

4 at your own place and time:地点和时间都随你自己定去。
5 but for this:if this condition etc. were absent 假使没有那么一回事。

Eustace Grey

At the head of the letter there was no address. "Eustace Grey" sounded uncommonly like a pseudonym. Altogether a very surprising sequel to the adventure of eight years ago. Was the writer man or woman? Impossible to decide from the penmanship, which was bold, careless, indicative of character and of education. As a man, at all events[1], the mysterious person must be answered, and curiosity permitted no delay. Where should the meeting take place[2]? He had no inclination to breathe the air of London just now, and a journey of twenty miles might fairly be exacted from a correspondent who chose to write in the strain of melodrama. Let "Eustace Grey" come hither.

With all brevity the poet invited him to take a certain train from Waterloo, which would enable him to reach the cottage at about four in the afternoon, on a specified day.

The appointed hour was just upon nightfall. With blind drawn, lamp lit, and a log blazing in the old fireplace, the poet awaited his visitor, who might or might not come, for no second communication had been received from him. If he came, he would doubtless take a conveyance from the railway station, a mile and a half away; a

---

1 at all events: certainly 无论如何。
2 to take place: to happen 举行。

尤斯退·格雷

信的顶端没有寄信人的住址。"尤斯退·格雷"念起来怪像个假名字。真是八年前的奇事的一个很奇怪的结果。写这封信的人是男是女呢？不能从笔迹上去决定，笔锋是大胆的，随便的，指示出刚毅的性格同良好的教育。诗人既是一个男子汉，无论如何，这个神秘的人总是要答覆的，好奇心使他不能迟延。相会要在什么地方呢？他现在正是不愿呼吸伦敦空气，二十哩的旅程可以很公平地索之于一个高兴用传奇的笔墨来写信的人。让"尤斯退·格雷"来这里罢。

极简短地诗人请他从滑铁卢搭某一次火车，那可以使他在说定的某一天下午四时左右到他的小屋。

约定的时间刚是快黑时候。百叶窗拉下，灯点着，一块木头在旧火炉里燃烧，诗人等候他的客人，那个人也许来，也许不来，因为从他那里没有得到第二封的信。若使他来，他一定从火车站，离这里有一哩半路，雇一辆车子；轮声会宣布他的

rumble of wheels would announce him. At a quarter past four no such signal was yet audible, but five minutes later it struck upon the listener's ear. He stood up, and waited in nervous expectancy.

The vehicle stopped by the door; a knock sounded. A tap at the door of the sitting-room, and there appeared, led by the servant, a tall lady. She was warmly and expensively clad; wraps and furs disguised the outline of her figure, and allowed but[1] an imperfect view of her features. In a moment[2], however, she threw some of the superfluities aside, and stood gazing at the poet, who saw now that she was a woman of not more than thirty, with a strong, handsome face, and a form that pleased his eye. She offered a hand.

"If I had known—"[3] he began, breaking the silence with voice apologetic. But she interrupted him.

"You wouldn't have brought me all this way. Never mind. It's better. I shall be glad to have made a pilgrimage[4] to the home of the celebrated author."

Her language and utterance certainly did not lack refinement, but she spoke with more familiarity than the poet was prepared for. He judged her a type of the woman that lives in so-called smart soci-

---

1 but: only.

2 in a moment: in an instant; very soon 顷刻间。

3 If I have known: 他想说的话是，假使我知道不是一个男子，我一定不会叫她这样跋涉长途。

来临。四点过一刻,还听不见这种记号,但是五分钟后,这声音打到静听着的人的耳鼓。他站起来,在神经震动的期望里等候着。

车子停在门口;来了一下敲门的声音。客厅的门上轻轻一敲,现出一位体格高的太太,仆人在前引着。她穿有暖和的,值钱的衣服;外套和皮围巾遮住她身体的轮廓,只让人们看见她一部分的形容。然而她立刻扔开一些多余的衣服,站着睨视诗人,他现在看见她是不过三十岁的女人,一副有毅力的,漂亮的脸孔,一个悦目的身材。她伸出一只手。

"假使我晓得——"他开始用道歉的口吻来破这寂默。但是她截断他。

"那么你不会叫我走这么多路。不要紧。这还好些。我很愿来参诣文豪的家。"

她的辞句同语调的确并不缺乏文雅,但是她说话的亲密态度是出乎诗人预料之外的。他认为她是那种在所谓时髦社会里

---

4 pilgrimage:参诣圣地,朝山进香之意。这是她恭维这位作家,说值得远道来顶礼。

ety. His pulses had a slight flutter; in observing and admiring her he all but[1] forgot the strange history in which she was concerned.

"The cab will wait for me, " she continued, "so I mustn't be long[2]."

"I'm sorry for that, " replied the poet, so far imitating her as to talk like an old acquaintance. "You shall have a cup of tea at once." He rang a hand-bell. "You've had a cold journey."

Whilst he spoke he saw her lay upon the table a rolled packet, which was doubtless his manuscript. Then she seated herself in an easy chair by the fireside, glanced round the room, smiled at her own thoughts, and met his look with steady gaze.

"Are you Eustace Grey?" he inquired, taking a seat over against[3] her.

"I chose the name at random[4]. My own doesn't matter. I am only an—an intermediary, as you would say in a book."

He searched her countenance closely, persistently, without regard to good manners. It was no common face. Had he ever seen it before? It did not charm him, but decidedly it affected his imagination. This could not be an ordinary woman of fashion. He knew little of the wealthy world, but his experience of life assured him that

---

1 all but: almost 几乎。
2 I mustn't be long: I must not stay for a long time 我绝不能久滞在这里。
3 over against: facing 对面。

过活的人。他的脉搏微有震动；一心去观察同赞美她，他几乎忘却和她相关的那段奇怪事情。

"马车等着我，"她继续说道，"所以我绝不能久坐。"

"我觉得怅然，"诗人答道，模仿她，说话像个老朋友样子。"你立刻有一杯茶喝。"他摇一个手铃。"你走了一个寒冷的旅程。"

当他说话时候，他看见她放一卷小包在桌上，那无疑地是他的诗稿。然后她自己坐在炉边一张舒服的椅上，向房子四周望一下，自己想笑起来了，用一种从容的凝视来抵住他的注视。

"你是尤斯退·格雷吗？"他问道，坐在她对面。

"我随便拣中这个名字。我自己的名字是毫无关系的。我只是一个媒介者——你在小说里会这样说。"

他仔细地，固执地，不顾礼貌地端详她的脸孔。那不是个普通的脸孔。他从前看见过吗？这脸孔并不使他入迷，但是的确打动了他的想像。这不会是个普通时髦女子。他不大知道有钱人家的事情，但是他的人生经验坚决地告诉他，"尤斯退·格

---

4 at random：at haphazard；without aim 随便；无目的。

"Eustace Grey" was not now for the first time engaged in transactions which had a savour of romance.

"Those are my verses?" He pointed towards the table.

"Exactly as they left your hands," she answered calmly.

"Or my portmanteau, rather."[1]

"Yes, your portmanteau." She accepted the correction with a smile.

Surely he had not seen her face before? Surely he had never heard her voice? At this moment the servant entered with a tea-tray. The poet stood up and waited upon[2] his visitor. As soon as the door had closed, she said:

"You are not married?"

"No—unhappily."

"Please don't add the word in compliment to me. I'm delighted to know that you keep your independence. Don't marry for a long time. And you live here always?"

"Most of the year."

"Ah, you are not like ordinary men."

"Nor you—I was thinking—like ordinary women."

---

1 诗人已有些猜到这个女子就是从前那个拿了他的房钱, 带去他的提包的人。所以用这些话来试她, 但是她饱历世变, 沧海曾经, 也就神色不动地暗暗承认一切, 只是不刺破这个假名字。

2 to wait upon: to attend upon 伺候; 干倒茶递饼这类的事情。

雷"现在不是第一次干带有浪漫意味的事情。

"那是我的诗稿吗?"他指桌上。

"正如它离开你的手时候,"她冷静地答道。

"也可以说离开我的手提包,还好些罢。"

"是的,你的手提包。"她以一笑接受这个更正。

他真的没有见过她的脸孔吗?他真的没有听过她的声音吗?这时仆人捧一个茶盘进来。诗人站起来,招待他的来客。门一关好,她就问道:

"你还没有结婚吗?"

"没有——不幸得很。"

"请你不要为着我加上这句恭维的话。我觉得高兴听到你保存有你的独立。在长时间之内请你不要去结婚。你总是住在这儿吗?"

"一年大半的时光。"

"啊,你不像普通的男人。"

"你也不像——我正想着——普通的女人。"

"Well, no; I suppose not." She looked at him with a peculiar frankness, with a softer expression than her face had yet shown, and, whilst speaking, she drew off her left-hand glove. A peculiarity in the movement excited her companion's attention; he saw that she wore two rings, one of them of plain gold[1].

"I like your books, " was her next remark.

"I'm glad of it."

"Have you good health? You look rather pale—for one who lives in the country."

"Oh, I am very well."

"To be sure you have brains, and use them. It's pleasant to know that there are such men." She sipped her tea. "But time is going, and the driver and horse will freeze."

"I have no stable," said the poet, "but the man can sit by the kitchen fire and have some ale. Anything to make your visit longer."

"Complimentary; but I am here on business[2]." She had grown more disitant. "Of course, you want to know how those papers came into my hands. I'll tell you, and make a short story of it[3]. I had them a year or two ago from a friend of mine—a girl, who died. She had

---

1 这指结婚戒指，因为照例都是没有雕花的。

2 on business: with a purpose relating to business 为着正经的事务的。

3 to make a short story of it: to tell it in a few words 简单说出来。

"不像；我想大概是不像罢。"她有一种特别坦白的态度望着他，脸上形容的和蔼是她脸上一向所没有表现过的，当说话时候，她脱下她左手的手套。这个动作的一个特别姿势引起她同伴的注意；他看见她戴两粒戒指，一粒是通常的金戒指。

"我喜欢你的书，"她又说道。

"我听着很高兴。"

"你健康吗？你脸色仿佛苍白些——就一个住在乡下的人而论。"

"啊，我身体很好。"

"你的确有脑筋，而且善用它们。这是一件乐事，知道世上尚有这样的人们。"她啜些茶。"但是时间快过去了，马夫同马会冻住了。"

"我没有马房，"诗人说道，"但是那个人可以坐在厨房火旁，喝点麦酒。怎么办都可以，总之使你多坐一会儿。"

"客气得很；但是我是来交代事情。"她变得冷淡些。"你自然想知道这诗篇怎么会落到我手里。我要告诉你，向你简短地说出那经过。一两年前我从我一位朋友那里得来——一个已经

stolen them."

The listener gave a start[1], and looked at the face before him more intently than ever. He detected no shrinking, but a certain suggestion of defiance.

"She was a girl who did what is supposed to be the privilege of men—sowed wild oats[2]. She came to an end of[3] her money, and found herself in a poor lodging—somewhere in the south of London—"

"Off Kennington Road, " murmured the poet.

"Very likely. I forget. She had got rid of all the clothing she could spare. She was a week behind with[4] her rent. Another day or two, and she would starve. No way of earning money, it seemed. Poor thing, she thought herself something[5] of an artist, and went about offering drawings to the papers and the publishers; but I'm afraid the work was poor to begin with, and got poorer[6] as she did. The desperate state of things made her fierce and ready for anything.

"However, she had a girl friend who wrote to her now and then[7], addressing to the name she had assumed. This friend lived far

---

1 to give a start: 吓得一跳。
2 to sow wild oats: to indulge in youthful follies 少年任情胡为。
3 to come to an end of: to spend all 用尽。
4 behind with: in arrear with 拖欠。
5 something: 多少；几分。

死了的女子。她偷来这诗稿。"

听的人吓了跳，比以前更注意地睋视在他面前这个脸孔。他寻不出退缩的神气，只是含有些抵抗的意思。

"她是一个干大家公认为男人专利的事情——过放荡的生涯——的女子。她弄得金尽了，自己住在一个可怜的寄宿处——伦敦南部邻近——"

"离肯宁顿路不远的地方，"诗人轻轻说道。

"大概是罢。我忘却了。她把她不必需的衣服全典卖完了。她还欠一星期的房租。再过一两天，她就得饿肚子了。好像无法可以攒钱。可怜人，她以为自己勉强可以算个艺术家，到处向报馆同书店卖画；但是我恐怕那玩意儿是不足靠以谋生的，她的确变得更穷了。绝望的环境使她横起心来，肯干任何事情。

"然而，她有一个女朋友，时时写信来给她，信封外面写交给她所假托的名字。这位朋友远处北方，自己谋生。一天下午，

---

6 第一个poor是"可怜的""不妙的"的意思；第二个是"贫"的意思。
7 now and then：occasionally 有时；时常。

away in the north, and earned her own living. One afternoon, just when things were at the blackest, there arrived a telegram: "If you come at once. I can promise you employment. Start immediately." All very well but how was she to raise fifteen shillings or so for her journey? Now it happened that at this moment she was the only person in the house. The landlady, she knew, would be away for two or three hours; the husband wouldn't be home till eight (it was now five), —and another lodger had just gone out. I mention this—you know why. Whilst she was still standing with the telegram in her hand, some one knocked. She opened the door. A young man, carrying a portmanteau—a very nice-looking young man, who spoke softly and pleasantly—had come for a lodging; he wanted one room. She let him in, and took him upstairs."

"She did, " murmured the poet, his eyes straying about the room.

"And you remember what followed? "

"Remarkably well. I can see—well. I'm not quite sure; but I think I can see her face."

"Can you? Well, until you had left the house, her intention was perfectly honest. She thought that, in return[1] for her service in letting the room the landlady might perhaps lend her money for the journey

---

1 in return: as requital 酬报。

刚刚当一切前途在最黑暗时候,来一封电报:"若使你立刻来,我能答应你找得到位置。请立即动身。"好极了,但是她怎能够筹出十五先令左右的款做旅费呢?这时候凑巧只有她一个人在屋里。房东太太,她知道,会在外面滞两三钟头;那个丈夫在八点钟以前不会回家(现在是五点),——另一个寄宿的人出去了。我说这句话——你知道是为什么缘故。当她还站着手里拿这个电报,有人敲门。她打开门。一个青年,带一只手提包——一个非常漂亮的年青人,轻轻地,可爱地说话着——来寻寄宿处:他要一间房子。她让他进来,引他到楼上去。"

"她的确是这样干,"诗人低声说道,他的眼睛随便望房里各处瞧。

"你记得后来的事情吗?"

"记得非常清楚。我现在能看见——呀,我不十分有把握,但是我想我现在能看见她的脸孔。"

"你能够吗?好罢,在你离那屋子之前,她的存心完全是诚实的。她想,为着报偿她租出房子这个情谊,房东太太也许肯

north, and trust for repayment. But as soon as you had gone the devil began whispering. Your money lay in her hand. Your portmanteau contained things that would sell or pawn. The chance of a loan from the landlady was dreadfully slight. You see? A man of imagination ought to understand."

"I do—perfectly."

"She tried her keys on the portmanteau. No use. But it was old and shaky. She pressed open the lock. What she found disappointed her; it wouldn't fetch many shillings. But she had taken the fatal step. No staying in the house now. She put on[1] her hat and jacket, stuffed into her pockets the few things still left to her, caught up the portmanteau—and away!"

The poet could not help a laugh, and his companion joined in it. But she was agitated, and her mirth had not a genuine ring.

"And how much were my poor old rags worth?"

"Five shillings."

"By Jove[2]! You don't say so![3]"

"She pawned them in a street somewhere north of the Strand. But this gave her only thirteen shillings. The she sold the

---

1 to put on: to wear 戴上去。

2 By Jove: Jove（Jupiter）天帝，by Jove是表欣欢的感叹词。

3 you don't say so!：你不是这样说吗！因为太惊骇了，就疑自己听错了，或者说话的人没有讲明白，所以这样追问一下。

借她到北方去的川资，相信她会寄还。但是你一走去，魔鬼开始耳语了。你的钱在她手里。你手提包里有可以卖或者典当的东西。从房东太太借到一笔款的可能性是少得可怕。你会意吗？一个有想像力的人应当会了解。"

"我会了解——十分了解。"

"她将她钥匙试开那手提包。没有用。但是那是个破旧摇动的提包。她压开那锁。她所看见的使她失望；那不会换得许多先令。但是她已经走了那不可挽回的步骤了。现在绝不能再滞屋里了。她穿上她帽子同短衣，将她还剩下的几件东西塞在衣袋里，抓起手提包——走矣！"

诗人免不了大笑一声，他的伴侣也附和着。但是她的心震动了，她的笑声缺乏真挚的音调。

"我那几件破衣服值多少？"

"五先令。"

"哈哈！难道你说的是真话吗！"

"她将它们押在斯徒莲北边的某一条街的当铺。但是这一起

portmanteau; that brought eighteen-pence. Fourteen shillings and six pence. Next she sold or pawned her jacket; it brought three shillings."

"Poor girl! With such a journey before her on a cold night! But the poems? "

"She looked at them, and was on the point of throwing them away, but she didn't. She read some of them in the train that night. And oh—oh—oh! How ashamed of herself she was then and for many a long day! So much ashamed that she couldn't even feel afraid."

"And she got the employment promised? "

"Yes. And sowed no more wild oats. It was a poor living, but she struggled on—until by chance[1] she met a very rich man, who took a fancy to[2] her. She didn't care for him. In her life she had only seen one man who really attracted her, but—well, she made up her mind[3] to marry the rich man; and then—she died. I knew her story already, and at her death she left your poems in my care, to be restored if possible. There they are."

With a careless gesture she rose.

---

1 by chance: accidently 偶然。
2 to take a fancy to: to take a liking to 喜欢。
3 to make up ones' mind: to determine 决定。

只给她十三先令。然后她卖去那手提包；这给她十八便士。总共是十四先令六便士。其次她卖掉或者典去她的短衣；这给她三先令。"

"可怜的姑娘！她面前还横有冷夜里这么一段旅程！但是那些诗稿呢？"

"她瞧一下，几乎要扔开了，但是她却没有扔开。那夜里火车中她念了一点儿。啊——啊——啊！那时她自己多么惭愧呀，有好几天都如是！她自惭到不能觉得害怕了。"

"她得到那个朋友答应她的那个工作吗？"

"是的。不再过放荡的生涯了。那是个可怜的位置，但是她奋斗下去——等到偶然她碰到一个很有钱的人，他喜欢她。她并不高兴他。一生里她只有一个真叫她心迷的男人，但是——好罢，她决心嫁给这个富人；然后——她死了。我早知道她的故事了，死时候她把你的诗稿交托我，若使能够就归还原主。现在这诗稿就在这儿。"

具一种随随便便的态度，她站起来。

"You are not going yet, " exclaimed the poet.

"I am; this moment. I have a train to catch."

"Hang the train! There's one at about nine o'clock. I shall send away your cab."

She looked at him very coldly.

"I am going at once, and you will be good enough to stay[1] where you are."

"You won't even tell me your name? "

"Not even that. Good-bye, poet! "

She gave him her hand. Holding it, he gazed at her with bright eyes.

"I do remember your friend's face. And how I wish she could have spoken to me that night! "

"The ideal is never met in life, " she answered softly. "Put it into your books—which I shall always read."

The door closed, and he heard the cab rumble away.

---

1 you will be good enough to stay：please stay 请滞在。

"你现在总不走罢,"诗人惊奇地说道。

"我走;就是此刻。我还要赶火车去。"

"该死火车!九点左右还有一次。我打发你马车走罢。"

她很冷淡地望着他。

"我立刻就走了,请你滞在你自己这地方罢。"

"你甚至于不肯告诉我你的名字吗?"

"甚至于名字也不肯说。再见,诗人!"

她向他伸出手。握着它,他眼睛奕奕地注视她。

"我真记得你朋友的脸孔。我现在多么希望那天晚上她会对我说话!"

"理想是绝不能在人生里遇见的,"她轻轻地说道。"把它放你书里罢——那我将永远念着。"

门关了,他听到马车辚辚的声音渐渐消灭了。

The Three Strangers

三个陌生人

（英汉对照）

T. Hardy 著
梁遇春 译注

"英文小丛书"之一，上海北新书局，1931年4月付排，1931年5月初版

Thomas Hardy
(1840—1928)

哈代是英国近代文坛上卓然自立，无懈可击的作家。他用简洁深刻的辞句传达出"自然"对于渺小的人类的调侃，隐隐地露出"怜悯"的福音。他觉得命运之神总是弄出种种把戏来跟我们捣乱，它有时赋我们以一个残缺的性格，那就足以叫我们颠连一生了。他看到人世上处处都是布满悲剧的空气，然而他却能镇定地将这些辛酸故事一一刻画出来，弄出个玲珑的布局，婉转地描状通常人们的心曲，自己在一旁冷笑着，但是又带了无限的慈祥，在这点上显出他那惊人的艺术天才。只有看透人世的幻象，整个身子都浸在悲哀里面的人才能有恬然的心境，才能将人生消息从笔尖上从容传出，所以悲剧在文学是格调最高的作品，所以只有心头上尝遍人世间苦味的人才能有近于涅槃的心境。哈代的杰作有 *Jude the Obscure*；*Tess of the d'Urberville*；*The Return of the Native* 等几本长篇小说，它们的题材都是"极小的生命"（infinitesimal lives）在这"满天星斗的宇宙这个巨大的背境上"（the stupendous background of the stellar universe）所演的惨剧。

他又善描写风景。利用地方色彩来渲染他的故事，使人们更深切感到"自然"的威力。他小说里所说的都是 Wessex 地方的事情，我们念起来仿佛亲临其地，而且觉得那地方有一种令人生无限感慨的空气。

哈代的短篇小说不如他长篇小说，没有那么有精彩。*Wessex Tales*，*Life's Little Ironies* 等集。我们这里所选的《三个生客》是在 *Wessex Tales* 里面的。但是这篇可以算做他的短篇杰作，几乎是大家公认的，是跟他的长篇小说同样不朽的作品。

末了，我们不要忘记他又是个诗人，而且有一些批评家说他的诗是比他的小说更伟大，预料将来人们也许把他当做诗人看。

The Three Strangers

Among the few features of agricultural England which retain an appearance but[1] little modified by the lapse of centuries, may be reckoned the high, grassy and furzy downs, coombs[2], or ewe-leases[3], as they are indifferently called, that fill a large area of certain counties in the south and south-west. If any mark of human occupation is met with hereon, it usually takes the form of the solitary cottage of some shepherd.

Fifty years ago such a lonely cottage stood on such a down, and may possibly be standing there now. In spite of its loneliness, however, the spot, by actual measurement, was not more than five miles

---

1 but: only 只；惟；仅。
2 coomb: a hollow in a hillside 山边凹下的地方；豁谷。

三个陌生人

英国的农业区域有几个特色还保留个本来面目,不大受时代递迁的影响,这几个特色中间的一个就是那些位于高处的,多草的,荆棘丛生的沙阜,也可以叫做豁谷,或者牧地,人们都是这样随便叫它们了,它们占了英国南部及西南部几个州里大部分的地面。若使在那里我们遇到什么,可以指出有人烟的东西,那常是牧羊人的孤独茅屋。

五十年前,有这么一个寂寞的茅屋站在这么一个沙阜上,也许现在还站在那儿。然而,不管它多么寂寞,那地方实在量起来跟一个州城相离不过五哩。但是这是无关紧要的。起伏不

---

3 ewe-leases:land for sheep to feed upon 牧地。

from a county-town. Yet that affected it little. Five miles of irregular upland, during the long inimical seasons[1], with their sleets, snows, rains, and mists, afford withdrawing space enough to isolate a Timon[2] or a Nebuchadnezzar[3]; much less, in fair weather, to please that less repellent tribe, the poets, philosophers, artists, and others who "conceive and meditate of pleasant things".

Some old earthen camp or barrow[4], some clump of trees, at least some starved[5] fragment of ancient hedge is usually taken advantage of[6] in the erection of these forlorn dwellings. But in the present case, such a kind of shelter had been disregarded. Higher Crowstairs, as the house was called, stood quite detached and undefended. The only reason for its precise situation seemed to be the crossing of two footpaths at right angles hard by[7], which may have crossed there and thus for a good[8] five hundred years. Hence the house was exposed to the elements[9] on all sides. But, though the wind up here[10] blew unmistakably when it did blow, and the rain hit hard whenever it fell, the various weathers of the winter season were not quite so

---

1 inimical seasons: hostile or harmful seasons 与人为敌的或为害甚烈的时季,就是指雨雪载途,寒风凛烈的时候。

2 Timon: 雅典一个爵爷,非常慷慨,后来弄穷了,从前受了他恩惠的人们却全不理他。他恨人们到极点,跑旷野去过原人的生活,不愿再同人类接近,后来寂寞地死了。

3 Nebuchadnezzar: 巴比伦的王,非常虔敬,喜欢静处默思。

齐的五哩高地，在悠长的冷酷季候里，连同雨雪雾霰，给人们以足够退隐的余地，就是一个泰梦或者一个尼布甲尼撒在那里也会觉得已经与人世绝缘了；在天气晴朗的时候，也是太远了，不能使那比较不大讨厌的人们喜欢，就是所谓诗人，哲学家，艺术家同其它"一切冥想可爱的事物"的人们。

建筑这类枯寂的住宅时常利用泥做的古垒，或者古冢，或者一丛树林，最少也要靠着古篱的零干残枝。但是，我们现在谈的这个茅屋却不用这些保护。亥儿·克洛斯腾尔思，这是那茅屋的名字，是完全无依无靠，也没有别的东西保护着，站在那里。它刚刚建于那个位置的惟一理由大概是两条小路在邻近成为直角地交叉，那也许在那里这样交叉了整整五百年。所以这个屋子四面都受风雨的侵蚀。但是，虽然当刮起风时，那上面的确有狂风吹着，每回下起雨时，也的确是暴雨；在沙阜上冬季里各种天气却没有像住在低地的人们

---

4 barrow：a large sepulchral mound，or tumulus 冢。

5 starved：withered 枯萎的。

6 to take advantage of：to use as a means of effecting one's purpose 借以实现个人的目的；利用。

7 hard by：near at hand 邻近；近旁。

8 good：full 整整的。

9 elements：atmospheric agency 空中的各种威力，如风雪雨霜等。

10 up here：因为是居于高处，所以用 up 字。

formidable on the coomb as they were imagined to be by dwellers on low ground. The raw rimes were not so pernicious as in the hollows, and the frosts were scarcely so severe. When the shepherd and his family who tenanted the house were pitied for their sufferings from the exposure, they said that upon the whole[1] they were less inconvenienced by "wuzzes and flames"[2] (hoarses and phlegms) than when they had lived by the stream of a snug neighbouring valley.

The night of March 28, 182*, was precisely one of the nights that were wont to call forth[3] these expressions of commiseration. The level rainstorm smote walls, slopes, and hedges like the clothyard shafts[4] of Senlac[5] and Crecy[6]. Such sheep and outdoor animals as had no shelter stood with their buttocks to the winds; while the tails of little birds trying to roost on some scraggy thorn were blown inside-out[7] like umbrellas. The gable-end of the cottage was stained with wet, and the eavesdroppings flapped against the wall. Yet never was commiseration for the shepherd more misplaced. For that cheerful rustic was entertaining a large party in glorification of the christening of his second girl.

---

1 upon the whole: all things considered 把一切情形归结看起来。
2 wuzzes and flames: 这是土话，就是 hoarse and phlegm 的意思。
3 to call forth: to elicit 引起。
4 clothyard shafts: arrow a yard long 有一码长的箭矢。

所忆想的那么十分可怕。那里的严霜也不像谷中的那么有害；结冰几乎也没有那么厉害。当人们可怜住在那屋子里的牧羊人和他的家庭，他们却说全部论起来在那里他们却比住在邻近温暖的山谷里河旁时少受声哑同多痰这两个毛病的打扰。

一八二〇年三月二十八日之夜正是一个常引起这些哀怜话的夜。平地的暴风雨打着墙，斜坡同篱笆，像森拉克同克勒西两次大战时所用的箭矢。无处可避的羊同其它野兽拿它们的臀部朝风站着；打算栖在瘦削的荆棘上的小鸟的尾巴吹翻过来，展开像伞一样。茅屋的三角墙顶端现出潮湿的痕迹，檐前的滴沥打到墙上。但是我不该哀怜这个牧羊人。因为这个快乐的乡下人正款待着许多人，庆祝他第二女孩的命名式。

---

5 Senlac：诺尔曼人（Norman）于一〇六六〈年〉征服英国本地的萨克森人（Saxons），他们的公爵威廉就成为英史中之征服者威廉 William the conquerer，当时大战的地点在 Hasting 邻近的 Senlac 山上。
6 Crecy：一三四六年英国 Edward Ⅲ 和法国 Philip 决战的地方。
7 inside-out：inside becomes outside 里面变成外面了。

The guests had arrived before the rain began to fall, and they were all now assembled in the chief or living room[1] of the dwelling. A glance into the apartment at eight o'clock on this eventful evening would have resulted in the opinion that it was as cosy and comfortable a nook as could be wished for in boisterous weather. The calling of its inhabitant was proclaimed by a number of highly-polished sheepcrooks without stems that were hung ornamentally over the fireplace, the curl of each shining crook varying from the antiquated type engraved in the patriarchal pictures of old family Bibles to the most approved fashion of the last local sheep-fair. The room was lighted by half-a-dozen candles, having wicks only a trifle smaller than the grease which enveloped them[2], in candlesticks that were never used but at high-days[3], holy-days, and family feasts. The lights were scattered about the room, two of them standing on the chimney-piece. This position of candles was in itself significant. Candles on the chimney-piece always meant a party.

On the hearth, in front of a backbrand to give substance, blazed a fire of thorns, that crackled "like the laughter of the fool".

Nineteen persons were gathered here. Of these, five women,

1　living-room: sitting room 与卧室相反的，是白天的居室。
2　这是讥笑牧羊人的节俭，蜡烛上几乎全是烛心，只有一点儿蜡。
3　high-days: a holy or feast day 圣日。见《圣经》："因那安息日是个大日。"(for that sabbath day was an high day)

在大雨开始下之前，客人都来了，他们现在全聚在屋里最重要的房子里，也可以说是起坐室。若使我们当这个多事的晚上八点钟时候向这房里瞧一下，就会认为在这风狂雨暴的天气里，我们不能希望有个再紧密温暖的，再安适的好所在了。住在里面的人的职业可以从许多擦得很亮的，没有杆的，挂在壁炉上当装饰品用的牧羊杖看出，个个明亮的杖的卷曲处有许多样子，从世家历代传下的大本《圣经》上族长图像里所画的古式一直到本地最近一次羊市里最受人们赞美的新式。房里有六枝蜡烛照着，烛心只比敷在上面的油小一点儿，插在除开在大日，宗教节同家宴日外绝对不用的烛台上。这几枝烛分散房里各处，有二枝放在火炉架上。蜡烛的位置本身就是有意义的。火炉架上放着蜡烛总是表示有个大宴会的意思。

火炉里面烧块木头，使火力实在些，炉边燃着荆棘，发出爆裂的声音："像傻子的笑声"。

有十九个人聚在这儿。这里面，五个女人，穿种种鲜明颜

wearing gowns of various bright hues, sat in chairs along the wall; girls shy and not shy filled the window-bench; four men, including Charley Jake the hedge-carpenter, Elijah New the parish-clerk, and John Pitcher, a neighbouring dairyman, the shepherd's father-in-law, lolled in the settle; a young man and maid, who were blushing over tentative pourparlers[1] on a life-companionship, sat beneath the corner-cupboard; and an elderly engaged man of fifty or upward moved restlessly about from spots where his betrothed was not[2] to the spot where she was. Enjoyment was pretty general, and so much the more prevailed in being unhampered by conventional restrictions. Absolute confidence in each other's good opinion begat perfect ease, while the finishing stroke[3] of manner, amounting to a truly princely serenity, was lent to the majority by the absence of any expression or trait denoting that they wished to get on[4] in the world, enlarge their minds, or do any eclipsing[5] thing whatever—which nowadays so generally nips the bloom and bonhomie[6] of all except the two extremes of the social scale[7].

---

1 pourparlers: informal opening of a question between diplomatists 外交官关于一个问题的非正式的谈判。这个字本来是法文。

2 was not: to be 有 to exist with reference to a certain place 在某一处之意,比如 to be here, 所〈以〉where she was not 就是"她不在那儿的地点"。

3 the finishing stroke: the stroke which finishes 最后的工作；完成一切的最后努力；使臻于尽美尽善地位的修饰润色之工。

色的外衣,坐在墙边的椅子上;害羞的和不害羞的少女占着窗子旁边的长凳;四个男人,包括专做栅栏的木匠查利·约克,教区的书记以利亚·纽,邻近牛奶场的主人、牧羊人的丈人约翰·匹舍尔,凭倚在高背长椅子上;一个年青人同一位姑娘关于终身伴侣这个问题正酝酿着试作非正式的谈判,坐在基角上碗碟柜的底下;一个五十岁了或者还要老些的订婚了的人不安定地从他未婚妻不在的地点走到他未婚妻所在的地点。大家都在享乐着,因为没有受世俗礼仪的种种束缚,所以更痛快些。绝对地相信彼此互有好感就产生了完全的自由自在,而使大多数人的态度臻于尽美尽善的地步,差不多做到王者的真正的安详雍容。这全因为他们都没有现出或者露出什么指明他们想在世界上谋发展,扩张他们自己的心境,或者干任一种损人利己的事情——这些心境现在摧残了一切人的温和偁傥,除开了社会阶级上的两个极端的人们。

---

 4 to get on:to make progress;to advance 有进步;前进。
 5 eclipsing:throwing into the shade 使变成隐晦。
 6 bonhomie:geniality 和蔼可亲。
 7 the two extremes of the social scale:指顶富的和顶穷的人们,有钱的人们处在安逸的环境里,对于人们常是温文有礼;穷光蛋与人无所争了,对于人们常具一种快乐伴侣的态度。

Shepherd Fennel had married well, his wife being a dairyman's daughter from a vale at a distance, who brought fifty guineas in her pocket—and kept them there, till they should be required for ministering to the needs of a coming family. This frugal woman had been somewhat exercised[1] as to the character that should be given to the gathering. A sit-still party had its advantages; but an undisturbed position of ease in chairs and settles was apt to lead on[2] the men to such an unconscionable deal of toping[3] that they would sometimes fairly drink the house dry. A dancing-party was the alternative; but this, while avoiding the foregoing objection on the score of good drink, had a counterbalancing disadvantage in the matter of good victuals' the ravenous appetites engendered by the exercise causing immense havoc in the buttery. Shepherdess Fennel fell back upon[4] the intermediate plan of mingling short dances with short periods of talk and singing, so as to hinder any ungovernable rage in either. But this scheme was entirely confined to her own gentle mind: the shepherd himself was in the mood to exhibit the most reckless phases of hospitality.

The fiddler was a boy of those parts, about twelve years of age,

---

1 exercised: worried 焦虑。
2 to lead on: to entice beyond the point contemplated 引诱使干出在意料之外的事情。

牧羊人樊纳尔娶一门很好的亲，他的妻子是跟这里相隔一些路的一个谷里牛奶场的主人的女儿，嫁给他时袋里带来了五十金币——还留在那儿，等将来大家庭需要这笔款时才用。这位勤俭的女人关于这次聚会应取那一种形式曾经用过苦心。坐谈不动的宴会有它的好处；但是舒服地，丝毫不动地坐在椅子上同高背的长椅子上容易使男子喝进多到没有道理的酒，他们常把家里的酒全喝干了。其它的方法就是跳舞会；但是当避免了前面所说的关于美酒的毛病，在佳美的食品上有一个相当的不利，运动后狼吞虎咽的食欲会使家中伙食房大受损失。牧羊妇樊纳尔只好靠个折衷的办法，把短时间的跳舞和短时间的谈话唱歌混在一起，为的是使在任一方面都不至于有过度难制的欲望。但是这个计划完全藏于她自己柔和的心里：牧羊人的心境是想表现出最豪爽的殷勤招待。

奏提琴的是本地一个小孩，十二岁左右，对于轻快跳舞曲

---

3 toping：drinking strong liquors to excess 喝进过量的烈酒。
4 to fall back upon：to have recourse to help 求助于；依赖。

who had a wonderful dexterity in jigs and reels, though his fingers were so small and short as to necessitate a constant shifting for the high notes, from which he scrambled back to the first position with sounds not of unmixed purity of tone.¹ At seven the shrill tweedle-dee of this youngster had begun, accompanied by a booming ground-bass from Elijah New, the parish-clerk, who had thoughtfully brought with him his favourite musical instrument, the serpent. Dancing was instantaneous, Mrs. Fennel privately enjoining the players on no account² to let the dance exceed the length of a quarter of an hour.

But Elijah and the boy, in the excitement of their position, quite forgot the injunction. Moreover, Oliver Giles, a man of seventeen, one of the dancers, who was enamoured of his partner, a fair girl of thirty-three rolling years, had recklessly handed a new crown-piece to the musicians, as a bribe to keep going as long as they had muscle and wind³. Mrs. Fennel, seeing the steam begin to generate on the countenances of her guests, crossed over and touched the fiddler's elbow and put her hand on the serpent's mouth. But they took no notice, and fearing she might lose her character of genial hostess if

---

1 这是笑他免不了弹出不纯的音调。因为他的手太短，转动不灵，所以弹起来，有时带了上一个的音调。

2 on no account: certainly not 绝不。

3 wind: power of respiration; breath 呼吸的能力。

同苏格兰跳舞曲有出奇的擅长，虽然他的手指是这么短小，使他奏高音时不得不常换个姿势，从那里他匆忙地回复起先的姿势时免不了带个不纯净的音调。七点钟，这个小孩提琴的尖锐声音就开始了，以利亚·纽隆隆的基本低音和着，这位教区里的书记思虑周到地把他所喜欢的乐器，蛇形喇叭，带来。跳舞立刻开始了，樊纳尔太太偷偷地嘱咐这班乐人无论如何不要让跳舞超过一刻钟。

但是以利亚同那小孩居于这种地位高兴得完全忘却这个命令了。而且，奥力味·斋尔兹，一个十七岁大的男子，跳舞的人们里的一个，被他的舞侣，一个过了三十三个流年的美丽姑娘，迷了，不愿利害地给音乐家一块新银币，算做一种贿赂，请他们筋肉气力还能支持时总是奏下去。樊纳尔太太看见她客人脸上都开始有蒸气了，就穿过房子，轻轻地碰一下奏提琴者的肘节，把她的手放在蛇形喇叭的嘴上。但是他们不理她。她恐怕若使太显明地干涉起来，会失掉她这温和女主人的身格，

she were to interfere too markedly, she retired and sat down helpless. And so the dance whizzed on with cumulative fury, the performers moving in their planet-like courses, direct and retrograde, from apogee to perigee[1], till the hand of the well-kicked clock at the bottom of the room had travelled over the circumference of an hour.

While these cheerful events were in course of enactment within Fennel's pastoral dwelling, an incident having considerable bearing on the party had occurred in the gloomy night without. Mrs. Fennel's concern about the growing fierceness of the dance corresponded in point of time with the ascent of a human figure to the solitary hill of Higher Crowstairs from the direction of the distant town. This personage strode on through the rain without a pause, following the little-worn path which, further on in its course, skirted the shepherd's cottage.

It was nearly the time of full moon, and on this account, though the sky was lined with a uniform sheet of dripping cloud, ordinary objects out of doors were readily visible. The sad wan light revealed the lonely pedestrian to be a man of supple frame; his gait suggested that he had somewhat passed the period of perfect and instinctive agility, though not so far as to be otherwise than rapid of motion

---

1 apogee: point in orbit of the moon that is farthest from the earth 月球轨道上与地球相距最远之点。perigee——point of the moon's orbit nearest the earth 月球轨道上与地球相距最近之点。

只好退去，无能为力地坐下。于是跳舞加倍猛烈地呼呼跳下去，跳舞的人们顺着他们行星般的轨道的转动，顺行同逆行，从远地点到近地点，一直等到房子边际大受震动的时钟走了一个钟头的圆周。

当这些盛事正在樊纳尔田舍里举行时候，一件与这宴会有重大关系的事件在外面黯然的夜里发生。樊纳尔太太忧虑跳舞的渐见热烈在时间上刚和一个人形从远镇那一方走上亥儿·克洛斯腾尔思里这孤寂的小山同时。这个人物在雨中踏着大步，毫不停留，顺着那不大磨损的路，这条路延长下去，缘着牧羊人的茅屋。

这差不多是月圆时节了，所以，虽然天是布满一片色调相同的雨云，户外普通的东西还是容易看出。黯默愁人的光线照出这个寂寞的步行者是一个体格柔软的人；他的步态使人们看出他已经有些过了出于本能的十分轻快活泼的时期，虽然当有必需时候，还能够急步前进，不至有什么狼狈的样

when occasion required. At a rough guess, he might have been about forty years of age. He appeared tall, but a recruiting sergeant, or other person accustomed to the judging of men's heights by the eye, would have discerned that this was chiefly owing to his gauntness, and that he was not more than five-feet-eight or nine.

Notwithstanding the regularity of his tread, there was caution in it, as in that of one who mentally feels his way; and despite the fact that it was not a black coat nor a dark garment of any sort that he wore, there was something about him which suggested that he naturally belonged to the black-coated[1] tribes of men. His clothes were of fustian, and his boots hobnailed, yet in his progress he showed not the mud-accustomed bearing of hobnailed and fustianed peasantry.

By the time that he had arrived abreast of the shepherd's premises the rain came down, or rather came along[2], with yet more determined violence. The outskirts of the little settlement partially broke the force of wind and rain, and this induced him to stand still. The most salient of the shepherd's domestic erections was an empty sty at the forward corner of his hedgeless garden, for in these latitudes the principle of masking the homelier features of your establishment

---

1 black-coat: a clergyman 教士。
2 to came along: to move on toward 向某处来；横来。

子。大约推测，他的年纪总在四十左右。看起来他是个高身量儿，但是一个招募新兵的军官同其它惯于靠眼睛去断定人们的高度的人们会看透多半因为他的瘦削，所以显出体格高。他实在不过五尺八九吋。

虽然他的步态是整齐的，但是含有一种谨慎的神气，好像精神上暗中摸索着的人的步态；他所穿的虽然不是黑色的衣服，或者任一种暗色的服装，可是他有一种态度，使人们觉得他天然是属于黑衣服那类的人们里面。他的衣服是柳条绒布制的，他的长靴钉有马蹄铁的钉子，然而他迈步前来时并没有现出穿柳条绒布的，钉有马蹄铁钉子的农夫的已惯泥泞的态度。

当他走到同牧羊人的屋子并肩时候，雨下得，或者可以说横冲来，比以前更坚决地有劲。这个小小居留地的边界可以稍杀风雨的暴力，这一点引诱他站在那里一会儿。牧羊人的住宅在建筑上最显著的地方是他那没有篱笆的园的前面基角上一个空猪栏，因为在这些区域里人们还不晓得用一个通俗的门面把

by a conventional frontage was unknown. The traveller's eye was attracted to this small building by the pallid shine of the wet slates that covered it. He turned aside, and, finding it empty, stood under the pent-roof for shelter.

While he stood, the boom of the serpent within the adjacent house, and the lesser strains of the fiddler, reached the spot as an accompaniment to the surging hiss of the flying rain on the sod, its louder beating on the cabbage-leaves of the garden, on the eight or ten beehives just discernible by the path, and its dripping from the eaves into a row of buckets and pans that had been placed under the walls of the cottage. For at Higher Crowstairs, as at all such elevated domiciles, the grand difficulty of housekeeping was an insufficiency of water; and a casual rainfall was utilized by turning out[1], as catchers[2], every utensil that the house contained. Some queer stories might be told of the contrivances for economy in suds and dishwaters that are absolutely necessitated in upland habitations during the droughts of summer. But at this season there were no such exigencies; a mere acceptance of what the skies bestowed was sufficient for an abundant store.

At last the notes of the serpent ceased and the house was silent.

---

1 to turn out: to move out of place 拿出去。
2 catchers: that which catches 承受之器具。

屋子里比较粗野的色彩遮住。这位行路人的眼睛因为这小房子上面湿瓦的灰色光辉，而注意到这个小房子。他走到路旁，看见里面是空的，就站在这单斜檐底下躲雨。

当他站在那儿，邻近屋里蛇形喇叭的隆隆同提琴的更细一点儿的声调传到那地点了，好像跟飞雨打到大地时的咝声，打到园里菜叶上同从路上可以窥见的八个或者十个蜂窝时更响的声音，以及雨水从檐前滴沥到放在屋外大墙底下的一排水桶同锅子里的声音相加。因为在亥儿·克洛斯腾尔思，像一切这样位于高处的住宅，家庭管理上最大的困难是缺水；偶尔下一回雨，就得把家里所有的一切器具都端出做盛水器，极力利用那雨水。关于肥皂水同洗碟水的经济办法，在高原上住宅里当夏旱时候那是绝对必须的，我们可以说出几个奇怪的故事。但是在这季里情形没有这么危急；单单把上天所赐的接收下来就足够藏着用许久了。

最后，蛇形喇叭的声音停了，屋子也归于寂静了。这个停

This cessation of activity aroused the solitary pedestrian from the reverie into which he had lapsed, and, emerging from the shed, with an apparently new intention, he walked up the path to the house-door. Arrived here, his first act was to kneel down on a large stone beside the row of vessels, and to drink a copious draught from one of them. Having quenched his thirst he rose and lifted his hand to knock, but paused with his eye upon the panel. Since the dark surface of the wood revealed absolutely nothing, it was evident that he must be mentally looking through the door, as if he wished to measure thereby all the possibilities that a house of this sort might include, and how they might bear upon[1] the question of his entry.

In his indecision he turned and surveyed the scene around. Not a soul was anywhere visible. The garden-path stretched downward from his feet, gleaming like the track of a snail; the roof of the little well (mostly dry), the well-cover, the top rail of the garden-gate, were varnished with the same dull liquid glaze; while far away in the vale, a faint whiteness of more than usual extent showed that the rivers were high in the meads. Beyond all this winked a few bleared lamp-lights through the beating drops—lights that denoted the situation of the county-town from which he had appeared[2] to come. The absence

---

1 to bear upon: to relate to 有关系。
2 to appear: to seem 好像。

止动作唤醒了这孤单单的步行者,他刚才沉到默想里去了,从棚底下出来,显明地具一个新的主意,他顺着路走到茅屋的门口。到了那里,他第一下动作是跪在那排瓮旁边的一块大石头上面,从一双瓮痛快地喝一满口水。解了他的渴了,他站起来,举手敲门,但是又停住,他的眼睛望着门上的嵌板。木头的黑色表面既然是绝对不能透露出什么,他分明一定是精神上看穿那个门,好像他想借此估一估这么一种屋子会包含有的一切可能的事情,以及这些事情对于他的走进去会有什么关系。

在他迟疑未决时候,他转过来,眺视四围的风景。无论那里都看不见一个人,园中的路从他的脚旁向下延长下去,发光着有如一只蜗牛走过后所留的痕迹;小井(当是干的)上面的屋顶,井盖,园门的上层栏杆,也具有同样暗淡的流动光辉;谷中的远处有比较宽些的一片微白,那指出几条河是居于牧场高处。在这一切之外,几个朦胧的灯光在雨中闪烁着——这些灯光指出州城的位置,他好像就是打那

of all notes of life in that direction seemed to clinch[1] his intentions, and he knocked at the door.

Within, a desultory chat had taken the place of movement and musical sound. The hedge-carpenter was suggesting a song to the company, which nobody just then was inclined to undertake; so that the knock afforded a not unwelcome diversion.

"Walk in!" said the shepherd promptly.

The latch clicked upward, and out of the night our pedestrian appeared upon the door-mat. The shepherd arose, snuffed two of the nearest candles, and turned to look at him.

Their light disclosed that the stranger was dark in complexion and not unprepossessing as to feature. His hat, which for a moment he did not remove, hung low over his eyes, without concealing that they were large, open, and determined, moving with a flash rather than a glance round the room. He seemed pleased with his survey, and, baring his shaggy head, said, in a rich deep voice, "The rain is so heavy, friends, that I ask leave to come in and rest awhile."

"To be sure, stranger," said the shepherd. "And faith[2], you've been lucky in choosing your time, for we are having a bit of a fling[3]

---

1 to clinch: to make conclusive 使确定。

2 faith: verily 真的。

3 to have a bit of a fling: to have some indulgence in impulse 稍些痛快玩一下。

里来的。那方面的毫无人声仿佛使他的主意更坚决，他于是敲门了。

屋子里面，随便的谈天代替了跳舞和音乐。做栅栏的木匠正向大家提议唱一首歌，那时却没有人愿意干，所以这个敲门给他们以快意的换口味。

"走进来！"牧羊人赶紧说道。

门闩向上啪嗒一声，我们这位步行者就从夜里现在门口的地席上面了。牧羊人站起来，把最近的两枝烛的烛花剪去，转过来瞧他。

他们的烛光照出生客的面色是棕黑的，脸貌并不讨厌。他的帽子，才进来时他没有脱开，低低地戴在他的眼睛上，却没有遮住，人们能够看见那坦白的，有毅力的大眼睛闪一闪，却不是溜一溜，看房子四围的情形。他观察的结果仿佛是满意的，他露出头发缠乱不清的头，用深沉响亮的声音说道，"雨下得这么大，朋友们，我请你们让我进来，歇一会儿。"

"当然可以，生客，"牧羊人说。"天呀，你的确运气好，拣这个时候来，因为我们正在作乐，为着一个可庆的原因

for a glad cause—though, to be sure, a man could hardly wish that glad cause to happen more than once a year."

"Nor less," spoke up a woman. "For 'tis best to get your family over[1] and done with[2], as soon as you can, so as to be all the earlier out of the fag o't."

"And what may be this glad cause?" asked the stranger.

"A birth and christening," said the shepherd.

The stranger hoped his host might not be made unhappy either by too many or too few of such episodes, and being invited by a gesture to a pull at the mug, he readily acquiesced. His manner, which, before entering, had been so dubious, was now altogether that of a careless and candid man.

"Late to be traipsing[3] athwart this coomb—hey?" said the engaged man of fifty.

"Late it is, master, as you say. —I'll take a seat in the chimney-corner, if you have nothing to urge against it, ma'am; for I am a little moist on the side that was next the rain."

Mrs. Shepherd Fennel assented, and made room for the self-invited comer, who, having got completely inside the chimney-

---

1 to get over: to finish（troublesome work）了结"麻烦的事情"。

2 to have done with: to have no further concern with 不再去理了。

3 traipsing: walking about in careless or thoughtless manner 随便胡里胡涂走动着。

——虽然，真的，一个人几乎也不会希望那可庆的原因一年里超过一次。"

"但是也不要更少，"一个女人说起来了。"因为最好是极力趁早把你儿女的事情了结，那么可以早些脱离劳苦。"

"请问这个可庆的原因是什么呢？"生客问道。

"生一个孩子，举行命名式。"

生客希望主人将来不会因为这类事情太常或者太稀而忧愁，主人做手势请他从有柄的杯呷一口酒，他慨然从命。他在进来之前是那么不放心的样子，现在却完全带个挂念的，坦白的人的态度了。

"这时穿过豁谷不是太晚一些吗？"五十岁了的订婚了的人说。

"先生，你说得不错，外面天色已晚了。——我想坐在火炉边上，若使你没有什么反对的理由，太太；因为我身上挨雨打的那一边有些潮湿了。"

牧羊妇樊纳尔答应了，腾出地方给这不速之客，他全身都

corner, stretched out his legs and his arms with the expansiveness of a person quite at home[1].

"Yes, I am rather cracked in the vamp." he said freely, seeing that the eyes of the shepherd's wife fell upon his boots, "and I am not well fitted either. I have had some rough times[2] lately, and have been forced to pick up what I can get in the way of wearing, but I must find a suit better fit for working-days[3] when I reach home."

"One of hereabouts[4]?" she inquired.

"Not quite that—further up the country."

"I thought so. And so be I; and by your tongue you come from my neighbourhood."

"But you would hardly have heard of me," he said quickly. "My time would be long before yours, ma'am, you see."

This testimony to the youthfulness of his hostess had the effect of stopping her cross-examination.

"There is only one thing more wanted to make me happy," continued the new-comer. "And that is a little baccy[5], which I am sorry

---

1 at home: at ease 安逸。
2 to have a rough time: to have suffered a great deal 饱尝艰苦。
3 working-day: a day on which work is done 工作的日子。
4 hereabouts: people in this vicinity 邻近的人们。
5 baccy: tobacco 烟。

在火炉边了，伸出他的腿同臂，那种从容舒展，完全是一个人十分舒适的样子。

"是的，我的鞋面皮有些破裂了，"他满不在乎地说道，看见牧羊妇的眼睛注视他的靴子，"我的衣服也不称身。近来我碰到不好的境遇，不得不勉强把能得到手的衣服穿上，但是我必定要找一套更宜于工作的衣服，当我到家时候。"

"也是这里邻近地方的人吗？"她问道。

"不能算做——却是更乡下些。"

"我早已看出了。我本来也是更乡下些的人；从你口音上看起来，你是生长在我的邻近地方。"

"但是你大概不会听到人们说我，"他匆忙地说道。"我是比你早得多，太太，你看。"

这样证明了他女主人的年青居然挡住了她的诘问。

"现在再有一个东西就可以使我十分高兴了，"新来的人又说道。"那是一些烟，我不得不说我的烟已罄了。"

to say I am out of[1]."

"I'll fill your pipe," said the shepherd.

"I must ask you to lend me a pipe likewise."

"A smoker, and no pipe about 'ee[2]? "

"I have dropped it somewhere on the road."

The shepherd filled and handed him a new clay pipe, saying, as he did so, "Hand me your baccy-box—I'll fill that too, now I am about it."

The man went through the movement of searching his pockets.

"Lost that too? " said his entertainer, with some surprise.

"I am afraid so," said the man with some confusion. "Give it to me in a screw of paper." Lighting his pipe at the candle with a suction that drew the whole flame into the bowl he resettled himself in the corner and bent his looks upon the faint steam from his damp legs, as if he wished to say no more.

Meanwhile the general body of guests had been taking little notice of this visitor by reason of an absorbing discussion in which they were engaged with the band about a tune for the next dance. The matter being settled, they were about to stand up when an interruption came in the shape of another knock at the door.

---

1 to be out of: to be in want of 缺乏。
2 'ee: thee; you 你。

"我可以把你的烟斗装好,"牧羊人说。

"我还要请你借我一只烟斗。"

"一个惯抽烟的人,身边没有带烟斗?"

"我把它掉在路上什么地方了。"

牧羊人将一个新的土烟斗装好,交给他,一面说,"把你的烟盒交我——我将把它也装满,现在我既然干这件事了。"

那个人做出向他自己衣袋里搜索的样子。

"那也掉了吗?"他的主人有些惊骇地说道。

"我恐怕是,"那个人微露慌张的神气说。"将烟放在纸卷里给我罢。"向蜡烛去点燃他的烟斗,深吸一口,将整个火焰都拖到烟窝里去了,他又自在地坐在炉边,俯视从他潮湿的腿所发的细微蒸气,好像他不愿意再说话了。

那时多半的客人不大注意这个来客,因为他们正在同乐队专心讨论下次跳舞所用的调子。这件事解决了,他们刚要站起来,又有一个打扰来了,那是门外又来个敲门的声音。

At sound of the same the man in the chimney-corner took up the poker and began stirring the brands as if doing it thoroughly were the one aim of his existence; and a second time the shepherd said, "Walk in!" In a moment another man stood upon the straw-woven door-mat. He too was a stranger.

This individual was one of a type radically different from the first. There was more of the commonplace in his manner, and a certain jovial cosmopolitanism sat upon his features. He was several years older than the first arrival, his hair being slightly frosted[1], his eyebrows bristly, and his whiskers cut back from his cheeks. His face was rather full and flabby, and yet it was not altogether a face without power. A few grog-blossoms marked the neighbourhood of his nose. He flung back his long drab greatcoat, revealing that beneath it he wore a suit of cinder-gray shade throughout, large heavy seals, of some metal or other that would take a polish, dangling from his fob as his only personal ornament. Shaking the water-drops from his low-crowned glazed hat, he said, "I must ask for a few minutes' shelter, comrades, or I shall be wetted to my skin before I get to Casterbridge."

"Make yourself at home, master," said the shepherd, perhaps a trifle less heartily than on the first occasion. Not that Fennel had the

---

1 frosted: turned white 变白。

听到这声音,坐在炉边的那个人拿起火钳,开始拨动燃木,好像澈底地干这件事就是他做人惟一的目的;牧羊人第二次说,"走进来!"一会儿另一个人站在门口草编的地席上面。他也是一个生客。

这个人是属于根本上跟第一个生客不同的那类人们里面。他的态度比较通常些,他的容貌具有欣欣然四海为家的神气。他比第一个来客老几岁,他的头发稍有变白的地方,他的眉毛粗硬,他的胡须从双颊向后反刮。他的脸近于丰满松弛,然而又不完全是个没有意志力的人的脸孔。几粒酒刺长在他鼻子旁边。他向后扔开他那长的褐黄色大衣,现出底下他穿一套全是灰色的衣服;厚重的大印章,可以擦亮的金属物制造的,从他的表袋垂下,那是他身上惟一的装饰品。把雨点从他那个帽顶不高的,有光泽的帽摇去,他说,"我必得请你们让我躲几分钟,同伴们,否则我将湿透了,在我到了喀斯忒布立治之前"。

"请你不要客气,先生,"牧羊人说,也许稍微没有第一次那么热心。并不是因为樊纳尔性情上有些吝啬的色彩;却是因

least tinge of niggardliness in his composition; but the room was far from large, spare chairs were not numerous, and damp companions were not altogether desirable at close quarters for the women and girls in their bright-coloured gowns.

However, the second comer, after taking off his greatcoat, and hanging his hat on a nail in one of the ceiling-beams as if he had been specially invited to put it there, advanced and sat down at the table. This had been pushed so closely into the chimney-corner, to give all available room to the dancers, that its inner edge grazed the elbow of the man who had ensconced himself by the fire; and thus the two strangers were brought into close companionship. They nodded to each other by way of breaking the ice[1] of unacquaintance, and the first stranger handed his neighbour the family mug—a huge vessel of brown ware, having its upper edge worn away like a threshold by the rub of whole generations of thirsty lips that had gone the way of all flesh[2], and bearing the following inscription burnt upon its rotund side in yellow letters:

THERE IS NO FUN UNTIL I CUM[3].

The other man, nothing loth, raised the mug to his lips, and drank on, and on, and on—till a curious blueness overspread the

---

1 to break the ice: to break through cold reserve 开口以破沉寂。
2 all flesh: whatever has bodily life 凡为血肉之躯者。
3 until I cum: until I come 乡下人不知实在的字母，所以乱写。

为房子绝不能说是大的，空椅子也无多，而且在拥挤的地方人们不愿有潮湿的伴侣，当妇人们和姑娘们都穿着鲜色的衣服。

然而，这位第二个来客脱下他的大衣，将他的帽子挂在天花板一根横梁上的一个钉子上，好像有人特别请他挂在那里，他就望〔往〕里面走，坐在桌旁。这张桌子推得这么靠近炉边，为着尽量腾出地方给跳舞的人们，以致桌子里面的边擦着自己隐在火旁的那个人的肘节；所以这两位生客弄得变成很接近的伴侣。他们互相点一下头，藉此冲破陌生人的隔膜，第一个生客交给他的邻人那世代相传的有柄酒杯——棕色的土制成的大杯子，它的上面边缘被历代干渴的嘴唇磨损了，和门限一样，这些嘴唇也已随肉体而俱亡了，杯子球形的边旁刻有底下这几个黄色的字：

我不来，就不好玩。

那个人，毫不推辞，举杯到唇边，喝着，喝着，喝着——

countenance of the shepherd's wife, who had regarded with no little surprise the first stranger's free offer to the second of what did not belong to him to dispense.

"I knew it!" said the toper to the shepherd with much satisfaction. "When I walked up your garden before coming in, and saw the hives all of a row, I said to myself, 'Where there's bees there's honey, and where there's honey there's mead.' But mead of such a truly comfortable sort as this I really didn't expect to meet in my older days." He took yet another pull at the mug, till it assumed an ominous elevation.

"Glad[1] you enjoy it!" said the shepherd warmly.

"It is goodish mead," assented Mrs. Fennel, with an absence of enthusiasm which seemed to say that it was possible to buy praise for one's cellar at too heavy a price. "It is trouble enough to make—and really I hardly think we shall make any more. For honey sells well, and we ourselves can make shift with[2] a drop o'small[3] mead and metheglin[4] for common use from the comb-washings."

---

1 glad: I am glad 我是喜欢。

2 to make shift with: to content oneself for want of something better with 没有更好，便满意于。

3 small: weak 弱的。

4 metheglin: a beverage fermented of honey and water 蜜同水制成的饮料。

一直等到牧羊妇的脸孔涌起一种奇怪的蓝色,她很觉得纳罕,看到第一个生客随便将不是属他去分配的东西呈献与第二生客。

"我早就知道有好酒了!"酒鬼很满意地向牧羊人说。"当我在进来之前,走过你的园,看见整排的蜂窝,我对自己说道,'有蜂的地方就有蜜,有蜜的地方就有蜜酒。'但是像这么一种真妙的蜜酒,我从前的确没有料到在我老年时还能遇见。"他又向酒杯呷饮,等到杯底反朝上,大有将罄之概。

"我觉得高兴,你喜欢它!"牧羊人热烈地说。

"这是很好的蜜酒,"樊纳尔太太也承认,可是讲话时态度冷淡,那仿佛说一个人也许出了太大的代价换来对于他的酒窖的赞美。"酿起来是够麻烦的——我恐怕我们今年真不能再酿了。因为蜜价现在很高!我们自己通常日用上有一些洗蜂房的水制成的弱蜜酒和蜜水就可以对付了。"

"O, but you'll never have the heart[1]!" reproachfully cried the stranger in cinder-gray, after taking up the mug a third time and setting it down empty. "I love mead, when 'tis old like this, as I love to go to church o' Sundays, or to relieve the needy any day of the week."

"Ha, ha, ha!" said the man in the chimney-corner, who, in spite of the taciturnity induced by the pipe of tobacco, could not or would not refrain from this slight testimony to his comrade's humour.

Now the old mead of those days, brewed of the purest first-year or maiden honey, four pounds to the gallon—with its due complement of white of eggs, cinnamon, ginger, cloves, mace, rosemary, yeast, and processes of working, bottling, and cellaring—tasted remarkably strong; but it did not taste so strong as it actually was. Hence, presently, the stranger in cinder-gray at the table, moved by its creeping influence, unbuttoned his waistcoat, threw himself back in his chair, spread his legs, and made his presence felt in various ways.

"Well, well, as I say," he resumed, "I am going to Casterbridge, and to Casterbridge I must go. I should have been almost there by this time; but the rain drove me into your dwelling, and I'm not sorry for it."

---

1 to have the heart to do something: to be unfeeling enough to do something 忍心去干某件事，居然硬心肠到肯干某件事。

"啊，但是你绝不会舍得把它卖去！"穿灰色衣服的生客第三次举起酒杯，剩个空杯放下，带责备的口气喊道。"我爱喝老到这样程度的蜜酒，正好像我爱在星期日到礼拜堂去，或者在星期里任一天救济穷人们。"

"哈，哈，哈！"坐在炉边的那个人喊着，他虽然因为抽那斗烟变静默了，却不能自制，或者不肯自制，就这样子稍稍证明他同伴的滑稽。

那时候的老蜜酒是用第一年的，或者可说初次的蜜酿制，每加伦的蜜酒用四磅的蜜——还杂有相当分量的蛋白，肉桂，姜，丁香，豆蔻花，迷迭香，和酵母，经过各种手续，制好后装进瓶子，放在酒窖里——这种酒喝起来味是非常烈的；但是它实在的性质是比它的味更烈。所以，不久，坐在桌边的那个穿灰色衣服的生客，因为酒力慢慢发作了，就解开他背心的扣子，躺在他坐的椅子上，伸长他的腿，种种方面使人们觉得有他这个人在那儿。

"好罢，我不是说过，我将到喀斯忒布立治去，我是一定要到喀斯忒布立治去。本来这时候我已经可以抵喀斯忒布立治了；但是雨把我赶到你们屋子里，我觉得这样也好。"

"You don't live in Casterbridge?" said the shepherd.

"Not as yet; though I shortly mean to move there."

"Going to set up in trade, perhaps?"

"No, no," said the shepherd's wife. "It is easy to see that the gentleman is rich, and don't want to work at anything."

The cinder-gray stranger paused, as if to consider whether he would accept that definition of himself. He presently rejected it by answering, "Rich is not quite the word for me, dame. I do work, and I must work. And even if I only get to Casterbridge by midnight I must begin work there at eight to-morrow morning. Yes, het[1] or wet, blow or snow, famine or sword, my day's work to-morrow must be done."

"Poor man! Then, in spite o' seeming, you be worse off[2] than we?" replied the shepherd's wife.

"'Tis the nature of my trade, men and maidens." 'Tis the nature of my trade more than my poverty... But really and truly I must up and off, or I shan't get a lodging in the town." However, the speaker did not move, and directly added, "There's time for one more draught of friend-ship before I go; and I'd perform it at once if the mug were not dry."

---

1 het: hot 热。这也是乡下人的土音。
2 worse off: in a worse condition 在个更坏的境况里。

"你不住在喀斯忒布立治吗？"牧羊人说。

"现在尚未；虽然我最近打算搬到那儿住。"

"大概去那儿开铺子吗？"

"不，不，"牧羊妇说道。"还是容易看出来的，这个先生有钱，用不着干什么事。"

穿灰色衣服的生客迟疑一会儿，好像考虑一下他接受不接受这个对他下的定义。他不久拒绝这定义，答道，"有钱这个字于我不十分合式，太太。我有工作，我非工作不可。甚至于假使我今晚午夜才到喀斯忒布立治，明早八时我必得在那儿开始工作。是的，不管冷暖，不管风雪，不管饥荒或者刀兵，明天我的工作是一定要干的。"

"可怜的人！那么，虽然外面看起来仿佛好些，你实在是比我们还不如呢？"牧羊妇答道。

"这种准时工作是我职业的性质，先生们，姑娘们。这是我职业的性质，不是因为我穷……但是我真真的确非动身出发不可了，否则我在镇里将找不到住宿的地方。"然而，这位说话的人并不动，立刻接着说道，"在我走之前，还有再饮一杯联欢之酒的时间；我会立刻饮尽这杯，若使这个杯不是已干了。"

"Here's a mug o' small," said Mrs. Fennel. "Small, we call it, though to be sure 'tis only the first wash o' the combs."

"No," said the stranger disdainfully. "I won't spoil your first kindness by partaking o' your second."

"Certainly not," broke in Fennel. "We don't increase and multiply every day, and I'll fill the mug again." He went away to the dark place under the stairs where the barrel stood. The shepherdess followed him.

"Why should you do this?" she said reproachfully, as soon as they were alone. "He's emptied it once, though it held enough for ten people; and now he's not contented wi' the small, but must needs call for more o' the strong! And a stranger unbeknown to any of us. For my part[1], I don't like the look o' the man at all."

"But he's in the house, my honey; and 'tis a wet night, and a christening. Daze it[2], what's a cup of mead more or less? There'll be plenty more next bee-burning[3]."

"Very well—this time, then," she answered, looking wistfully at the barrel. "But what is the man's calling, and where is he one of, that he should come in and join us like this?"

"I don't know. I'll ask him again."

---

1 for my part: so far as concerns me 至于我。
2 daze it: confuse it 管它呢! 一种近乎发誓的话。
3 bee-burning: 取蜜时先用烟熏蜂巢，将蜂赶走，以便取蜜。

"这儿有一杯弱蜜酒,"樊纳尔太太说,"我们叫它做弱的,其实这只是第一次洗蜂窝的水。"

"不,"生客藐视样子说道。"我不肯接受你这次的盛意,而变成破坏了你第一次的盛意。"

"绝对不,"樊纳尔突然插嘴说道。"我们不是天天添人口,我将把那杯再注满。"他走向楼梯下暗处去,酒桶就站在那儿。牧羊妇跟着他。

"你为什么这样干呢?"她责备他道,一当他们单独在一块儿时候。"他已经喝干一回了,虽然里面盛有足够十人喝的酒;现在他还不满于弱蜜酒,一定指明要强的!而且是我们全不认得的一个生客。至于我这方面,我绝不喜欢这个人的神气。"

"但是他现在是我们的客,我的甜蜜人儿;这又是个风雨夜,行命名式的日子。管它的,多一杯蜜酒,少一杯蜜酒,这有什么要紧?下次取蜜蜂时候,我们还可以有许多哩。"

"也好——那么,只限这一下,"她深思地望着酒桶说道。"但是这个人的职业是什么,他是属于那里的人,居然进来,这样加入我们作乐?"

"我不知道,我将再问他一下。"

The catastrophe of having the mug drained dry at one pull by the stranger in cinder-gray was effectually guarded against this time by Mrs. Fennel. She poured out his allowance in a small cup, keeping the large one at a discreet distance from him. When he had tossed off his portion the shepherd renewed his inquiry about the stranger's occupation.

The latter did not immediately reply, and the man in the chimney-corner, with sudden demonstrativeness, said, "Anybody may know my trade—I'm a wheelwright."

"A very good trade for these parts," said the shepherd.

"And anybody may know mine—if they've the sense to find it out," said the stranger in cinder-gray.

"You may generally tell what a man is by his claws," observe the hedge-carpenter, looking at his own hands. "My fingers be as full of thorns as an old pin-cushion is of pins."

The hands of the man in the chimney-corner instinctively sought the shade, and he gazed into the fire as he resumed his pipe. The man at the table took up the hedge-carpenter's remark, and added smartly, "True; but the oddity of my trade is that, instead of setting a mark upon me, it sets a mark upon my customers."

No observation being offered by anybody in elucidation of this enigma, the shepherd's wife once more called for a song. The same obstacles presented themselves as at the former time—one had no

整杯的酒被穿灰色衣服的生客一口饮尽的危险，这次樊纳尔太太澈底地预防了。她将给他喝的酒斟在一个小杯里，把大酒杯放在离他相当远的地方。当他举杯饮尽他份下的酒，牧羊人重新询问生客的职业。

他不立刻答应，坐在炉边那个人，忽然间露出头角，说道，"谁也可以知道我的职业——我是一个轮匠。"

"在这里这是个很有用的职业，"牧羊人说道。

"谁也可以知道我的——若使他们聪明，能够观察出来，"穿灰色衣服的生客说道。

"你们普通可以从一个人的手看出他是干什么的，"做栅栏的木匠说，瞧着自己的手。"我的手指满是荆棘，正好似一个旧的针毡满插着针。"

坐在炉边的那个人的手不自觉地隐在暗处了，他望着火，当他又抽起他的烟斗。坐在桌旁的人跟着做栅栏的木匠的话，巧妙地说道，"不错；但是我的职业的奇怪处是不把标记打我身上，却打在我的顾客们身上。"

谁也没有说什么话，来解释这个谜，牧羊妇又提议唱一首歌。跟上次同样的障碍又来了——一个人嗓子坏，另一个忘却

voice, another had forgotten the first verse. The stranger at the table, whose soul had now risen to a good working[1] temperature, relieved the difficulty by exclaiming that, to start[2] the company, he would sing himself. Thrusting one thumb into the arm-hole of his waistcoat, he waved the other hand in the air, and, with an extemporising gaze at the shining sheep-crooks above the mantelpiece, began:

"O my trade it is the rarest one,

Simple shepherds all—

My trade is a sight to see;

For my customers I tie, and take them up on high,

And waft 'em to a far countree[3]!"

The room was silent when he had finished the verse—with one exception, that of the man in the chimney-corner, who, at the singer's word, "Chorus!" joined him in a deep bass voice of musical relish—

"And waft 'em to a far countree!"

Oliver Giles, John Pitcher the dairyman, the parishclerk, the engaged man of fifty, the row of young women against the wall, seemed lost in thought not of the gayest kind. The shepherd looked meditatively on the ground, the shepherdess gazed keenly at the singer, and with some suspicion; she was doubting whether this

---

1 working: active 活动的。
2 to start: to cause to act 使动作；发动。
3 countree: country 国土。

第一段的歌词。坐在桌旁的生客,他已醉到很想发作的程度了,救济这个困难,说道,为着使大家唱起来,他愿自己先唱。一只大姆〔拇〕指插在背心的胳肢窝那里,另一只手在空中摇动,直着眼睛望火炉架上的明亮的牧羊杖,带一种临时编歌的神气,开始唱道:——

"啊,我的职业是最稀奇,

老实的牧羊人们呀——

我的职业是值得看的;

因为我把我的主顾们扎起,拿他们到高处,

送他们到辽远的一个国土!"

房子里面是静寂的,当他唱完这第一段歌——只有一个例外,坐在炉边的那个人听到唱歌者说出"合唱"这个字,就用一种悦耳的深沉低音和他:

"送他们到辽远的一个国土!"

奥力味·斋尔兹,牛奶场的主人约翰·匹舍尔,教区的书记,已经订婚了的五十岁的人,靠着墙边的一排年青姑娘,好像都正沉思个不大高兴的事情。牧羊人用种冥想的神气瞧着地面,牧羊妇眼睛锐敏地,有些怀疑地望着唱歌者;她正猜着到

stranger were merely singing and old song from recollection, or was composing one there and then for the occasion. All were as perplexed at the obscure revelation as the guests at Belshazzar's Feast[1], except the man in the chimney-corner, who quietly sad, "Second verse, stranger," and smoked on.

The singer thoroughly moistened himself from his lips inwards, and went on with the next stanza as requested:

"My tools are but common ones,

Simple shepherds all—

My tools are no sight to see:

A little hempen string, and a post whereon to swing.

Are implements enough for me!"

Shepherd Fennel glanced round. There was no longer any doubt that the stranger was answering his question rhythmically. The guests one and all started back with suppressed exclamations. The young woman engaged to the man of fifty fainted half-way, and would have proceeded, but finding him wanting in alacrity for catch-

---

1 Belshazzar's Feast: feast before trouble and sorrow as in the case of Belshazzar who was proud an did not believe in God. When he gave a big feast, a hand appeared writing on the wall. The prophecy foretold of the downfall of Babylon of which Belshazzar was king. 有烦恼同悲哀跟着来的宴会。巴比仑王Belshazzar骄傲，不信上帝，一天举行大宴会，忽然有一只手在墙上写字，预言巴比仑的覆灭。

底这位生客只是凭着记忆唱一首旧歌呢,还是特地为着当时需要此刻此地编出一首呢。大家听到这难解的自白都迷惑得像伯沙撒的宴会的来客,除开坐在炉边那个人,他安详地说道,"唱第二段罢,生客,"就继续抽他的烟。

唱歌者缩进嘴唇好好地润一下口,应那个人的请求继续唱下段:

"我的工具只是普通的东西,

老实的牧羊人们呀——

我的工具是不值得看的:

小段麻绳,一根可以把东西吊在上面的柱子,

这两件工具就足够我的使用了!"

牧羊人樊纳尔向四面望一望。现在用不着再怀疑了,这个生客的确是用韵语来答复他的询问。客人们都发出低声的惊呼,吓得望〔往〕后退,跟五十岁的人订婚的那位年青姑娘晕了一半,正想继续晕下去,可是看到他来救助并不敏捷,她就

ing here she sat down trembling.

"O, he's the—!" whispered the people in the background, mentioning the name of an ominous public officer, "He's come to do it! 'Tis to be at Casterbridge jail to-morrow—the man for sheep-stealing—the poor clockmaker we heard of, who used to live away at Shottsford and had no work to do—Timothy Summers, whose family were a-starving[1], and so he went out of Shottsford by the high-road, and took a sheep in open daylight, defying the farmer and the farmer's wife and the farmer's lad, and every man jack[2] among 'em. He (and they nodded towards the stranger of the deadly trade) is come from up the country to do it because there's not enough to do in his own county-town, and he's got the place here now our own county man's dead; he's going to live in the same cottage under the prison wall."

The stranger in cinder-gray took no notice of this whispered string of observations, but again wetted his lips. Seeing that his friend in the chimmey-corner was the only one who reciprocated his joviality in any way[3], he held out his cup towards that appreciative comrade, who also held out his own. They clinked together, the eyes

---

1 a-starving：a等于in, on, at等字，表示"正在"的意思。

2 every man jack：every one个个人。jack这个字本来是John的昵称，因为普通名做"约翰"的人很多，所以"个个约翰"说是"个个人"的意思。

3 in any way：to some extent多少有些。

浑身发抖地坐下。

"啊,他是——!"居于后面的人们耳语道,说出一个不祥的公吏的名字。"他是来干那件事!那件事明天将在喀斯忒布立治执行——那个人因为偷羊而处死刑——我们所听说的那个钟表匠,他常在叔提斯福特地方住,找不到工作——他叫做提摩太·散麦斯,他家里人饿着,于是他从大路离开叔提斯福特,光天化日之下拿去一只羊,公然反抗农夫,农夫的妻子,农夫的孩子,以及他们里面个个人。他(他们点头指着这个干杀人生意的生客)从乡下来干这事,因为在他本州县里没有什么生意,现在我们这里的刽子手死了,他就接他的空缺;他将住在牢墙底下从前那个人住的小屋子里。"

穿灰色衣服的生客不去理这一串耳语,却又润一下他的嘴唇。看到只有坐在炉旁的他那位朋友是可算做响应他的诙谐的人,他举起酒杯向着这位有同情的伴侣,他也举起酒杯向着他。他们碰杯饮祝,房里其余人们的眼睛都钉〔盯〕着唱歌者的行

of the rest of the room hanging upon the singer's actions. He parted his lips for the third verse; but at that moment another knock was audible upon the door. This time the knock was faint and hesitating.

The company seemed scared; the shepherd looked with consternation towards the entrance, and it was with some effort that he resisted his alarmed wife's deprecatory glance, and uttered for the third time the welcoming words, "Walk in!"

The door was gently opened, and another man stood upon the mat. He, like those who had preceded him, was a stranger. This time it was a short, small personage, of fair complexion, and dressed in a decent suit of dark clothes.

"Can you tell me the way to—?" he began: when, gazing round the room to observe the nature of the company amongst whom he had fallen, his eyes lighted on the stranger in cinder-gray. It was just at the instant when the latter, who had thrown his mind into his song with such a will that he scarcely heeded the interruption, silenced all whispers and inquiries by bursting into his third verse: —

"To-morrow is my working day,

Simple shepherds all—

To-morrow is a working day for me:

For the larmer's sheep is slain,

动。他打开嘴唇来唱第三段歌,但是在这时候人们听到门外又有一个敲门的声音。这一次的敲门是低音的,犹豫的。

房里人们好像吓住了;牧羊人惊慌地望着门口,他费了些劲,才能拒绝他那受惊了的妻子的抗议眼神,第三次说出那欢迎的话,"走进来!"

门轻轻地开了,一个人站在门口的席上。他,跟比他先来的那几个一样,是一个生客。这回是一个体格短小的人,面貌文雅,穿一套整齐的黑衣服。

"你们能够告我到——?"他开始说,一面注视四周,看一看他碰到了那一种人们,这时他眼睛落到穿灰色衣服的生客身上。刚好在这时候,这位被人注目的生客——他是这么一心一意地把精神全搁在他的歌上面,几乎没有去睬这个打扰——唱出第三段的歌,因此压下了一切的耳语和询问了。

明天是我工作的日子,

老实的牧羊人们呀——

明天是我工作的一个日子:

因为农夫的羊被人杀死了,

干这件事的孩子抓到了,

and the lad who did it ta'en[1],

And on his soul may God ha' mercy!"

The stranger in the chimney-corner, waving cups with the singer so heartily that his mead splashed over on the hearth, repeated in his bass voice as before: —

"And on his soul may God ha' mercy!"

All this time the third stranger had been standing in the doorway. Finding now that he did not come forward or go on[2] speaking, the guests particularly regarded him. They noticed to their surprise that he stood before them the picture of abject terror—his knees trembling, his hand shaking so violently that the door-latch by which he supported himself rattled audibly: his white lips were parted, and his eyes fixed on the merry officer of justice in the middle of the room. A moment more and he had turned, closed the door, and fled.

"What a man can it be?" said the shepherd.

The rest, between the awfulness of their late discovery and the odd conduct of this third visitor, looked as if they knew not what to think, and said nothing. Instinctively they withdrew further and further from the grim gentleman in their midst, whom some of them seemed to take for the Prince of Darkness[3] himself, till they formed

---

1 ta'en: taken 抓到了。
2 to go on: to continue 继续。
3 the Prince of Darkness: the devil 魔鬼。

愿上帝垂怜他的灵魂!"

坐在炉边的生客顺着唱歌者的音调这么高兴地摇他的酒杯,以致他的蜜酒泼到炉边,跟前次一样地用他的低音和道:——

"愿上帝垂怜他的灵魂!"

这些时候里,第三个生客老站在门口。看到他现在既不走前,也不继续说话,客人们就特别注意他。他们真觉得奇怪,看见他站在他们面前吓得沮丧不堪的样子——他的双膝发抖着,他的手额动得这么猛烈,他所倚靠的门闩都响出声了;他那一双白嘴唇打开了,他的眼睛盯着房子中间那个快乐的法吏身上。再一会儿,他转过身,将门关好,逃跑了。

"这个到底是那一种人呢?"牧羊人说。

其余的人们被他们最近的可怕发现和这位第三个生客的奇怪行为弄糊涂了,现出一种傻神气,仿佛他们不知道怎么想好,一个字也没有说。他们出乎本能地渐渐退后,远离在他们中间的那个凶猛的先生,他们里面有些人仿佛认他为魔鬼本身,等

a remote circle, an empty space of floor being left between them and him—

...circulus, cujus centrum diabolus. [1]

The room was so silent—though there were more than twenty people in it—that nothing could be heard but the patter of the rain against the window-shutters, accompanied by the occasional hiss of a stray drop that fell down the chimney into the fire, and the steady puffing of the man in the corner, who had now resumed his pipe of long clay.

The stillness was unexpectedly broken. The distant sound of a gun reverberated through the air—apparently from the direction of the county-town.

"Be jiggered[2]!" cried the stranger who had sung the song, jumping up.

"What does that mean?" asked several.

"A prisoner escaped from the jail—that's what it means."

All listened. The sound was repeated, and none of them spoke but the man in the chimney-corner, who said quietly, "I've often been told that in this county they fire a gun at such times; but I never heard it till now."

---

1 ...circle, whose center is diabolical 一个圆周，它的中心是属于魔鬼的。
2 be jiggered 这是一种咒诅，没有意义的。

到末了他们做成一个大圈子，在他们同他之间剩下一大片空地板——

……一个圆周，它的中心是鬼气森森的。

房里是这么静寂——虽然里面有二十多人——什么声音都没有，只听到雨打窗板的滴嗒声，此外还有从烟囱落到火里的飘零雨点的咝声，和坐在炉边，现在又抽起泥制长烟斗的人阵阵吐烟的嘘声。

这个寂静是出乎意表地打破了。远处的枪声经过空中回响着——分明是从州郡那一方发出来。

"糟了！"唱那首歌的生客跳起来喊道。

"这枪声含有什么意义？"好几个人问道。

"一个囚犯从狱里逃出了——这是它所含的意义。"

大家都静听着。枪声又响起来，他们没有一个人说话，除开坐在炉边那个人，他安详地说道，"我常听人们说在这个州里有这类事情发生时候他们放枪；但是一直到现在我还没有听过这种枪声。"

"I wonder if it is my man?" murmured the personage in cinder-gray.

"Surely it is!" said the shepherd involuntarily. "And surely we've zeed[1] him! That little man who looked in at the door by now, and quivered like a leaf when he zeed ye and heard your song!"

"His teeth chattered, and the breath went out of his body," said the dairyman.

"And his heart seemed to sink within him like a stone," said Oliver Giles.

"And he bolted as if he'd been shot at," said the hedge-carpenter.

"True—his teeth chattered, and his heart seemed to sink; and he bolted as if he'd been shot at," slowly summed up the man in the chimney-corner.

"I didn't notice it," remarked the hangman.

"We were all a-wondering[2] what made him run off in such a fright," faltered one of the women against the wall, "and now 'tis explained!"

The firing of the alarm-gun went on at intervals, low and sullenly and their suspicions became a certainty. The sinister gentleman in cinder-gray roused himself. "Is there a constable here?" he asked,

---

1 zeed: saw, 乡下人把see念作zee, 用于过去时候又把它加上一个d字。
2 a-wondering: 参观第304页注1。

"我纳罕逃的是不是'我'的人？"穿灰色衣服的先生喃喃地说道。

"一定是！"牧羊人自然而然地说出。"我们一定看见了那个人！刚才从门口望〔往〕内瞧，当他看见你，听到你的歌词，颤动得像一个树叶子的那个短小的人！"

"他的牙齿颤震作声，身里一点气力都没有，"牛奶场的主人说道。

"他的心仿佛跟一块石头一样沉下去了，"奥力味·斋尔兹说。

"他飞奔去，好像他中了子弹，"做栅栏的木匠说。

"不错——他的牙齿颤震作声，他的心仿佛沉下去了；他飞奔去，好像他中了子弹，"坐在炉边的人慢慢地把这几句话总括起来。

"我并没有注意到，"绞刑吏说。

"我们都正在纳罕什么使他这样吓得不得了跑去，"靠着墙边的女人里有一个犹豫地说道，"现在这得到解释了！"

警炮的鸣放继续着，隔一会儿就放一声，声音是低的，凄惨的，他们的猜想变成真实了。穿灰色衣服的不祥先生振作起来。"这里有一位警吏吗？"他用含糊的声调问道，"假使有，

in thick tones. "If so, let him step forward."

The engaged man of fifty stepped quavering out from the wall, his betrothed beginning to sob on the back of the chair.

"You are a sworn constable? "

"I be, sir."

"Then pursue the criminal at once, with assistance, and bring him back here. He can't have gone far."

"I will, sir, I will—when I've got my staff. I'll go home and get it, and come sharp[1] here, and start in a body[2]."

"Staff!—never mind your staff; the man'll be gone! "

"But I can't do nothing without my staff—can I, William, and John and Charles Jake? No; for there's the king's royal crown a painted on en in yaller and gold[3], and the lion and the unicorn, so as when I raise en up and hit my prisoner 'tis made a lawful blow thereby. I wouldn't 'tempt[4] to take up[5] a man without my staff—no, not I. If I hadn't the law to gie[6] me courage, why, instead o' my taking up him he might take up me!"

---

1 sharp: punctually 准时。

2 in a body: all together 大家一起。

3 a painted on en in yaller and gold: painted on it in yellow and gold 黄金色的, 画在上面。

4 'tempt: attempt 试。

5 to take up: to arrest 拘留。

6 to gie: to give 给。

请他走出来。"

已订婚了的五十岁的人战栗地从墙旁走出来,他的未婚妻开始靠着椅背呜咽。

"你是个宣誓过的警吏吗?"

"我是,先生。"

"那么立刻带同帮手去追赶那犯人,带他到这儿来。他不至于跑到很远了。"

"我一定要去追他,先生,我一定要去追他——当我拿到了我的棍子。我现在回家去拿它,立刻就到这儿来,结队出去。"

"棍子!——千万不要管你的棍子;那个人将逃掉了!"

"但是没有我的棍子,我什么事也不能做——我能够吗,威廉,约翰,查理斯·约克?不;它上面画有当今圣上的金黄色的皇冕,和狮子同独角兽,所以当我举起它,打我的囚犯时,那个打击因此是合法的。我不肯没有带着我的棍子,试去抓人——不,我不肯。若使没有法律来壮我的胆量,嗳呀,我不单是抓不到他,他还会把我抓去!"

"Now, I'm a king's man myself, and can give you authority enough for this," said the formidable officer in gray. "Now then, all of ye, be ready. Have you any lanterns?"

"Yes—have ye any lanterns?—I demand it!" said the constable.

"And the rest of you able-bodied—"

"Able-bodied men—yes—the rest of ye!" said the constable.

"Have you some good stout staves and pitchforks—"

"Staves and pitchforks—in the name o'[1] the law! And take 'em in yer hands and go in quest, and do as we in authority tell ye!"

Thus aroused, the men prepared to give chase. The evidence was indeed, though circumstantial, so convincing, that but little argument was needed to show the shepherd's guests that after what they had seen it would look very much like connivance if they did not instantly pursue the unhappy third stranger, who could not as yet have gone more than a few hundred yards over such uneven country.

A shepherd is always well provided with lanterns; and, lighting these hastily, and with hurdle-staves[2] in their hands, they poured out of the door, taking a direction along the crest of the hill, away from the town, the rain having fortunately a little abated.

---

1 in the name of: denoting the use of another's name to give authority to one's act.用别人的名义，使一个人有干某件事的权限。

2 hurdle-staves: hurdle, a movable frame for folding sheep 可以移动的羊栏，hurdle-stave 是插闭这种羊栏的门的棍子。

"你看，我个人也是皇上底下的人，很能够给你权力去干这件事，"穿灰色衣服的可怕法吏说道。"来，你们一切人们，预备好。你们有灯笼吗？"

"是的——你们有灯笼吗？——我要它！"警吏说道。

"你们这班好汉子——"

"好汉子——是的——你们这班人！"警吏说道。

"你们有坚固的好棍子和叉耙——"

"棍子和叉耙——我用法律的名义要这些东西！把它们拿在你们手里，去寻找囚犯，照我们这班有权力的人们告诉你们的话做去！"

这样鼓励之后，人们预备去追赶。虽然只有情况证据，但是这证据是如是令人相信的，用不着多少唇舌就可以使牧羊人的客人们看出他们既见了这个情况，那么很像是有意纵容，若使他们不立刻去追赶这位不幸的第三个生客，他在道路这么不平的乡下里，此刻顶多不过跑了几百码。

一个牧羊人总是预备有不少的灯笼；赶紧把它们点好，手里拿着栏插，他们涌出门外，向山顶走去，朝着跟市镇相反的方向走去，幸而雨势已经稍弱一些了。

Disturbed by the noise, or possibly by unpleasant dreams of her baptism, the child who had been christened began to cry heart-brokenly in the room overhead. These notes of grief came down through the chinks of the floor to the ears of the women below, who jumped up one by one, and seemed glad of the excuse to ascend and comfort the baby, for the incidents of the last half-hour greatly oppressed them. Thus in the space of two or three minutes the room on the groundfloor was deserted quite.

But it was not for long. Hardly had the sound of footsteps died away when a man returned round the corner of the house from the direction the pursuers had taken. Peeping in at the door, and seeing nobody there, he entered leisurely. It was the stranger of the chimney-corner, who had gone out with the rest. The motive of his return was shown by his helping himself to a cut piece of skimmer-cake that lay on a ledge beside where he had sat, and which he had apparently forgotten to take with him. He also poured out half a cup more mead from the quantity that remained, ravenously eating and drinking these as he stood. He had not finished when another figure came in just as quietly—his friend in cinder-gray.

"O—you here?" said the latter, smiling, "I thought you had gone to help in capture." And this speaker also revealed the object of his return by looking solicitously round for the fascinating mug of old mead.

被这些噪杂声音所惊，或者也许是被她自己受洗礼的恶梦所惊，这位已受过洗礼的小孩开始在楼上房里痛哭。这些悲音从地板的罅隙传到下面女人的耳朵里，她们一个个跳起来，好像很高兴有这个借口，可以上去安慰小孩，因为最近半小时里的事变使她们很觉得烦闷。于是二三分钟之内底下一层的房子里面的人们全走空了。

但是这种荒凉的情况继续不久。她们脚步的声音几乎还没有完全消失，就有一个男人从追踪者所走的方向缘着屋角回来。在大门外偷望一下，看到里面没有人，他从容地进来。这个人就是坐在炉边的那个生客，他起先跟其它人们一同出去。他回来的动机可以从他自己把从前他坐的地方旁边架子上一块切下的薄饼，那分明是他忘却带走了，吃下去这一点看出。他又从剩下的蜜酒里倒出半杯，站着一面鲸吞虎咽地食着喝着。他还没有完了，另一个人同样安静地进来——穿着灰色衣服的他的朋友。

"啊呀——你也在这儿？"这位朋友微笑地说道，"我还以为你已去帮他们捕犯人了。"这个说话的人也露出他回来的目的，因为他焦虑地回顾寻找那迷人的老蜜酒的酒杯。

"And I thought you had gone," said the other, continuing his skimmer-cake with some effort.

"Well, on second thoughts, I felt there were enough without me," said the first confidentially, "and such a night as it is, too. Besides, 'tis the business o' the Government to take care of its criminals—not mine."

"True; so it is. And I felt as you did, that there were enough without me."

"I don't want to break my limbs running over the humps[1] and hollows of this wild country."

"Nor I neither, between you and me[2]."

"These shepherd-people are used to[3] it—simple-minded souls, you know, stirred up to anything in a moment. They'll have him ready for me before the morning, and no trouble to me at all."

"They'll have him, and we shall have saved ourselves all labour in the matter."

"True, true. Well, my way is to Casterbridge; and 'tis as much as my legs will do to take me that far. Going the same way?"

"No, I am sorry to say! I have to get home over there" (he nodded indefinitely to the right), "and I feel as you do, that it is quite

---

1 hump: protuberance 凸处。
2 between you and me: in confidence 私下的；秘密的。
3 used to: accustomed to 惯于。

"我也以为你已去了，"那个人答道，有些费劲地继续吃他的薄饼。

"回头一想，我觉得没有我人也足够了，"第一个说话人秘密地说道，"又是这么一个晚上。而且，那是政府的事情，当心看守它的囚犯——并不是我的。"

"不错；的确是。我跟你一样地觉得，没有我人也足够了。"

"我不愿跑过这荒凉乡下里高高低低的地方，弄得跑断我的腿子。"

"我也不愿，这话我只好私下告诉你。"

"这班牧羊人是惯于跑这种路——你知道，他们都是老实的人们，一下子就可以激他们去干任何种事情。他们会把他抓到，预备明早我来下手，一点都不要我麻烦。"

"他们会把他抓到，我们关于这件事尽可以替自己省力气。"

"是的，是的。好罢，我是到喀斯忒布立治去的；我的腿力也只够带我到那儿去。你也是走这条路吗？"

"不，对不住！我要回家到那儿去"（他渺茫地点头指着右方），"我跟你一样觉得要我的腿力支持到上床的时候已经

enough for my legs to do before bedtime."

The other had by this time finished the mead in the mug, after which, shaking hands heartily at the door, and wishing each other well, they went their several ways.

In the meantime the company of pursuers had reached the end of the hog's-back elevation which dominated this part of the down. They had decided on no particular plan of action; and, finding that the man of the baleful trade was no longer in their company, they seemed quite unable to form any such plan now. They descended in all directions down the hill, and straightway several of the party fell into the snare set by Nature for all misguided midnight ramblers over this part of the cretaceous formation. The "lanchets"[1], or flint slopes, which belted the escarpment at intervals of a dozen yards, took[2] the less cautious ones unawares, and losing their footing on the rubbly steep they slid sharply downwards, the lanterns rolling from their hands to the bottom, and there lying on their sides till the horn was scorched through.

When they had again gathered themselves together, the shepherd, as the man who knew the country best, took the lead, and guided them round these treacherous inclines. The lanterns, which seemed rather to dazzle their eyes and warn the fugitive than to

---

1 lanchet：flint slope燧石斜坡。
2 to take：to catch绊着。

是不容易了。"

那个人这时已经把杯中的蜜酒饮罄了,喝完在门口诚恳地握手着,互相祝福,他们各走各的路了。

当时追赶的人们已走到高据沙洲之上的猪背形小山的尽头了。他们没有决定出一个一定的计划;看到干不祥生意的那个人不在他们里面,他们现在好像不能弄出这么一个计划来。他们顺着各方向分散走下山去,立刻里面就有几个人掉进"自然"在这片白垩质构成的地面上所安下给午夜不识路的游荡者去摔交〔跤〕的陷阱里去。绕着峻崖的燧石斜坡,那是隔十几码就有一个,使不大小心的人们上当,他们在那陡坡站不住脚后,就一下子滑下去,灯笼从他们手上滚到崖底,躺在那儿,一直等到明角全烧焦了。

当他们又聚在一起时候,牧羊人算是最懂得那里地势的人,就当领袖,引他们缘着这阴险的斜坡走。灯笼好像反使他们目眩,而且给逃囚一个警告,并不能帮助他们进行访查,他们于

assist them in the exploration, were extinguished, due silence was observed; and in this more rational order they plunged into the vale. It was a grassy, briery, moist defile, affording some shelter to any person who had sought it; but the party perambulated it in vain, and ascended on the other side. Here they wandered apart, and after an interval closed together again to report progress. At the second time of closing in they found themselves near a lonely ash, the single tree on this part of the coomb, probably sown there by a passing bird some fifty years before. And here, standing a little to one side of the trunk. As motionless as the trunk itself, appeared the man they were in quest of, his outline being well defined against the sky beyond. The band noiselessly drew up and faced him.

"Your money or your life!" said the constable sternly to the still figure.

"No, no," whispered John Pitcher. "'Tisn't our side ought to say that. That's the doctrine of vagabonds like him, and we be on the side of the law."

"Well, well," replied the constable impatiently; "I must say something, mustn't I? And if you had all the weight o' this undertaking upon your mind, perhaps you'd say the wrong thing too!—Prisoner at the bar, surrender in the name of the Father—the Crown, I mane[1]!"

---

1 I mane: I mean 我的意思是。

是把它们灭了，保守个应有的静默；在这个更合理的秩序之下他们冲到下面的谷里。那是一个多草多荆棘的潮湿狭路，想躲避在那里面的人很有藏身的地方；但是这一队人们白巡行了，又登上对面的山坡。到那里时他们分开去找，过一会儿又聚一起来报告进行情形。第二次聚合时候，他们所站的地方邻近有一棵寂寞的槐树，那是这块沙阜上惟一的树，也许是五六十年以前一只过鸟种下的。这儿，站在稍近树的一旁，跟树干一样的不动，现出他们所寻找的那个人，他的轮廓被远天衬着显出很分明。这一队人无声地走上前，面对着他。

"拿你的钱出来，否则拿出你的命！"警吏严厉对这木立不动的人说道。

"不，不，"约翰·匹舍尔低声说。"我们这面人不该说这种话。这是像他这样流氓们的主意，我们是站在法律这边。"

"算了罢，算了罢，"警吏不耐烦地说道，"我总得说些话，是不是？假使这件事全部都压到身上，也许你也会讲错话！法庭里的囚犯，我用上帝的名义——不，我说的是用皇帝的名义——叫你屈服！"

The man under the tree seemed now to notice them for the first time, and, giving them no opportunity whatever for exhibiting their courage, he strolled slowly towards them. He was, indeed, the little man, the third stranger; but his trepidation had in a great measure gone.

"Well, travellers," he said, "did I hear ye speak to me?"

"You did, you've got to¹ come and be our prisoner at once!" said the constable. "We arrest 'ee on the charge of not biding in Casterbridge jail in a decent proper manner to be hung to-morrow morning. Neighbours, do your duty, and seize the culpet²!"

On hearing the charge, the man seemed enlightened, and, saying not another word, resigned himself with preternatural civility to the searchparty, who, with their staves in their hands, surrounded him on all sides, and marched him back towards the shepherd's cottage.

It was eleven o'clock by the time they arrived. The light shining from the open door, a sound of men's voices within, proclaimed to them as they approached the house that some new events had arisen in their absence. On entering they discovered the shepherd's living room to be invaded by two officers from Casterbridge jail, and a

---

1 to have go to: to be obliged to; to have to; must 不得不。
2 culpet: culprit 犯人。

站在树下的人好像现在才见到他们,没有给他们以表示他们勇敢的机会,他向他们从容地慢步走来。他的确是那个矮小的人,那个第三位生客;但是他的惊恐却大半已过去了。

"哦罢,旅客们,"他说,"我刚才听到的是你们向我说的话吗?"

"对的,你得立刻来做我们的囚人!"警吏说道。"我们拘捕你,你的罪名是不肯规规矩矩地滞在喀斯忒布立治狱里,让人们明早把你绞死。邻人们,尽你们的责任,来抓这个罪人!"

听到这个罪名,那个人好像明白了,一句别的话也没有吐,有礼得出奇地顺从这个搜察队的命令,他们手上拿着棍子,四面围着他,押他回到牧羊人的茅屋里。

他们到的时候是十一点钟了。从打开的大门射出的灯光和里面男人们说话的声音指出给他们看,当他们走近那屋子时候,在他们出去之后有些新事情发生。走进去,他们看见牧羊人憩息的房子里面有两个从喀斯忒布立治狱来的狱吏同一个住在离

well-known magistrate who lived at the nearest country-seat, intelligence of the escape having become generally circulated.

"Gentlemen," said the constable, "I have brought back your man—not without risk and danger; but every one must do his duty! He is inside this circle of able-bodied persons who have lent me useful aid, considering their ignorance of Crown work. Men, bring forward your prisoner!" And the third stranger was led to the light.

"Who is this?" said one of the officials.

"The man," said the constable.

"Certainly not," said the turnkey[1]; and the first corroborated his statement.

"But how can it be otherwise?" asked the constable. "Or why was he so terrified at sight o' the singing instrument of the law who sat there?" Here he related the strange behaviour of the third stranger on entering the house during the hangman's song.

"Can't understand it," said the officer coolly. "All I know is that it is not the condemned man. He's quite a different character from this one; a gauntish fellow, with dark hair and eyes, rather good-looking, and with a musical bass voice that if you heard it once you'd never mistake as long as you lived."

"Why, souls— 'twas the man in the chimney-corner!"

---

1 turnkey: one in charge of the key of a prison 狱里管钥匙的人。

这儿最近的别墅里的官吏，逃犯这个消息已传到四处了。

"先生们，"警吏说道，"我把你们的人带回来了——并不是毫无危险的；但是个个人总得尽他的责任！他就在这班能干的人们里面，他们给我以很有用的帮助，这真是难得的，我们一想到他们是不懂皇家公事的。好汉们，把你们的犯人带出来！"第三个生客就被引到光亮的地方。

"他是谁？"一个狱吏说道。

"那个人，"警吏说。

"绝不是，"管牢狱锁匙的人说；那一个狱吏也证实他的话。

"但是，怎么会不是呢？"警吏问道。"否则他看到坐在这儿那位法律的歌颂者时怎么会吓得那么厉害呢？"他于是说出第三个生客当绞刑吏唱歌时走进屋子后的奇怪行为。

"我不知道，"狱吏冷淡地说。"我所晓得的是这个并不是那判定了死刑的人。他是跟这个很不相同的一个人；一个瘦削的汉子，头发同眼睛的颜色都是棕黑色的，都还漂亮，有一种悦耳的低音声调，假使你听到了一回，那么你一生也不会认错。"

"嗳吓，人们——这就是坐在炉边那个人！"

"Hey — what?" said the magistrate, coming forward after inquiring particulars from the shepherd in the background. "Haven't you got the man after all?"

"Well, sir," said the constable, "he's the man we were in search of, that's true; and yet he's not the man we were in search of. For the man we were in search of was not the man we wanted, sir, if you understand my every-day way; for 'twas the man in the chimney-corner!"

"A pretty kettle of fish[1] altogether!" said the magistrate. "You had better start for the other man at once."

The prisoner now spoke for the first time. The mention of the man in the chimney-corner seemed to have moved him as nothing else could do. "Sir," he said, stepping forward to the magistrate, "take no more trouble about me. The time is come when I may as well speak. I have done nothing; my crime is that the condemned man is my brother. Early this afternoon I left home at Shottsford to tramp it all the way to Casterbridge jail to bid him farewell. I was benighted, and called here to rest and ask the way. When I opened the door I saw before me the very man, my brother, that I thought to see in the condemned cell at Casterbridge. He was in this chimney-corner; and jammed close to him, so that he could not have got out if

---

1 a kettle of fish: a confused state of affairs 一榻〔塌〕胡涂。

"呀——什么?"官吏在后面向牧羊人打听详细情形后走向前说道。"你们到底抓到那个人没有?"

"唉,先生,"警吏说,"他是我们所要寻找的人,不错;然而他不是我们所寻找的人。因为我们所寻找的人不是我们所要寻找的人,先生,也许你听得懂我这种平常说话的口气;因为他是坐在炉边那个人!"

"简直是一大锅杂鱼搅在一起!"官吏说。"你们还是立刻去追赶那个人罢。"

囚人现在第一次说话了。人们提起坐在炉边的人好像感动他强过任何其它的东西。"先生,"他走前对着官吏说道,"不要再为我麻烦。我说话的时候也到了。我没有犯什么罪;我的罪是那个判定死刑的人是我的兄弟。今天下午很早时候我离开叔提斯福特我的家,步行到喀斯忒布立治去和他诀别。天已经黑了,我到这儿来休息一下和问路。由我打开门,我看见在我面前的就是那个人,我的兄弟,我起先以为将在喀斯忒布立治死囚牢里会见的。他就坐在这个炉边;紧紧地同他挤在一块就是

he had tried, was the executioner who'd come to take his life, singing a song about it and not knowing that it was his victim who was close by, joining in to save appearances[1]. My brother looked a glance of agony at me, and I knew he meant, 'Don't reveal what you see; my life depends on it.' I was so terror-struck that I could hardly stand, and, not knowing what I did, I turned and hurried away."

The narrator's manner and tone had the stamp of truth, and his story made a great impression on all around. "And do you know where your brother is at the present time?" asked the magistrate.

"I do not. I have never seen him since I closed this door."

"I can testify to that, for we've been between ye ever since," said the constable.

"Where does he think to fly to? —What is his occupation?"

"He's a watch-and-clock-maker, sir."

"'A said 'a[2] was a wheelwright—a wicked rogue," said the constable.

"The wheels of clocks and watches he meant, no doubt," said Shepherd Fennel. "I thought his hands were palish for's trade."

"Well, it appears to me that nothing can be gained by retaining this poor man in custody," said the magistrate; "your business lies

---

1 to save appearance: to keep up a fair outward show 保持个外观。
2 'a: he 他。

那个刽子手，所以假使他想走出也是办不到的，这个刽子手是来要他的命，唱一首关于这件事的歌，却不知道他的受害者就在身旁，和唱他的歌，免露马脚。我的兄弟向我沉痛地望一眼，我知道他的意思是，'不要说出你看见的人是谁；我的生命是决于这一点。'我吓得几乎站不稳脚，不知道我干的是什么，我回身逃跑。"

说话人的态度和声音带有真实的色彩，他的叙述给旁边一切人们以一个很深的印象。"你知道你兄弟此刻在什么地方吗？"官吏问道。

"我不知道。我关门以后就没有看到他了。"

"我能够证明这点，因为以后我们老居于你们中间，"警吏说。

"他想跑到那儿去？——他的职业是什么？"

"他是个钟表匠，先生。"

"他说他是一个轮匠——一个坏流氓，"警吏说。

"他一定是指钟表的轮，"牧羊人樊纳尔说。"我起先想他的手色灰白，不像干那职业的。"

"据我看，把这个可怜的人拘禁起来是无补于事的，"官吏

with the other, unquestionably."

And so the little man was released off-hand; but he looked nothing the less sad on that account, it being beyond the power of magistrate or constable to raze out the written troubles in his brain, for they concerned another whom he regarded with more solicitude than himself. When this was done, and the man had gone his way, the night was found to be so far advanced that it was deemed useless to renew the search before the next morning.

Next day, accordingly, the quest for the clever sheep-stealer became general and keen, to all appearance at least. But the intended punishment was cruelly disproportioned to the transgression, and the sympathy of a great many country-folk in that district was strongly on the side of the fugitive. Moreover his marvellous coolness and daring in hob-and-nobbing[1] with the hangman, under the unprecedented circumstances of the shepherd's party, won their admiration. So that it may be questioned if all those who ostensibly made themselves so busy in exploring woods and fields and lanes were quite so thorough when it came to the private examination of their own lofts[2] and outhouses. Stories were afloat of a mysterious figure being occasionally seen in some old overgrown trackway or other,

---

1 hob-and-nob: in close companion ship 亲昵。
2 loft: an attic of a barn 仓库的顶楼。

说,"你们的事情无疑地是关于那一个人。"

于是这位矮小的人随便释放了;但是他并不因此而减轻他的愁容,那是在官吏同警吏的能力之外,把印在上面的烦恼从他脑子里擦去,因为这些烦恼是为一个他觉得比他自己更关切的人。当人们把他释放了,他也上路了,夜已经是这么深,大家认为在天亮以前再出发去寻觅是无用的。

第二天,寻找这个伶俐的偷羊人于是变为普遍的,严厉的举动了,最少表面上是如此的。但是起先定下的责罚太残酷了,与他所犯的罪很不相称,那地方里面许多的乡下人都同情于逃犯。而且,在牧羊人宴会里那种空前的奇怪环境之下,他那惊人的冷静和敢同绞刑吏弄得那么亲昵,这两点得到乡下人们的赞美。所以,那是个疑问,那班外表上这么勤于搜索森林,田地同小巷的人们有没有这么澈底,当去检查自己的仓库顶楼同外屋时候。有些谣言,说人们间或在远离有关栅的大路的一些野草蔓生的古路上看到一个神秘的人;但是当在这些任一个有

remote from turnpike roads; but when a search was instituted in any of these suspected quarters nobody was found. Thus the days and weeks passed without tidings.

In brief, the bass-voiced man of the chimney-corner was never recaptured. Some said that he went across the sea, others that he did not, but buried himself in the depths of a populous city. At any rate, the gentleman in cinder-gray never did his morning's work at Casterbridge, nor met anywhere at all, for business purposes, the genial comrade with whom he had passes an hour of relaxation in the lonely house on the coomb.

The grass has long been green on the graves of Shepherd Fennel and his frugal wife; the guests who made up the christening party have mainly followed their entertainers to the tomb; the baby in whose honour they all had met is a matron in the sere and yellow leaf [1]. But the arrival of the three strangers at the shepherd's that night, and the details connected therewith, is a story as well known as ever in the country about Higher Crowstairs.

---

1 in the sere and yellow leaf: in old age 老年。这里是拿一年四季里树叶的荣枯来比人们的年纪。

嫌疑的路上举行搜查时,并没有找到什么人。于是乎一天一天,一礼拜一礼拜没有消息地过去了。

总之,坐在炉边的低音的人永远没有再抓到。有人说他飘海它去,有人说他没有渡海,却自己隐在人烟稠密的城市里的深处。无论如何,穿灰色衣服的人第二早在喀斯忒布立治没有干他的工作,也没有为生意起见在任何地方遇到这位同他在沙阜上寂寞屋里休息一个钟头的良伴。

牧羊人樊纳尔和他节俭的妻子填上的草久已青了;受名式宴会上在场的许多客人多半都随他们的主人到坟里去了;他们那天聚会所庆祝的小孩子已是个走进黄色枯叶的时代里的一个老太婆了。但是那天晚上牧羊人家里三个生客的来临同其它连带的细节是亥儿·克洛斯腾尔思乡里还是跟从前一样的谁也知道的一个故事。